The Green Valley

Unexpected events force Dan to live by the gun that he had hoped to leave behind.

James Oliver Virmala

Edition 1

Cover Photo By Gloria Virmala

"Elk In Meadow"

ISBN: 978-0-9972536-9-6

DEDICATION

To Richard, my close friend and hunting companion.

CONTENTS

BOOKS BY THE AUTHOR

Oli's Gold Book One
Search For Oli's Gold Book Two
Return To Oli's Gold Book Three
To Be A Mountain Man
Trouble On The Kansas Plains
Frontier Justice
Return Of The Mountain Man
The Tall Man
The Prospector
The Green Valley
Twilight Of The Mountain Man
The Mother Lode
Quest Of The Mountain Man
Journey's End
Rufus Pike
Rufus And The Pup
The Winding Trail Home
Rufus The Lost Years
The Kankakee Kid
Bogus Island
Tyler Tomas The Brothers' War
War of 1812 The Choice
Kyle Oliver The Next Horizon

ACKNOWLEDGMENTS

Six years ago, Tom was crossing a highway and was the victim of a hit and run driver. Severely brain damaged, the road back and been painfully slow. Untold hours have been devoted by his mother with her only reward being small acts that let her know he was aware and has some memory. Tom remains unable to swallow, talk, walk and has limited expressions accept for fear or sadness. Recently a humorous thing happened when I was trying to get a hook out of a fish and Tom broke into a broad smile. Inside I know he was *laughing out loud* at his uncle. Just one more sign to let his mother know that with her help, he is fighting to come back. I would like to thank her for sharing my books with him as part of his recovery.

CHAPTER ONE

The sun was bright in the green valley. Dan August sat in the ranch house kitchen, reading the newspaper he'd gotten while picking up supplies in Casper. The headlines screamed out *"Bannock Indians Massacre Entire Town!"*

Snorting, the broad-shouldered rancher called to his wife, Mary, "The newspapers will print the darnedest things. We heard when the army got to the place, they found all was peaceful."

Mary wiped the bread flour from her hands and picked up Joanie, their two-year-old daughter. They had named her after Dan's mother. "We have never had trouble with the Bannock. They have hunted elk in our valley and even shared some of the meat with us when we first arrived here."

It was 1895 and the summer was almost over. The ranch house sat on a rise, overlooking a large pond fed by the melting snowcap of the mountains rising on the north side of the valley. Five years earlier, Dan and

Mary had ridden into the valley planning to raise cattle. The green valley had been visited by Dan's grandfather, Oli. He had written about the beauty of the valley in his ledger.

Dan and two of his cousins had used the ledger to find Spanish gold left behind by their grandfather. This gold had made the building and stocking of the ranch possible. The herd had grown with the help of mild winters. As the ranch had grown, Dan had taken on two ranch hands, Curly Wells and Lars Hanson.

Dan emerged from the house and squinted his gray eyes as he looked at the stream flowing from the pond. It wound down the valley floor and disappeared between red cliffs west of the ranch. Beyond the cliffs the valley widened again, offering good grazing for the cattle during the winter. He and Mary would sit on the porch during the evenings and watch the sun set, enjoying the view and peacefulness of their valley.

The tall rancher pushed back his curly brown hair before placing his curved rim hat on his head. He strapped a Colt .44 on his narrow hips. After adjusting it for comfort, he stepped off the porch and headed for the corral.

As he walked he shook out the loop of his lasso. Dropping it over the head of his chestnut, Dan led the horse to the barn. Once it was saddled, he swung onto the animal and rode out of the lush valley. Prior to the trip to Casper, he had sent the hands to push the cattle grazing east of the valley closer to the ranch. He was bringing some of the supplies to them.

It took three hours before Dan reached the roundup. The cattle had spent the summer grazing freely over the plain, gaining weight and raising their calves. It would take hard work to convince them that they had to leave the place they thought of as home.

For years ranchers had left the cattle to graze on the open plains year-round, with good success. The drought in 1886, followed by one of the coldest and snowiest winters on record, killed as much as a quarter of the cattle left on the plain.

Then there was the Johnson County War in 1892. It was fought between the large and smaller ranchers, leaving many of the smaller ones out of business. It was these types of events that convinced Dan that it was best to keep tighter control of the herd.

Curly and Lars were sitting around a fire, making a small midday meal before continuing their work, when the ranch owner spotted them.

Dan rode up and called out, "Are the critters giving you trouble?"

Curly walked up and took the bag of supplies from the boss. "You'd think we were driving them to the stock pens in Casper, the way they've been balking."

The cowhand walked with a limp. He had told Dan that it was because he was born with one leg shorter than the other. The sandy-haired Curly loved to eat, and the stomach that hung over his tight belt was proof of his appetite. He had an infectious laugh and a constant twinkle in his eyes. When it came to herding cattle, Curly was a top hand.

Lars was busy poking at the side meat browning in the blackened frying pan. He was short and barrel-chested. He wore a rabbit skin hat, summer and winter. Unlike the other hand, Lars was serious and unaffected by Curly's humor.

He looked up at Dan and Curly. "You guys best get over here before the meat turns to char."

Lars was a fair cow hand, but could build or fix almost anything. He was the son of a smithy and had learned to work iron. Much of the building on the ranch had been with the help and skill of the Swede.

After eating and stowing their gear, the three men continued to push cattle out of the many ravines and thickets in the foothills. Shortly before dark, they arrived at the canyon that was being used as a collection point for the cattle. Next to it was a line shack. Extra horses were kept in the pole corral behind the shack.

A wash pan on a rock near a small stream was used for cleaning the dust and sweat from the day's work. There was a pot of rice sitting on a six-plate stove. The stove had been filled with wood, and the rice was put on before leaving for work in the morning. Now, after a little heating and some honey or canned fruit, they had a fine supper.

The line shack had two upper and lower bunks. A table and four stools sat next to the door. Dan planned to keep it occupied during the winter once his herds got too large for the green valley as winter pasture. The cattle would then be left to graze in the foothills and the plain under a watchful eye.

Dan was sitting at the table while Lars stirred honey into the rice, when Curly came in. "Someone is killing some of our cows. I found a pile of guts and other parts of a heifer. I figured the poacher quartered the animal and hauled it away."

Rolling a cigarette and lighting it, Dan thought about what his cowhand had found. "Was it Crow or

Bannock?" he asked.

"I can't be sure. It was late and I was pushing six critters toward the shack," Curly replied. "All I can tell you is it was fresh. Wolves or coyotes hadn't found it yet."

Hanging on a peg behind Dan was his Colt .44, and leaning against the wall was his Winchester Model 1892. Both weapons used the same caliber ammunition. Curly also had a Colt .44 and an older Winchester Model 73. Lars just had a Colt Cavalry model with a longer barrel. He often carried the revolver in a holster he had mounted on his saddle. He didn't like the way a gun belt would restrict his movement while working cattle.

After finishing their bowls of rice along with cups of strong coffee, the three men sat down to card playing. After a couple hours of low stakes poker, it was time to call it a night. Dan went out to check on the stock. The night was cool, with a cloudless sky. The stars of the Milky Way washed across the sky.

He could hear the bawling of some of the young stock in the canyon after they'd been separated from their parent. Out on the plain were the howls of wolves tracking prey. The chestnut whinnied when he approached the corral. Grabbing a pitchfork, Dan threw some more hay to the horses.

He rolled another cigarette while listening to the night sounds. The shriek of a fisher cut through the night. Tomorrow he would have to try to find out who was killing the stock. A rancher could expect to lose a few animals to those who needed the meat, but it was not wise to ignore the losses.

Sunrise found the men saddling their horses.

They wore coats to ward off the morning chill. By noon they would be stripped down to their long john tops in the high desert heat. Dan chose a round-bellied mustang. The animal had to have the kinks taken out of it before it settled down to being ridden. After a few stiff-legged bucks, Dan got the animal's head up and it stood snorting clouds of steam into the morning air.

"Work the drifts south of here." Dan instructed. "I will check out the kill found yesterday and then drive whatever I find back with me."

While he watched the hands ride away, he drew his Colt .44 and checked it over. He then made sure that the Winchester was fully loaded. As he rode away from the line shack, he was confident that there wasn't too much danger to be found in the killing of the heifer. Just in case he was wrong, Dan wanted to be ready. He drew the Colt once more before putting the loop over the hammer. Then he tapped the flanks of the mustang, bringing it to a trot.

He backtracked the trail left by the cattle Curly had driven in. The remains of the butchered animal were not hard to find. They had been spread by scavengers from the night before. Dan tied the mustang to a low bush and began to circle the area, looking for sign. There were the boot prints of one man and the hoof prints of at least four small animals. They led away in a northerly direction, paralleling the base of the foothills.

It had taken Dan just over an hour to ride here and check out the sign. He tilted his hat back and looked in the direction of the tracks. "Well, it weren't Indians," he muttered. Swinging onto the mustang, he patted the animal's neck. "Let's go find out who the hell it was."

For the next three hours he followed the trail. The tracks were easy to see and Dan was able to keep the mustang at a trot. He had spotted a few of his cattle during the first hour and planned to come back this way to drive them to the line shack. Dan stopped with the sun high in the sky. He began to wonder if it was worth continuing. Whoever had killed the animal would be unlikely to make the long trek back to take any more. He was now well beyond the range his cattle grazed on.

Dan looked at a red cliff to the west. It was all of a hundred feet high and appeared to have access from the south. He decided to ride to the top to see if any trace of the thief could be seen. He led the mustang up the last of the grade to save its strength for the ride home. Gaining the top, he dropped the horse's reins.

The view across the plain was breathtaking. The vast expanse of golden fall grass was punctuated by dark green trees. To his back were the mountains. The hugeness of everything around him made Dan feel very small.

All of a sudden, he spotted smoke coming from beyond a ridge to the north. Then, as quickly as he'd seen it, it was gone. He estimated that it was two miles away. Taking up the reins, he said, "We came this far. We might as well meet the eaters of our beef."

Dan rode ahead slowly, watching for any sign of danger. The loop was off his Colt and the Winchester was carried across the front of his saddle. The mustang was a good cutting horse and the slightest pressure of his knees was all that was needed to guide it.

The first sign of his quarry was the back of a log cabin. A clay and stick chimney ran up the wall. Beyond the building was the source of the smoke. Dan used the cabin for cover as he closed in. Beyond the cabin and to the right he could see the green of gardens.

His rifle at the ready, he guided the horse around the end of the building. There was a threatening snarl and the mustang reared, sending Dan out of the saddle and into a heap on the ground. The horse wheeled and ran, almost hitting him as it put distance away from a vicious, growling yellow dog.

Dan lay on top of his Colt. The Winchester had landed out of reach. He put his arm up, expecting to feel the savage bite of the angry dog in the next moment. Then there was a shout. "Sam! Sam, stay!"

Looking in the direction of the voice, Dan saw two young Mexican girls and a young man. All three were holding rifles. In front of them the dog stood, ready to lunge. The boy raised his muzzle loader into the air and fired a shot. Lying helpless, the sound of the gunshot sent chills up Dan's spine.

Sitting up slowly, so as not to cause the dog to attack, he said, "My name is Dan August. I have a ranch about a half-day's ride south of here."

"You are a long way from home," the shorter girl said, staring coldly at him.

Taking a chance, Dan said, "I lost some beef and have been following the trail to find it."

Before the three could respond, a short, balding Mexican man hurried around the corner.

Hesitating to take in the scene before him, he then spoke to the three younger ones in rapid Spanish. The two girls stepped back, still holding their rifles, while the young man grabbed the growling dog and pulled it toward the other side of the cabin.

The elder man rushed up to Dan and offered a hand to help him up. "Señor, you must excuse my children. We live far from others in this place and must be careful of strangers. Our dog was just doing its job, warning us of anyone coming in."

Standing and dusting himself off, Dan replied, "I understand your concern of strangers. My ranch is also isolated and we must be careful."

He then extended his hand, "My name is Dan August, owner of the Circle A ranch."

Accepting the hand, the elder man said, "I am Juan Torres." Pointing to the shorter girl, he said, "This is my daughter Karla. The other is Diana. My son brought the dog away. He is Ricardo. My wife, Teresa, is near the barn, milking the goats."

With introductions completed, Dan was anxious to get to the reason he was here. He glanced and saw that the mustang had stopped a short distance away. Picking up the rifle, he turned back to Juan. "One of my heifers was killed." He noticed that the two girls were still holding the rifles. Making no sudden moves, he continued. "I followed the trail of whoever took the meat here."

Nodding, Juan said, "The tracks were made by my son. Ricardo was coming back from selling our cheese. He told me that he had come across the animal. It had been attacked by a big cat and was injured. He shot it and rather than leaving the meat to spoil, he brought it here."

Juan said something in Spanish to the girls and they left to put the rifles away. Then to Dan he said, "Let me show you."

On a frame in front of the cabin was the heifer's hide. The skin from the hind quarters showed evidence of ragged tears from the claws of the big cat. Additional frames had the meat drying above smoky fires. Movement caught Dan's attention. It was Teresa coming out of the barn with a clay jug full of goat's milk.

Dan was impressed with what Juan and his family had done. There was a full-length porch along the front of the cabin with an inlaid stone floor. There was a small barn and a corral. Six donkeys stood eating hay that had been forked in for them. The valley behind the cabin was irrigated with water flowing from the foothills. The fertile land was covered with vegetables, beans and corn. They had stick pens that held the goats. Chickens ran free around the front of the barn, chasing grasshoppers and looking for seeds.

Realizing that his long ride had been for nothing, it was time to head for the line shack. "You have a nice farm and family here. Your son did what was best with the heifer. I'll get my horse and head back."

"Señor Dan, we were about to eat. Please stay and share our meal. Ricardo will get your horse, water it and give it some grain."

Before he could object, Karla and Diana appeared from the cabin carrying chopped greens and sliced beef. Two flat skillets had been heated over one of the smoky fires. They quickly fried the beef and heated the corn tortillas. A hand-made table surrounded by benches stood in front of the cabin. The food was placed on it, along with chopped peppers and cheese. A glass of fresh goat milk was placed next to Dan.

Following the others' example, Dan filled his warm tortilla with beef and vegetables. He also added a generous slice of goat-cheese. He watched as the family added ample chopped peppers to their tortillas. Karla smiled and tossed one of the peppers into her mouth, followed by a bite of her tortilla.

The milk was sweet and creamy. Dan couldn't remember the last time he had drank milk. The meal was tasty and the fresh vegetables were a treat. He made himself another tortilla, adding just a few of the chopped peppers. It burned his mouth and he took a quick drink of milk.

Diana giggled and said, "You are brave, taking the ones with seeds."

Sweat was breaking out on Dan's forehead as he chewed on the tortilla. He would have to remember to stay away from the pepper seeds. With the meal finished, he drank water from the clay búcaro hanging from the porch. Ricardo brought the mustang to him.

Tied to the saddle horn was a bag filled with vegetables and rounds of cheese. Dan took the reins and looked at Juan. "We have your beef to enjoy," Juan said. "You have something in return from us."

Dan rode away with a good feeling knowing that he had neighbors like the Torres family. The sun told him that it would be six hours before dark. He decided that he would push any cattle he came across closer to the line shack. Then, tomorrow, he could return for them.

It was dark when Dan rode up to the line shack. Lars and Curly were next to the corral, saddling up two horses to come looking for him. Hearing the approaching mustang, Curly turned and yelled, "Dan!"

"Sorry I got back so late," the rancher apologized. "I met a fine family that gave me this big bag of cheese and vegetables that slowed me down."

Curly ran forward to take the bag. "Did you say *cheese*?"

CHAPTER TWO

Two weeks later the three men rode toward the green valley, pushing almost 1,000 cattle. They were met by some hands Dan had hired while getting supplies in Casper. Two of the men had worked for him previously. One man was new but came highly recommended by a cattle buyer who used the railroad from Casper to ship the cows.

Ralph, a lean, stoop-shouldered hand who wore a wide-brimmed hat and scarred leather vest, had helped with three roundups. Kelly, a redheaded Irishman who liked a derby to shade his freckle-covered face, had worked the past two years. The new man was John Hurley. He had silver-blond hair that he wore shoulder-length. He had a flat-brimmed leather hat and used a buckskin jacket to keep the morning chill off.

All three of the men carried Colts on their hips. Only Hurley had a rifle in a scabbard on his saddle. The men met them five miles out from the valley and immediately proved their worth helping to drive the cattle into the valley.

Dan had a bunkhouse that could lodge six hands. There was a potbelly stove for heat and making coffee. A sturdy table with benches was used to play cards or other tasks. The ranch house had a large kitchen where the hands ate breakfast and supper. Jerky or leftover bread was chewed on during the day.

They also had the help of a trapper and his Crow wife who had a cabin a half day's ride southwest of the valley. His name was George and his wife had taken the name of Ella. George would help by keeping the branding fire going and castrating bulls. Ella helped Mary with the meals. They slept in a canvas tent that George had erected near the pond.

Mary had a meal of roast venison, boiled potatoes and beet greens from her kitchen garden waiting for the men when they finished settling the herd down. Kidding and laughing, the men washed up for supper in basins located in front of the bunkhouse.

Once the meal was done, the men headed down to the bunkhouse for some cards. Lars had some things he needed to do, so he went into the tool shed and fired up the forge. Soon the ranch yard rang with the sound of his hammer on iron.

Dan and Mary sat drinking coffee while little Joanie played near them. Ella was putting the last of the dishes away. "I am glad we were able to get George and Ella again this year," he told Mary. He had noticed that his wife looked tired when he got back from rounding up the cattle. It wasn't good when he had to leave her alone at the ranch. Being responsible for all the day-to-day chores, plus taking care of a child, would leave anyone tired.

Ella left to go down to her tent. She knew that her husband would spend time in the bunkhouse playing cards. She nodded at Lars as he left holding the repaired branding iron. It would not be long before all of them would be in their beds. They would be up before daylight, getting ready for the first day of branding.

By noon the next day, branding and castrating were in full swing. Dan oversaw the operation while Curly, John, and Kelly cut the animals they wanted out of the herd. They went through several horses during the process. It seemed like the only break the men got was when they were switching saddles to a fresh mount.

Dan estimated that it would take just over a week to finish branding. The work area had been churned to mud. Heavy clouds had come in, threatening to make it even worse. Curly tossed his loop around the back legs of a young bull. Kelly had a loop over its head. Stretching the animal out, it was brought down and dragged near the fire.

George handed the branding iron to Lars, bent down, and with a quick cut he castrated the animal. Then, making room for Lars, the barrel-chested man stepped in and burned the Circle A brand on the flank. The stink of burning hair clung to the men's clothing.

The routine was repeated time after time as the men worked. Once, an animal was dropped and George stepped in to castrate it. Snorting, he stood up. "Damn, heifer! I almost cut the tits off it!"

Dan wasn't sure, but he could have sworn that he saw a smile on Lars' face as the trapper stomped away. The Swede finished the brand and tossed the iron back into the fire. Once the heifer was back on its feet, Dan pushed it back to the herd.

They had a total of just under 300 that would need branding. Most were year-old animals or younger. A few had been missed during past years and their larger size made a dangerous job even worse.

Keeping the men fed was a full-time job for the women. The smell of burned hair and cow dung seemed to stick to everything in the kitchen. Mary couldn't wait until it was over so she could give the house a good scrubbing and airing out.

The rain that had threatened for two days finally came in late afternoon on the fourth day. Dan had the men quit early, giving them time to take care of personal items that they had been neglecting. Water was heated on the forge in the tool shed and some of the men took advantage of it and bathed.

Once supper was done, a few of the hands decided to play cards. Dan sat on the porch of the ranch house and watched the rain. All of a sudden there was a shout, and then a shot, coming from the bunkhouse. Dan was running toward the building when two men tumbled out the door. It was Lars and John! The two men were rolling around on the ground, unable to gain footing in the mud. The ranch owner ran over and grabbed the cocked arm of John and pulled the two men apart.

"The next one that throws a punch can pack their gear and ride the hell out of here!" Dan threatened.

The two men lay on their backs in the muddy yard with the rain pouring down on them. Lars was the first to speak. "Sorry, boss. It weren't nothing."

"Me and him was just unwinding a bit," John explained.

"Who the hell fired a gun?" Dan demanded.

Curly was standing in the door and explained. "They were discussing a hand of cards. The gun got knocked to the floor and went off. Nobody got hurt."

If it wasn't for the need of manpower, Dan would have sent John packing that night. Lars was a good worker and he would have stayed. Instead, he had to keep both men until the branding was done.

"No more cards until the branding is done. Any more fighting and I will be kicking some ass," Dan warned the men. He then headed for the ranch house, soaked to the skin from the rain. He saw his wife on the porch holding their child.

Following him into the house, Mary put down their daughter. She poured him coffee with a shot of rye. Accepting the steaming cup, Dan sat at the table, still feeling the tension from the confrontation. Mary sat next to him and took his hand, grinning. "I don't think your mother would like hearing you talk like that."

"No, I don't believe she would," Dan said, laughing. Mary always knew how to make him relax.

The rain had ended and the men went to work the next morning like nothing had happened. John Hurley was sporting a black eye and Lars had a cut on his cheek. The mud was now soup. Once George had the fire going and the iron red-hot, they were ready to go. The cattle were grazing further down the valley, so it was taking more time to cut the unbranded animals and push them toward the fire.

All day long ropes snaked out, dropping loops over the horns or heads of the cattle. Snugging the other end to the saddle horn, they were led to the branding area. One of the bulls attacked Curly and his horse. The quick-thinking hand kicked his boot out of the stirrup and raised his leg just in time to avoid the horn. The animal put a severe gash in the mustang Curly was riding.

John charged in and dropped a loop over the bull and pulled it away before it could do anymore damage. Dragging the resisting animal to the branding fire, Kelly rode up and got a rope around one of its back legs. The stubborn animal was brought to the fire.

After branding and castrating the animal, they shook the ropes off. It stood, blood running down its back legs, with its head down, snorting at the men. Lars waved the hot branding iron at the animal and shouted. "Come on, if you want another on your damn nose!" Unnerved by the display of the barrel-chested Swede, the steer turned and ran down the valley, tail in the air.

On the sixth day, Dan noticed that there was a heifer standing three-legged near the west end of the pond. Swinging onto the chestnut, he rode down to check it out. The front leg was broken. More than likely it had stepped into a prairie dog hole.

Tying the chestnut to a cedar tree, he pulled his Colt and put a bullet into the forehead of the injured animal. The heifer tried to step back, and then collapsed. He then cut its throat to let it bleed out. George came running from the fire.

"You want me and Ella to butcher the animal?" he asked. "Lars can cut a few nuts while we do it. I should have it all cut up in about an hour."

"You got it, George," Dan agreed. "Put a rope around its horns and I'll drag it to the barn."

Dan knew that George had hunted buffalo before trapping. Skinning and cutting was a way of life for the trapper. The fresh meat would help to feed the crew.

That evening, George didn't show up for supper. Dan asked Curly if he had seen him. "I sure did, boss. He's down by his tent, cooking the liver and tongue over his fire."

"Well, he is going to miss the custard pie I made for dessert," Mary called out.

The last couple days of branding yielded few animals. Dan paid Hurley and sent him back to Casper. The blond man seemed surprised to be let go. It appeared that he had hoped to spend the winter at the ranch.

Ralph and Kelly stuck around for a week after branding, helping with the driving of the cattle to winter pasture. Across the valley one could see haystacks that had been piled over the summer. The stacks would help feed the cattle during the worst of the winter.

George and Ella packed up their tent and headed west toward their small cabin. Mary was looking pale and was running a slight fever. The Crow woman offered to stay a little longer and help, but Mary insisted that she go. "I am just a little tired from roundup," she said. "In a couple days I will be all rested up."

Dan was mending a harness in front of the barn, after paying Ralph and Kelly and promising them work the following year. Looking up, he saw someone coming through the valley mouth. He recognized Ricardo, Karla, and Diana. They were leading three donkeys packed with supplies.

"We bring you corn and cheese from our father," Diana called out.

Mary was resting on the porch while watching Joanie. She got up and stood with Dan in the center of the ranch yard as the group approached. "These are Juan's son and daughters that I told you about," he said to his wife.

They stopped in the yard and Ricardo walked back to the packs. "There are also some melons. Where would you like me to unload the packs?"

Karla smiled and said, "I wanted to bring you more peppers, but my mother told me I shouldn't."

"Dan will help you unload them on the porch," Mary offered. "I have some beef stew on the stove. You must stay the night before heading back home."

Lars came out of the tool shed and Curly out of the barn to see who had come into the yard. "Did they bring more of that good cheese?" Curly inquired.

The rest of the day's work was forgotten. The girls visited with Mary and played with Joanie, while Ricardo rode with Dan around the valley. His father, Juan didn't believe riding horses was necessary. You had a team for plowing or pulling a buckboard or wagon. Donkeys could carry your packs and could forge on the roughest areas. God gave man legs so he could lead the pack animal. The young Mexican enjoyed riding the bay Dan had saddled for him.

The following morning Dan walked part of the way to the mouth of the valley with Juan's children. When they stopped to say their goodbyes, Karla stood looking back toward the green valley.

"This must be what heaven looks like," she said.

"Next time we come, maybe our father will join us," Diana said.

Ricardo wrapped his hand around the lead donkey's halter rope. Smiling at Dan, he said, "I know mother would want to come, but she has the goats. I want to thank you for letting me ride the bay. Some day when I save enough money, I will come to talk to you about buying a horse."

With that, the three young Mexicans headed for home. Dan had tried to send something to their parents, but Ricardo insisted the things they brought were for the animal he had killed. Dan walked back toward the ranch house, hoping his daughter grew up with some of Juan's children's qualities.

CHAPTER THREE

Dan stopped by the corral and pitched some hay to the horses before returning to the ranch house. Curly and Lars were already gone to separate the cattle. The older animals would be driven to the western end of the valley while the younger ones would be kept closer to the ranch.

He tossed a couple handfuls of corn to the chickens. He saw Mary leaning on the door jamb of the ranch house. He waved to her and suddenly realized that she was hanging on to the jamb for support. Dropping the bag of corn, he ran toward the house.

"Mary! Mary, what's the matter!" he shouted.

Reaching the porch, she collapsed in his arms. He lowered her to the porch floor. "What is it?" he asked. His wife's face was ghostly white.

"My stomach, it hurts," Mary whispered, hardly able to speak.

Dan picked her up and carried her to their bed.

She felt hot. He turned to get some towels and water to bathe her forehead. Behind him, he heard the sound of retching. Mary was throwing up.

For the next hour he changed her sheets and bathed her with cool water. The stomach pain ran from the lower right to the back. He remembered that his cousin Zac's mother had died of a burst appendix. Finally, Mary slept. The vomiting had taken down her temperature.

Dan's mind raced as he tried figure out what he should do. They were days away from any doctors. If it was Mary's appendix, she would die without being taken to the doctor. If it was the grippe, she would most likely get better right here on the ranch.

The ranch owner made his decision. He would take her to Casper. The town had a doctor. If it was the grippe, Mary should be well when they got there. They could spend a couple days and then head back.

Dan rode the chestnut down the valley to find Curly or Lars. They could run the ranch until he got back, even if their stay was longer. Most of the winter supplies were in. The men could butcher a beef once it got cool enough.

He saw Curly pushing a small bunch of older cattle to the west. Dan fired a shot to get his attention. The cowhand abandoned the animals and rode to meet Dan.

"Mary is real sick," Dan blurted out. "I'm going to take her to Casper. You and Lars will have to take care of the ranch until we get back."

"She has been tired," Curly admitted. "I thought it was just the long hours during roundup."

"So did I," Dan said. "We're going to leave as quickly as we can. If we need to be gone more than a couple weeks, I'll send word to let you know."

With that, Dan wheeled the chestnut and galloped back to the house. It took just over an hour to get the things they would need together. Curly had followed him back and hitched the team to the wagon. Mary was still sleeping. He wrapped her in a blanket and carried her to the wagon. There was hay in the back for her to lay on.

She had awoken and was looking up at Dan. "Just give me a couple days in bed right here. I will be okay, Dan," she pleaded.

"If you would be alright here," Dan said, "then you will be the same in Casper. We will treat ourselves to a couple days in town, and then come back home."

Hurrying back into the ranch house, he picked the napping child up. Startled, Joanie began to cry. Trying to shush her, he closed and locked the door. He put the child next to Mary in the wagon.

Casper was two days by wagon. Dan couldn't take the shortcuts that riding a horse would allow. He took most of the melons and vegetables that the Torres kids had brought. While driving the wagon, Dan cut up one of the melons. The sweet taste of the white flesh was lost on him due to worry. Mary shook her head when he offered her some. "You have to eat something, Mary," he urged her.

Taking a slice, she took small bites, sharing it with little Joanie. By evening they were over halfway to Casper. Dan stopped at a grove of oak trees with a clear running stream. He stopped the wagon near past fire pits made by himself and others.

After getting a fire going and putting on a pot of water to heat, Dan unhitched the horses, watered them and gave them some corn before picketing them on some brown grass.

Mary sat on a windfall while her husband made soup. The campfire licked the sides of the blackened pot while Dan cut up some of the vegetables into the steaming water. He had taken the fresh chicken that his wife had been planning for the evening meal and cut it up into the boiling cook pot.

Dan heated water for coffee. He poured a cup of hot water and added tea leaves to it for Mary. He then added grounds to the coffee pot for himself. He watched as his wife sipped the tea. He was thankful that it was staying down. Much of the day, riding in the wagon, he had prayed that the Lord would get them through this crisis.

Joanie, unaware of the seriousness of her mother's condition, played at the campsite, picking up sticks and running to bring them to her father for the fire. Dan would thank her and take them. He would toss them into the fire. Then the youngster was off to find more.

Mary drank the broth from the soup. Dan broke up chicken and mashed some of the vegetables for the child to eat with a cup of water to drink. He wished that he had thought to take some of the canned milk for Joanie. While drinking his coffee, he would let the youngster have sips. Each time she would wrinkle her nose and shake her head at the taste of the bitter brew. Soon, Joanie would be back for another taste.

Dan made his wife and child a bed under the

wagon. It was parked close to the fire and offered some heat to temper the night's chill. He sat next to the wagon with a blanket around his shoulders. Dan kept feeding the fire throughout the night, dozing off and on. He listened to the groans of his wife as she tried to sleep.

After a quick breakfast of warmed soup, Dan hitched up the team and they were on their way. Mary insisted on sitting on the wagon seat with her husband. She said that the nausea was less when sitting up. They rode with Joanie between them.

As they approached the town they passed a man herding some sheep, some oil derricks, and two freight wagons. The railroad had brought business to the town of Casper. Oil, logs, coal, and beef were shipped out from the town. Supplies for the army and the inhabitants of Carbon County came in by train.

Dan stopped the wagon in front of the mercantile. The doctor had an office in the building next to the store. Angie Hartwick, the merchant's wife, was sweeping the front porch. Dan called out to her, "Mrs. Hartwick, Mary is ill. Can you watch our child while I take her to the doc's?"

The plump woman hurried over to the wagon still holding the broom. "Give me the little one. Do you want Bert to help you with Mary?"

Handing Joanie to the woman, he replied, "No, I can carry her. Thank you."

Helping Mary down from the wagon, he picked her up against her protests and carried her up the steps to the doctor's office.

Doctor Morgan had the door waiting open for him. "Heard you telling Angie that Mary was sick."

Pointing toward the back of his office, he said, "Set her down on the bed over there."

Dan lay his wife on the bed and turned to tell the doctor what was wrong. "Shush, I'll get the information from her." With that, he had Dan wait on a chair by the door. Pulling a curtain across the back, he began his examination.

For the next half-hour Dan sat on the uncomfortable, straight-backed chair and strained his ears to hear what was being said in the back. They spoke too quietly and he caught only a word here and there. One of the words he did hear was appendicitis. Twice, Mary groaned loudly, making it difficult for Dan to remain seated. Memories of Zac's mother Carroll crying with pain as she died haunted him.

At last the doctor came out from behind the curtain. The old white-haired medical man sat on a chair next to Dan and removed his spectacles. The expression on his face gave Dan very little hope.

"What . . . what did you find?" Dan asked, struggling to keep his voice even.

"It is the appendix," Dr. Morgan began. "I can't tell how far along it is. If it leaks, there is not much anyone can do."

Dan sat gripping his hat brim, his knuckles white. "You can operate and remove it before that happens, can't you, doc?"

Looking away, the elderly doctor said, "I can set bones, lance things, even remove a leg or arm if necessary." Looking back at Dan with sad eyes, the doctor continued. "I can't do what Mary needs. The closest place would be Cheyenne."

"Cheyenne . . .?" Dan gasped.

Dr. Morgan placed his hand on Dan's shoulder, "The train to Cheyenne leaves in just over an hour. You will be there by morning. They have fine surgeons that do this type of operation all the time."

Standing, the doctor led Dan to his wife. Mary was sitting on the edge of the bed, her face pale and fear in her eyes.

Dan helped his wife finish getting dressed. He forced a smile and said, "We are going to Cheyenne. After they fix you up, I am going to take you shopping for a brand-new dress and we will celebrate."

To himself he thought, *With God's help, we'll get there in time.*

CHAPTER FOUR

The next hour was a blur of activity. Mrs. Hartwick, being childless, was delighted to take care of Joanie for a few days until Dan could come back and get her. He expected to be back in a week or less. Dan had money in the Casper bank. He went and withdrew some to cover travel and medical expenses. Dr. Morgan made arrangements for train tickets and got Mary to the station, and Bert Hartwick took care of the wagon and team. They would be kept in his own stable behind the mercantile.

Breathless from running around, Dan made the station less than 10 minutes before the train's departure. Mary was already seated on the train. She had tears streaming down her face.

"Everything will be fine," Dan promised her.

"I should have stayed in Elkader instead of coming out west," she cried. "I have brought all this trouble on you. And . . . and I will never see my baby again." The tears turned to wracking sobs.

Dan was unprepared to face such open emotion. Awkwardly, he put his arm around his wife and held her. Mary buried her face in his chest and continued to weep.

"As soon as the surgery is over and the doctor says you are okay, I will come right back to Casper and get Joanie," Dan assured her. "Our baby will be back in your arms before you know it."

Suddenly, she began to vomit what little she had consumed the past day. Dan watched helplessly as the pungent liquid ran down the floorboard and under the seat in front of them. He was thankful when the porter came to their rescue with towels.

The train lurched forward, jostling the passengers as it moved out of the station. Mary, seated next to Dan, sagged heavily against him, too weak to remain upright. Exhausted from the lack of sleep the night before, he held his wife, sitting with his eyes closed.

Mary was unable to walk to the dining car and Dan could not leave her side. He explained this to the helpful porter and asked him to bring them two cups of clear soup. Dan doubted that his wife would be able to drink any, and if she did, it would probably come back up.

The rhythm of the train wheels on the tracks reminded him of the trip from Elkader to New Mexico with his cousins. They had answered an ad to work on a cattle drive. When the soup came, Mary drank just a little. She asked for water and once again, the porter got this for them.

Mary seemed to revive just a little and sat up on the seat. "I need to use the toilet," she whispered.

The two of them slowly walked to the back of the car. Mary was unable to stand up straight and leaned on Dan as they moved down the aisle. A single toilet was used by all passengers in the car. He helped her in and then stood outside waiting. A tap on the door let him know that she was done.

Once back at the seats, they tried to get some sleep. Dan closed his eyes and prayed for the strength to face the coming days. Each time the train stopped at a station, they were jolted awake to face the reality of their situation. It was still dark when the train pulled into Cheyenne.

The two of them sat alone in the Cheyenne train station waiting for the sun to come up. They made promises to each other, many of which were not in their power to keep. Mary talked about her family in Elkader. She talked about her parents coming to America through Canada, about aunts and uncles still in Europe. It seemed important for him to know this. It scared him that she did not believe she was going to survive the operation.

When daylight came, Dan heard a carriage approaching the station. The carriage was for hire and had brought a passenger to the train station. They were able to engage it to bring them to the hospital. As they rode, Dan watched the city slowly coming to life. The smell of breakfasts being made and coal-fired stoves warming the homes filled the air.

When they reached the hospital, the driver carried their bags into the building while Dan helped Mary. The antiseptic smell greeted them as they entered the waiting room. A woman in a dark dress and a white, lacy head cover sat behind a desk.

"Can I help you?" she asked.

Dan sat Mary in a chair near the desk and replied, "My wife is sick. The doctor in Casper told us it was appendicitis. It has been several days since it started."

Looking at the disheveled couple, she said, "It will be at least an hour before she can be seen. The doctors are making rounds right now. Please take a seat, and as soon as someone if free I will let you know."

Dan felt the anger rise as he stared at the lady behind the desk. He realized that there was no way she could fathom what he and Mary had been through the past three days, but the thought of having to wait another hour was the last straw.

Clenching his fists at his side, Dan turned to face the woman. Before he had a chance to speak a door behind him opened. Dan looked and a kindly looking man in a white coat had entered.

The man addressed the woman behind the desk, "Let me know when Henry Walls arrives."

"Yes, doctor," she replied.

He turned to leave when Dan spoke to him. "Please wait, my wife is very sick." The desperation in his voice stopped the medical man.

The doctor looked at Mary. The expression of shock crossed his face. He turned to the lady behind the desk and said, "Get some orderlies to take this woman back, right now."

"Her name is Mary . . ." Dan said as the man in the white coat disappeared through the door.

Mary was quickly taken back, leaving Dan

alone in the waiting room with only the woman behind the desk for company.

"My name is Anna Johnson," the woman said. "I am sorry. I didn't realize how sick your wife was."

"Dan August, is my name," he said. "My wife . . ."

Anna Johnson interrupted him, "Doctor Walters is one of our best. You wife Mary is in good hands."

Miss Johnson disappeared for a few minutes and returned with a cup of hot coffee for Dan. "The doctor will be out shortly to give you an update."

Dan was just finishing the coffee when Dr. Walters came back. "Your wife is being prepped for the operation. She is weak. We are getting liquids into her. Miss Johnson can show you to a room where you can wait. I will talk to you when we're finished."

Dan sat in a pale green room with large, curtain less windows. He noticed that it was raining outside. After a while two men came in, and later a woman. They all sat quietly with their own thoughts and worries. A man entered, wearing a white, blood-stained coat. He called one of the waiting gentlemen over. Dan heard a gasp from the gentleman.

The man was led out of the room. It was obvious that whoever he was waiting for had not done well. Dan did not need to witness the man being told. He prayed that when the doctor came to talk to him the news was better.

He was sitting in a chair with his eyes closed and his head tilted back, almost asleep, when the sound of a door opening brought him upright. It was Dr.

Walters. A smile on the doctor's face sent a wave of relief over Dan.

"Are you hungry, Mr. August?" the doctor asked him. Without waiting for an answer, he said, "Let's go to the dining room."

Dan suddenly realized that it was noon and he hadn't eaten since the broth last night. He was starved. The dining room was small and apparently set up for the doctors only. There were sweet breads, sandwiches, a pitcher of water, and coffee on the sideboard.

The lack of urgency for Dr. Walters to start talking with him told Dan that the surgery had to have gone okay. He helped himself to a roast beef sandwich and a cup of coffee, then joined the doctor at one of the small square tables.

Dan let the sandwich sit while he waited for the doctor to start talking. Finally, Dr. Walters was ready. "First, Mr. August, the surgery went well. Your wife must have had an angel sitting on her shoulder. She had an abscessed appendix. It created scar tissue that formed a wall and prevented the infection from the appendix from getting into the rest of her body. Now, that is the good news," the doctor said. "Now for the not-so-good. Your wife is very weak and might still be in danger. Her recovery will take several months."

Dan's mind raced as he listened. "We have a child, doctor," he said. "I have to go to Casper to get her."

"I would wait a couple days, maybe a week before doing so. Then, with help, the child could be beneficial to your wife getting well," Dr. Walters advised. "Now eat up, help yourself to another if you would like."

An hour later, Dan sat by his wife's bedside. The room had several beds, most of them empty. Mary was groggy and kept dozing off. The doctor had warned him of this and that she might not even remember his visit tomorrow.

After staying for a while, a nurse came over and told him that he would have to leave. He could come back at 6 p.m. that evening. Dan found their bags and went out to find a hotel. Two blocks away there was a boarding house run by two sisters, Clara and Martha. He explained his situation and was told that there was a room available. Dan paid $7 for the first week. Breakfast was included in the price.

The room was on the first floor. It had a double bed, a chair, and a side table. The window faced the street. There was a bathroom down the hall with water for washing supplied by a tank on the second floor. There were places in Cheyenne that already had electric lights powered by batteries, but the boarding house still used kerosene lamps.

Dan stored the bags under the bed and left the boarding house to walk around the town. It had grown over the past five years since he had last been here. He left his gun in the carpet bag, remembering that carrying firearms was against the town ordinance. It had been made clearly evident by Sheriff Kent on a previous visit.

He wondered if a hostler named Carlos was still around town. The cousins had first met him in St. Paul and then again here in Cheyenne. Dan remembered the man's bushy eyebrows, salt and pepper hair, and the broad shoulders showing years of hard work. The livery that he had worked at was on the other side of Cheyenne. Dan decided to look Carlos up later in the week.

That evening, Mary was more alert. She did not remember his earlier visit. Truth was, she remembered little from the time they had left the train station. Dan could only imagine how much pain she had been in. Her face was still pale and her eyes were hollowed out, with dark rings around them. She had a bulky bandage on her right side.

Dan told her about the boarding house he had gotten a room in and about the doctor sharing a meal with him. The hospital had Mary on thin soup. She had been able to eat and keep it down. She asked about Joanie. Dan promised to go pick the baby up as soon as possible. He didn't tell her, but he wanted to wait until Dr. Walsh told him that Mary was out of immediate danger.

The week passed slowly. He was only allowed to visit Mary twice a day for an hour each time. The rest of the time he walked around the town. On the third day, he found the livery stable. Walking in, he recognized his bushy friend.

"Carlos, it has been too long," Dan called to him.

The old man hesitated a moment and then a broad smile spread across his face. "Is it Vic, or Dan?"

"It's Dan, you old codger."

"Well, hell," he said, "what brings you to Cheyenne?"

Dan quickly brought his old friend up to date. Carlos shook his head. "Lordy, you and the Missus sure were lucky."

"We're not out of the woods yet," Dan said, "but each day things get better."

Dan sat in the hostler's office and drank coffee. It was the most comfortable he had been since leaving the ranch.

At the end of the week, Dr. Walsh said Mary needed another two to three weeks in the hospital before transferring to a place where she could rest and regain her strength. Dan mentioned the boarding house as a place to go after the hospital. The doctor was familiar with the place and agreed that it would be good. It turned out that Martha knew of a young girl who could watch the baby while Dan visited the hospital.

Dan took the train back to Casper to pick up little Joanie, even though they wouldn't allow Mary to see the child for another week at the earliest. The train arrived in Casper in late afternoon. While leaving the station, Dan ran into J.P. Burdick, the cattle buyer who had recommended John Hurley.

"How did my boy work out for you?" J.P. called out, smiling broadly.

Shaking the outstretched hand, Dan replied, "He was a top hand, but had a bit of a temper."

"Many a good man has those traits," the cattle buyer admitted.

"I hate to rush, but I got to pick up my youngster at Hartwick's," Dan apologized.

"I had heard your wife was ill," J.P. said. "I hope she is better."

"It will take time, but I think she will be fine."

Before J.P. could reply, Dan nodded and headed up the street.

As he stepped onto the porch, Dan heard the squeal from little Joanie. Stepping inside the store, he saw her sitting on the counter, sucking on a peppermint stick. When the youngster saw her father, she reached out for him to pick her up.

The Hartwicks were happy to learn that Mary was on the mend. They offered to let the family stay with them in Casper while Mary regained her strength.

Dan thanked Angie and Bert for all of their help. He asked them to send word to the ranch, if anyone was going that way, to let Curly and Lars know that it could be a few months before he would be back.

The train station was busy when Dan entered. Standing in line, he looked around the crowd. Most were men traveling alone. One tired man sitting next to two leather bags looked like a drummer. He wondered what it must be like traveling from town to town, seldom seeing your family.

After purchasing the ticket, Dan carried Joanie to a bench away from the rest of the crowd. She climbed up and down from the bench, then would run a few steps away and then back to her father. Dan wished that he could be young again, without a care in the world.

The station manager called out that it was time to board. Dan picked up the baby and her stuff. The Hartwicks had been very generous with gifts. Loaded with luggage and the child, he headed for the train. He was anxious to get back to Cheyenne and check on Mary.

The trip took 12 hours and they arrived early

the next morning. After dropping Joanie's things off at the boarding house, Dan decided that he would try and see if Mary could see the baby. He carried her into the hospital and stopped in front of Miss Johnson's desk.

"This is our daughter, Joanie. I was wondering if there was any way Mary could see her?" he asked.

"I'm sorry, Mr. August," she apologized. "The hospital policy does not allow children to visit."

"Maybe for just a moment? I am sure it would help her recovery," Dan said, trying to sway the stern woman.

He wasn't ready to give up and leave. Setting Joanie on one of the waiting room chairs, he sat next to her. He hoped that the doctor would come in and okay the visit.

"Mr. August," Miss Johnson said. "I need to leave for a bit. If someone comes in, could you let them know that I'll be right back?"

Without waiting for an answer, the woman put on her shawl and left the hospital. For a moment, Dan sat wondering what was so urgent that took her away. Then he realized that he was in charge.

"Time for new rules," he told little Joanie.

Picking his daughter up, he took her to the back to see her mother. Mary's face lit up when she saw Dan and the baby walking towards her. Joanie wanted her mother to take her, but Dan knew that it could injure the incision area. Setting the child gently next to her mother, Dan let them visit. He could have sworn that the hollowness of her eyes disappeared right in front of him when Mary smiled from ear-to-ear.

After a short visit, Dan told Mary that he'd best get the youngster out before Anna Johnson returned.

"Thank you for bringing her in, Dan," Mary told him. With a tear in her eye, she gave the baby another kiss before they left.

Dan returned to the seat he had been sitting on. Within a minute, Miss Johnson returned. Hanging her shawl on the back of her chair, she turned to Dan. "Thank you for watching the front for me. Maybe you could do so again soon."

"Thank you, thank you very much. I will," he said. Then, scooping Joanie up, he left the hospital.

Holding the baby close he said, "That Miss Johnson is a very nice lady."

* **

For the next two weeks the kind Miss Johnson had Dan watch the lobby when he had Joanie with him. While Mary remained weak and pale, her attitude was very good. Dr. Walsh told him that the surgery area was almost healed and now it was a matter of time for her strength to return.

Dan visited Carlos most days. Several times he had borrowed a horse and explored the countryside around Cheyenne. He would wear the Colt .44 and practice. Once, a partridge was flushed. He'd drawn and fired, knocking it out of the air.

The leaves were in full color. Soon, snow would be blowing across the open plain. Dan had borrowed a sorrel and was returning to the livery. He removed the gun belt and put it into a bag hanging from the saddle horn before entering the city.

He saw a man talking with Carlos, whom he recognized as Sheriff Kent. Swinging down from the horse in front of the livery, Dan led the animal toward the door. Carlos and the sheriff followed him into the livery. Carlos poured the lawman a cup of coffee while Dan removed the saddle and groomed the horse.

Finishing up, he helped himself to some coffee. The sheriff tilted his flat-brimmed hat back and looked at the bag Dan was carrying. "I imagine you got a revolver in that bag."

"As a matter a fact, I do," Dan admitted.

"And no doubt you were planning on heading straight to my office to drop it off," Sheriff Kent said.

Dan stared at the stern-faced lawman without answering. He was remembering six years ago, when one of the Alan brothers had shot at him. The only weapon they'd had was the derringer Vic was carrying. The sheriff had shown up and taken the derringer from them, leaving the three cousins defenseless.

Gripping the bag tighter, the ranch owner said, "It is my revolver and I will be damned if I am going to turn it over to you."

"Then there is only one thing I can do," Sheriff Kent concluded.

Dan waited for the verdict. He noticed that Carlos was smiling. The sheriff adjusted his gun belt and took a deep breath. "I will have to deputize you or arrest you."

Carlos laughed, "It's my fault that the sheriff is here. He needs three deputies and one of them got married and moved away. He had mentioned it to me. I knew you were going to be in town for a while and would make a damn fine deputy."

Dan shook his head no. "I couldn't do the job. I have the baby to take care of and Mary needs me. Not only that, I will be going back to my ranch soon."

"Well, either way, stop by the office. Bring me your weapon, or pick up your badge." Confident that he was in control, the white-haired sheriff left the livery.

Carlos picked up the coffee pot and poured the remaining brew into their cups. "You might want to consider that deputy position," the hostler recommended.

"I don't like that man," Dan replied.

"Well, you are wrong about your opinion of the sheriff," Carlos said. "He is a good and fair man. Cheyenne was a dangerous cow town before he came. I remember when he ordered you and your cousins to take the fight with the Alans out of town. Gun play in the streets get innocent people killed. You might not have agreed with him, but the folks pay him to keep the town quiet."

Dan knew that he had too much time on his hands in Cheyenne. Curly and Lars could take care of the ranch. The hardest winter work was cutting wood to keep warm. With the cattle in the valley, they would be easy to keep an eye on. Soon, Mary would be moving to the boarding house. The deputy job would help pay for their room.

"Well, Carlos. I am not going to give up my gun, so I have no choice. I will tell the sheriff that I'll take the job. He'll have to understand that if Mary improves sooner than expected, I will be heading back to the valley."

Dan glanced down the street. The sheriff had just gone inside. As he walked toward the jail, Dan thought about the jobs he'd had over the years. Being a deputy would be a new experience. At least he would be able to wear the Colt in town.

Sheriff Kent was sitting behind a scarred oak desk. The office smelled of pipe tobacco. A corn cob pipe sat in a chipped bowl on the desk. Along the wall to the left, a rack held three rifles and two double-barrel shotguns. Several gun belts hung from pegs behind the desk. The barred cells were off a hall to the back.

"Come to bring me your revolver?" the sheriff asked.

Dan removed the gun belt from the bag and slung it around his hips. Fastening the buckle, he adjusted the Colt in its holster. He looked at Sheriff Kent. The lawman had his hand on a gun laying on the desk.

"You won't need that, sheriff," Dan said. "I'm here to get the badge."

Reaching into his desk, Sheriff Kent took out a badge and tossed it to his new deputy. "Wearing this badge means you will uphold and enforce the laws of Cheyenne. And, most important, you will follow my orders without question."

"That should not be a problem. You said there were two other deputies. When do I meet them?" Dan asked.

"They're out tracking a hombre that shot the

dealer at the Cattlemen's Saloon," Kent said.

The sheriff asked Dan to make the rounds with him. They walked past the stately brick and stone homes of the wealthy cattlemen. The street was surfaced with paving bricks. Dan was struck by the difference between all of this and the part of town where the cow hands stayed. Or for that matter, the rest of Wyoming.

Several blocks later, they crossed the tracks and turned down a dusty street lined with saloons and brothels. There was noisy music and the raucous laughter of the patrons. In the distance he could see the cattle pens. They were now in the world of the cowboys.

The sheriff took his time, stopping at each establishment and checking the patrons. They collected three gun belts, which Dan carried over his shoulder. Dusk was settling in. The front of the businesses were lit by smoky lanterns while the streets were dark, giving seclusion for those, good or bad, who didn't want to be seen.

At the cattle pens, they crossed the tracks again and headed back uptown. Dan and Sheriff Kent walked on the well-lit, paved street, isolated from the world of the cowboys. The sheriff stopped in front of an impressive dwelling with columns supporting a porch that was as large as Dan's home back in the valley.

"I brought you here to meet Jonas Wallace," the lawman said.

Adjusting the Colt on his hip, Dan looked up at the enormous house. "Are we here to arrest or help this man Wallace?"

"To help," the sheriff laughed. "We're not here because Mr. Wallace has done something wrong, quite the contrary. Jonas Wallace has been wronged."

"Before we go in, I better bring you up to date. Wallace's son has been kidnapped. I was talking about it with Carlos, and he recommended that I make you a deputy to help get him back."

Dan envisioned what Mr. Wallace must be feeling. If his daughter Joanie was taken, he would stop at nothing to get her back. He tilted his hat back and turned to Sheriff Kent. "How old is the boy?"

The lawman cleared his throat before speaking. "Well, I figure the boy is about 17. Yes, I am sure of it."

Dan's jaw dropped. "The boy is 17? Crying out loud, he is a man, not a boy."

"I don't disagree, Dan. But none the less, the young man was taken against his will," the sheriff said.

The sheriff's earlier words suddenly dawned on Dan. "What did you mean, Carlos said you should get me? I don't know nothing about kidnapping. That is, if it was kidnapping. Maybe the boy is ready to be on his own?"

A look of displeasure crossed the lawman's face. As quickly as it came, it disappeared. "The boy is being held for ransom. The men that took him are asking for $15,000 for the kid's safe return."

Still confused as to why this would be his problem, Dan asked, "Wouldn't your other deputies, or even you, be able to take care of this? By the looks of this house, that sum of money shouldn't be a problem for them to pay to assure getting the boy back."

Now Dan could tell that he had strained the patience of Sheriff Kent. The street light shined in the red face and tight jaws of the man.

Taking a deep breath, the lawman explained, "You may be right. This might not be a job for you and they might be best served by paying the ransom. The problem is, the boy may have gone voluntarily. He was seen with Jon Kidman the night he went missing."

"Would that be Kid Jonny?" Dan asked, recognizing the name.

"Yes it would. It is said he has killed a dozen men. A year ago, it was suspected that he lured a young woman named Honey from Medicine Bow. Her father had railroad money. Everyone figured she went willingly, until the request for ransom came in. At that point it made no difference if Honey went or was taken."

The sheriff paused as though reliving a painful memory. Finally, he continued. "Money was sent to the kidnapper by messenger as requested. Later, the man carrying the ransom was found shot in the back and there has been no knowledge of her whereabouts."

Looking at Dan with a drawn, face he said, "It is believed she is dead somewhere in the Dakotas. The Kid was suspected of taking her, but there was no proof." Clearing his throat again, he added, "She was my brother's daughter."

"I am sorry for your brother's and your loss. I take it you want me to carry the ransom for the boy?" Dan asked.

Nodding, the sheriff looked at the door.

"Carlos figured if anyone can get the boy back without taking a bullet, it would be you."

"Before we go in, I want you to understand," Dan said, "that I am in Cheyenne with a sick wife and a child that needs taking care of. Truth is, I took the badge from you tonight so I wouldn't have to turn in my gun. By going in with you, it doesn't mean I will take the money for the boy."

"Understood," the sheriff said. "Now, don't get the wrong impression by the Wallace's house here. Jonas struggled and fought to build his ranch. Everything he has, he earned with sweat and blood."

Dan set the gun belts down on the porch as the two men walked up to the door. It opened for them before they could knock. A stocky, white-haired man stood just inside. "Come on in, Bernard," he said in a booming voice. "I was wondering if you were stopping or not." Mr. Wallace turned, motioning them to follow.

"Bernard?" Dan asked.

Snorting, the lawman said, "Sheriff Kent to you."

They were led into a large office off the foyer. Jonas Wallace sat on a stuffed leather chair and pointed to two comfortable-looking chairs across from him. "I was just about to have a cigar and brandy after dinner. Please join me."

The words were barely out of his mouth when a slightly built, elderly Chinaman came into the room carrying a tray with a decanter of brandy, glasses, and a box of cigars. He set it down on a side table, nodded at Jonas, and left.

Dan noticed as the rancher poured the brandy that he had little use of his right arm. The shoulder on that side was lower than the left. Jonas apologized for taking so long to serve the brandy. "I took an arrow in the shoulder years ago. Chen says I should let him serve the brandy, but when a man can't pour his own drink, it is time to give it up."

Dan sat quietly sipping the brandy and smoking his cigar. Both were the best he could remember having. The sheriff and the rancher made some small talk about the condition of the herds and what was expected the coming winter.

Finally, Jonas Wallace addressed Dan. "Did Bernard tell you about my boy?"

"Yes, he did," Dan acknowledged. "I am very sorry about the taking of your son."

"I thank you for your concerns," Jonas said, his stiff stature seeming to fall a bit. "I was too busy when I started ranching to have time to take a wife and start a family. I met Stella here in Cheyenne. She had come from the east and was teaching school. When I was in Cheyenne I would try and get to church. I met her at one of the picnics and I guess it was love the first time I saw her."

"We were married and moved to the ranch. Our boy, Jonas, we called him Junior, was born. He meant everything to Stella. Cholera took her from me when Junior was only five. I threw myself into building the ranch to help forget what I had lost and kind of left it up to others to raise the boy."

"Like most boys, he got into trouble now and then. I must admit, I made excuses for him. Then I got word that he was missing and had been seen running with Kid Jonny. At first we feared he had taken up and gone with the Kid and his crew. Then we got a note demanding money. The boy had been gone for almost a month."

"Was the note from the Kid?" Dan asked.

"It wasn't signed," Mr. Wallace said. "At first I thought it was someone trying to make some easy money. Someone that didn't even know where the boy was. I talked with Bernard and he told me about his niece."

"The note arrived two days ago," Sheriff Kent said. "I was planning on looking for a hired gun or bounty hunter to go find the boy, then Carlos suggested you."

Feeling a sudden burn of anger, Dan replied, "If you're looking for a hired gun, I am sure as hell not your man. I have a ranch and family." Setting the drink and cigar down, he stood up to leave.

"Sit back down, for Christ's sake," the sheriff said. "I made you a deputy and you will make a hell of a lot less than a hired gun. I chose you because you came highly recommended as a good and honest man."

Feeling awkward now, Dan sat back in the chair and tossed down the rest of the brandy he had been sipping.

Mr. Wallace got up and refilled his guests' glasses. Sitting heavily in the overstuffed chair, he said, "The boy is the only thing I have left of Stella. He has her eyes and smile. Unfortunately, the rest of him is more like me."

Sheriff Kent took a long drag on his cigar before leaning forward in his chair and saying, "Jonas here wants you to take the ransom to Ardmore in the Dakotas. You would be gone two weeks at the most."

"My wife and child need me in Cheyenne," Dan said. "I wish that I could help you, but I don't see how I can."

"I will open my home to your family. I will make sure your wife gets the best care possible," Mr. Wallace offered.

Sheriff Kent stood and hitched up his pants. "I think we need to give Dan the night to think it over. However he decides, I will have someone here in the morning to bring the ransom."

The two men were escorted to the front door by Jonas Wallace. Dan noticed that the man had lost some of the self-assurance that was evident when they arrived. Without talking, Dan and Sheriff Kent walked back to the office. The sheriff sat down behind his desk while Dan hung the guns on the pegs. Deep in thought, the sheriff ignored his new deputy.

After a few moments, Dan removed the badge and his gun belt and placed them on the desk. Seeing them, the sheriff looked up in surprise. "What the hell is this?"

"I assumed when I didn't say yes to bringing the ransom, I no longer had the deputy job."

"Damn it, man," the sheriff blustered. "I hired you because I need a good man to help me. Get your stuff off my desk and put them back on."

Dan picked up his gun belt and badge. He sat on a bench along the wall near the desk, placing the items on his lap. "Who are you going to send with the ransom?" he inquired.

"I will take the money. You will stay here and watch over the office. My other deputies, Topper and Peck, know their job, but aren't leaders. You'll have no problem with them accepting you as the acting sheriff," the lawman said. "I will be leaving early in the morning. Meet me at 9:00 a.m. in front of Jonas'. I will give you the keys to this place. Now, you best head back for the boarding house and get some sleep."

Leaving the office, Dan went down the alley, taking a shortcut to the boarding house. He checked on his sleeping daughter before pulling off his boots and sitting on the edge of his bed. The face of Jonas Wallace kept flashing before his eyes. He could hear the even breathing of Joanie.

Dan couldn't fathom the pain the rancher must be feeling knowing that his son's life hung in the balance. He thought of the sheriff's niece. The demand had been met, yet her whereabouts were still unknown.

Sunrise found Dan already awake. He dressed quickly before checking on Joanie. Clara was already in the kitchen, mixing up a batch of biscuits. She pointed to the coffee pot on the back of the stove. "Help yourself to a cup. If you have to leave before breakfast, I can make you something to take with you."

He left the boarding house chewing on a thick ham sandwich. The sun was still low in the eastern sky, casting long shadows as he walked toward the hospital. The waiting area was empty when he arrived, so he went straight into the ward to talk with Mary.

CHAPTER FIVE

The sheriff was putting his bedroll and saddle bags on a long-legged black with a white blaze on its forehead when he paused, hearing footsteps behind him. Turning, he saw Dan wearing a fleece-lined coat to ward off the morning chill. He was carrying his gear for traveling.

"Is that the horse I will be using to ride to Ardmore?" the deputy asked.

"It is," Sheriff Kent answered. "It is one of the fastest horses Jonas has."

"Good," Dan said. "Now get your stuff off it so I can get ready to ride."

Smiling, the sheriff pulled his saddle bags and blanket roll off the horse. "You had me scared. I'd bet Jonas $10 that you would go."

"Well, Bernard," Dan said, smiling, "the town needs you here more than me. And, to be truthful, Mary will be much better off at Mr. Wallace's house than in the boarding house."

"I am sure you meant to say Sheriff Kent," the

white-haired lawman said, pretending to frown. "I agree with you about your wife."

The next couple hours were busy making arrangements to have Mary and little Joanie moved and filling Dan in on the ransom drop arrangements. He was to stop at the general store in Ardmore and pick up a letter addressed to Jonas Wallace. In the letter would be instructions for the exchange.

Dan sat near Mary in the hospital, with Joanie on his lap. He could see the worry on his wife's face. "I promise that I won't take any chances. In the Dakotas, my badge doesn't have any authority. My job won't be to arrest those that took the boy. I will just be bringing them the money."

"I still think he could have sent someone else. It isn't your responsibility to go," she said with tears in her eyes.

"Tomorrow, Dr. Walters will have you brought to the Wallace home and Clara from the boarding house will bring this here little one to you," he said, tickling Joanie and making her squeal.

It was noon before Dan rode out of Cheyenne. The black had a smooth gait. Sitting square in the saddle, Dan looked to the northeast. He hadn't told Mary about Sheriff Kent's niece. For all he knew, the men who had Jonas boy were totally different. Then again, if it was Kid Jonny, all bets of a smooth exchange were off.

Dan carried the Winchester in the scabbard of the saddle. On his hip rested his trusty Colt. Under his blue woolen shirt, he had a money belt with the ransom. The bills made the thick belt a little cumbersome, but he didn't want the money left out of his reach at any time.

It was the first week of October. Today the sky was clear and blue. The sunshine warmed his back as he rode. Winding rivers and streams could be traced across the plain by the trees and brush that grew alongside. The trees had few brown leaves left on them. "Damn near stick season," he said, rubbing the black's neck.

The open plain appeared to be empty of other travelers, but Dan knew better. An army of trouble makers could hide in the dips and valleys of the rolling grasslands. Dan could not afford to be careless on this trip. The money he carried was a sum many would kill for. Many people in Cheyenne knew of the disappearance of Junior Wallace. He was sure that the word was out that a ransom was requested and would be paid.

He rode well after dark, hoping to reach the Little Horse Creek. The constant wind blowing across the plain had Dan chilled to the bone by the time he reached the creek. Collecting some kindling, he started a fire before stripping the gear from the black. Putting water on to heat for coffee, he then pulled the saddle off the horse. Picketing the horse near the camp, he huddled next to the fire for the warmth.

Bushed from the long day, Dan crawled under his blankets right after a meal of biscuits with cheese and coffee. The crisp night air made the hunters of the night more active. The high-pitched cries of the coyotes split the night as they closed in on prey. The lonely howls of wolves and the hoot of an owl joined in the nocturnal sounds.

The sleeping man was unaware of the sounds.

His Colt was within reach under his saddle and the rifle under the edge of his blanket. The glowing coals of his fire reflected off the relaxed features of his face.

Dan awoke to heavy frost. The grass on the plains was white and crisp. The breath from the black came out in frozen clouds. He took the black down to the creek. While the horse drank, he filled his canteen with fresh water. Washing the sleep off his face with the brisk water, he returned to his camp, tying the black to a tag alder.

After starting the fire, he added some more water to last night's coffee grounds. Selecting a green branch, he poked it through two biscuits and held them over the fire to warm them up. Rinsing the coffee pot and his tin cup at the creek, Dan dipped the cup in and drank, washing the taste of the unsatisfying morning coffee out of his mouth.

The black was eager to be off. Dan kept to the lower areas along the creek. It was noon when he reached Horse Creek. Stopping, he loosened the horse's cinch and let it have a breather while he relieved himself and chewed on a piece of elk jerky.

A flash of light to the south caught his attention. The plain rose in that direction. As he slowly chewed the jerky, Dan watched. Again, he saw a flash of light. Someone was traveling across the rolling grass land. Dan wondered if his fellow traveler was also heading north.

While he had seen the flashes of light, he didn't catch sight of the traveler. Anxious to continue, Dan tightened the black's cinch and continued at a trot. Clouds began to come in from the northwest. The wind was cooler. He turned the collar of his sheepskin coat up to protect his neck.

That night, Dan camped away from Horse Creek. He kept his fire small and ate jerky broth and coffee. With the darkness to hide him, he climbed to a rise and sat near a gnarled pine tree. Digging in his coat pocket, he took out some wild plums he had picked near the creek. He sat chewing the tart fruit while he watched. The flicker of a campfire caught his eye.

Dan climbed into his blankets that night knowing that he wasn't alone on the plain. Whether or not the fellow traveler was a danger was uncertain, but he would have to continue watching for him. He had spread his bedroll away from the campfire in case unwanted company came prowling. Unable to sleep with the money belt around his waist, he kept it close to him under his blankets.

There were no additional sightings of the mysterious rider. He did pass a wagon loaded with supplies heading for a line camp. He ate his noon meal with them, accepting their offer of canned beans and cornbread. Wishing them well, he continued toward the town of Torrington.

It was said a man from Connecticut had named the Wyoming town after the place where he had grown up. It was a stop for the Chicago, Burlington and Quincy Railroad to take on water and coal. The town had grown to several businesses and a post office.

Dan arrived in Torrington in mid-afternoon. It was too early to quit for the night. He stopped at the livery to have them brush the black and give it some grain while he went into a saloon for a drink. The establishment had several tables for card playing.

There was a stage on the west side of the room for entertainment, and a long bar adorned with brass hardware on the south wall. A large mirror was hung over the back bar.

Walking across the sawdust-covered plank floor, Dan stepped up to the bar. There were several customers already having drinks or playing cards. Dan ordered a rye, then leaning with his back to the bar, he watched the patrons. It was a cool, cloudy day and the rye warmed him. He finished the drink and ordered another. There was bread, cheese and ham sliced at the end of the bar for the customers. Before leaving he made himself a sandwich.

Dan chewed on the sandwich as he walked back to get his horse. The black was tied to the rail near the livery. He stuffed the last bite of bread and meat into his mouth and found the hostler. He paid him for taking care of the horse. Before swinging into the saddle he asked the man, "Have you noticed any strangers come through town the last couple days?"

The bewhiskered old man spat a stream of tobacco juice on a post near the building and gave Dan a wide, toothless smile. "Well, you are a stranger. I see'd you."

Smiling at the comical old man, Dan asked, "Have there been any others than me?"

"A fellow came in about two hours ago riding a mustang. He, had been pushing the animal pretty good. Had a shoe come loose and needed the smithy," the hostler said. "Course, he ain't quite a stranger. Been around town for a couple, maybe three weeks."

"Where is the smithy?" Dan asked.

"On the street behind here," the old man said,

pointing over his shoulder.

"Has Kid Jonny been around Torrington?" Dan inquired.

The smile left the old hostler's face. "You'll find him in the Dakotas. He a friend of yours?"

"No," he assured the hostler. Showing him the badge under his coat, Dan said, "I have some questions for him."

Shaking his head, the hostler said, "You best be careful how you ask the questions. He'd shoot you without blinking an eye."

"I'll keep your warning in mind."

With concern on his whiskered face, the hostler cautioned, "I heard Doc Middleton was the law up in Ardmore. Called himself Texas Jack at one time. Watch yourself with him also."

"My badge is no good out of Wyoming," Dan said. "I have heard of Middleton. My hope is to spend little time in Ardmore."

Dan had already spent too much time in Torrington. He swung onto the black. Looking down at the old man, he said, "Hope to see you when I come back this way. If anyone should ask, I would appreciate you not mentioning my coming through."

Without answering, the old hostler turned and headed back into the livery. Dan rode past the smithy behind the building and saw the blacksmith working on the mustang's shoe. He did not recognize the horse or its brand. He did notice the silver trim on the Spanish saddle.

Following the railroad tracks for a distance, Dan then turned north. He planned to be in Harrison,

Nebraska by the next evening. He would spend the night there before making contact with the kidnappers. It would be a day's ride from Ardmore and away from anyone watching.

After a short night's sleep and a long day of riding, he arrived in Harrison. The town looked dreary in the overcast afternoon. He passed the depot with a prominent sign saying *Fremont, Elkhorn, & Missouri Valley Railroad*. Down the muddy street he saw a two story hotel called the Harrison House. Dan had ridden the last three hours in a cold rain. His slicker had offered some protection from the weather. He stopped in front of the hotel and pulled his saddle bags off the horse.

The clerk pushed the registry log toward the dripping customer and turned to get a skeleton key for the room. Turning back, he said, "The room is at the top of the stairs. We offer a breakfast from 6 until 8 in the morning. That will be ten bits per day in advance."

Dan paid, and asked about accommodations for his horse. The clerk put the money in a drawer under the counter and then answered, "There is a barn in the back with a couple empty stalls. No charge if you take care of the animal, or four bits per day if we take care of it."

Dropping the saddle bags off in the room, Dan went down to take care of the black. The mud alongside the hotel created sucking sounds with each step as he led the horse toward the barn. Two of the eight stalls in the barn were occupied. The barn was clean, with fresh bedding in the empty stalls.

He would have to wait for the black to dry off before he could brush it. While he pitched hay into the stall for the horse, it snorted and rubbed against the side. Glancing around, Dan saw some oats and a nose bag. He put some grain into it for the black and let it eat while he dried and cleaned the saddle.

It was dark when he finished taking care of the horse. Dan stopped briefly in the outhouse before going back to his room. Knocking as much mud off his boots as possible, he crossed the lobby with his rain slicker over one arm and the Winchester cradled in the other. The clerk was eating his supper behind the counter.

Entering his room, he leaned the rifle next to the door and dropped the slicker and hat at the end of the bed. There was a cast iron grill in the floor to allow the heat from the stove on the first floor to rise, warming the room. It wasn't doing the job, so he kept his coat on. The room had a single bed, a sideboard with a basin and pitcher, and a stand next to the bed with a kerosene lamp. The window facing the street had crisp white curtains.

The hotel didn't offer an evening meal. Dan had noticed a small café next to the depot. Glancing out the window, he saw that the rain had stopped. The café was run by Ma Harper. The plump woman welcomed him with a broad smile.

"I got beef stew tonight," she said. "If that don't fill ya, I still have some apple pie."

Dan took a seat and was soon enjoying the hardy beef stew. It was served with a cold mug of hard cider. Pie and hot coffee topped off the meal. He sat finishing his cup while thinking about his next move. Ardmore was only 30 miles from Harrison.

He figured that someone would be watching

the general store for the person who picked up the letter. All strangers in town would be suspect. He figured to make the Harrison Hotel his point of operation. Once he got Junior, they could leave by train. It would be safer than the open plain.

There were large snowflakes falling as he walked back to the hotel. Lights from the late night businesses made the flakes look like diamonds floating down from the heavens. The night's chill stiffened the mud on the streets, making walking easier.

Dan noticed that some of the room doors were open to allow more heat in from the first floor stove. He entered his room and was greeted by the nippy air. Having the money with him, he didn't dare leave his door ajar. Removing his boots, and gun belt, he lay on the bed fully dressed and with his coat on. With the help of the blanket, he was warm enough to sleep.

He awoke to sun streaming through the frosted window. Rising from the bed, he peered out the window. It was Sunday and the snow-covered town was quiet. There was a single set of tracks in the fresh snow on the street. He went to the sideboard. A layer of ice covered the water pitcher. Dan could hear somebody downstairs putting wood into the stove.

After pulling his stiff, cold boots on, he left the room to search out the warmth of the stove and some breakfast. The rising heat hit Dan as he descended the stairs. There was a pot of coffee on the potbelly stove. Pouring himself a steaming cup, he sat at one of the tables next to the kitchen and listened to the sounds of the food being prepared.

The grandfather clock in the lobby told him that it was 7:30 a.m. as he left the hotel. He headed back toward the barn to get the black. The sun had started melting the snow clinging to the buildings. There was the sound of water dripping as he walked on the frozen clods of mud alongside the hotel.

He carried his rifle cradled in his left arm. The Colt .44 was in its holster. The sheepskin coat hung over the revolver, to protect it from the weather. He planned to get the rest of his gear after saddling the horse. As Dan passed the outhouse between the barn and the hotel, something struck him on the lower back followed by the sound of a gunshot.

The impact knocked the wind out of him and forced Dan headlong, with him striking his chin on the frozen mud. Dan struggled to regain his breath. He realized that he had been shot in the back. Running footsteps came toward the fallen rancher. Rough hands rolled him over and began to rip open his coat. Dan's arms flailed, trying to fend off the attacker.

The person bending over him wore a wide sombrero, which shadowed his features. Dan could feel the hot breath of the man as he tore open the green shirt, popping its buttons. The man was after the money belt. As the money belt was being pulled off his body, Dan's hand fell on the Colt.

As the belt came free, the attacker stepped back. Pulling the Colt, Dan raised it at the looming man and fired. The thief howled and stumbled back, landing against the outhouse wall. Dan rolled to his side to fire again. Pain in his back from the gunshot tore through his body. He gasped and collapsed, unable to hold himself up. Fighting to remain conscious and expecting another bullet from the attacker, he fought to raise the Colt. The sounds of voices coming closer were the last thing he remembered before slipping into darkness.

Dan opened his eyes. He was in the hotel lobby, lying on a carpet. A white-haired man with a kindly face was kneeling over him. The clerk was standing behind the man. Dan tried to sit up.

"Stay down. I'm a doctor, let me check you over," the kindly man said as he placed his hand on Dan's shoulder.

"I . . . I have to get the man who shot me," he stammered.

"The man ain't going anywhere," the clerk piped up. "You shot him through and killed him."

"My money belt?" Dan asked.

The doc reached back and held the money belt up. "It's a heavy one, and you're lucky it was. The back pouch stopped the bullet. You will have a nice bruise for a while and be sore. You might even piss a little blood, but other than a gash on your chin, you got no holes in you."

Dan reached for the belt and held it close. The doctor and clerk helped him up and into a chair. Any movement caused spasms in his back. A large man entered the room. Looking over, Dan saw a star on the man's coat.

"This is Marshal Rennie," the doctor said. "I was coming for breakfast at the hotel when we heard the shots."

The sheriff took a chair next to Dan. He reached over and turned the belt, exposing the entry point of the bullet. "You're a lucky hombre."

"So I've been told."

Marshal Rennie brushed back his moustache. "The man you killed was Mexican Bob. We found his horse tied just up the street. Looks like he'd been waiting a while for you to come and get your animal. He was close when he shot you, and must not have expected you to be able to do much while he stripped your belt."

"Well, Mexican Bob damn near got what he was after. Was his horse a mustang with a Spanish saddle?"

"Why, yes. Did you know him?" the surprised marshal asked.

"I believe he has been following me since I left Cheyenne."

"There are a couple of other things I need to know," Marshal Rennie inquired. "You're carrying a badge that says 'Cheyenne Deputy' on it. Also, this belt is filled with a hell of a lot of money."

Dan explained the kidnapping and his purpose for being in Harrison. He told the marshal that he suspected that Mexican Bob was part of the Kid Jonny gang.

Shaking his head, the marshal disagreed. "Mexican Bob didn't run with anyone. He generally worked as a hired gun. Either that, or he found out you were carrying the ransom and decided to take it."

This knowledge created a new concern for Dan. If someone in Cheyenne had sent the Mexican to take the money, were there more?

Marshal Rennie was satisfied with the explanation and left the hotel. The clerk headed for the kitchen to help the cook. Sitting on the chair, Dan watched the doctor close his bag. Turning to his patient, he said, "You were fortunate that the bullet hit the belt at an angle. A square impact would have penetrated the belt. Course, the bullet ripped the heck out of the bills in that pouch."

Chuckling at his joke, the doc left the hotel. Dan's tried to pull his shirt together. Four of the buttons were missing. He saw his mud-covered rifle leaning against the wall next to his chair. Grasping the barrel, he pushed himself upright.

Rotating his waist, he found his mobility was better than he had expected. He climbed the stairs to his room and removed the damaged shirt. Pulling down the top of his long johns, Dan inspected his back. The large bruise looked worse than it felt.

The bullet had hit only inches to the left of his spine. Everyone was right. He had been lucky. While he changed shirts, a thought crossed his mind. The messenger for the kidnapped girl had been found shot in the back. Could it have been Mexican Bob, or someone like him? Maybe the kidnapper never received the ransom. Thinking they had been double crossed, they would have killed the girl. When he got back to Cheyenne, Dan would run the theory by Sheriff Kent.

After washing the blood off his whisker-covered chin, he cleaned and oiled both of his guns. His back was sore, but tolerable. It was still early enough to make Ardmore before dark. Carrying his gear on the way out of the hotel, he picked up his sheepskin coat that had been left in the lobby. He looked at the neat bullet hole in the back. Tossing the key onto the counter, he stepped outside.

The snow was gone and the wind felt warm. Dan watched and listened for any danger as he went to the barn and saddled the black. When he rode away from the barn, he used the alleys between the buildings rather than the main street. Two miles out of town he picked up Sowbelly Creek and used the sparse cover along the creek.

He was told that as he followed the creek he would ride through a depression named Sowbelly canyon. In the distance he saw sandstone cliffs as he rode. Dan was thankful that the black had a smooth gait. When the horse went in and out of washes, jolts of pain would shoot through the muscles in his back.

He had ridden over a grass and sagebrush-covered rise when the lights of Ardmore came into view. The sun had set about an hour earlier. Dan had been depending on the keen senses of the horse to avoid obstacles in the dark.

He walked the black into town using the shadows of the buildings for cover. A smoky lantern illuminated the porch of the general store. A barrel holding ax handles, rolls of barbed wire and other various items sat under the sloping roof. The proprietor was busy emptying the contents of a wooden box onto the shelves.

Tying the horse to one side of the store, he stepped onto the porch and entered the building. The owner called over his shoulder, "Just a couple more things and I'll be right with you."

"Thanks, no hurry."

Dan browsed the bolts of cloth, tea sets, and hats on display. He hoped to bring Mary a gift when he returned to Cheyenne. He continued past these and looked at hinges, latches, rope, sickles, mallets, and other items that could be used around a ranch.

The store owner set the empty box down and cleared his throat. Dan turned and walked over to the counter. "You have a letter addressed to Jonas Wallace that I'm supposed to pick up."

The apron-clad owner scratched his head and thought a minute. "Jonas Wallace? Just a moment, let me check." He bent down behind the counter and shuffled through some papers. "I got one for Junior Wallace. Could that be the one?"

"Yes. Yes, it would," Dan said, reaching for the piece of mail.

"This letter was left under my door. There was no postage on it. This was the official post office until they opened the new one. There is postage due," the proprietor stated.

"How much?"

"Let's see. It was left here two weeks ago. I kept it even though postage was due." Looking at Dan, he pointed out, "I could have thrown it away, you know."

Dan thought twice about purchasing anything from this store. "Yes, I know you could have thrown it out."

"That will be two bits."

Fishing out a coin from his coat pocket, Dan placed it on the counter. Accepting the letter from the proprietor, he left the store. "Is nothing going to be easy on this trip?" he asked the dozing horse.

The air was much warmer than the night before. High clouds masked the stars and trapped the more temperate air. Stuffing the letter into his coat, Dan rode out of town. He had passed an abandoned cabin just the other side of the rise and planned to sleep there.

The moon was near full, and enough light penetrated the cloud cover to make out landmarks. Dan's back was stiffening up. He had found it painful when climbing into the saddle next to the store. Arriving at the cabin, he sat on the black, waiting for a wave of spasms to subside. Leaning forward, he dragged his leg over the black's rump to dismount.

Dan stood inside the aging building and took a candle out of his saddle bag. Striking a match, he lit it. Dripping some melted wax onto a dusty saucer on the table, he affixed the candle to the plate. He looked around his temporary quarters. The cabin was made from pine logs. The door sagged but remained on its hinges. The roof had a hole on the back side. Dan could roll out his bedroll near the front. A rusty six-plate stove stood in the middle of the cabin, its stove pipe going through the roof at a slight angle.

Some previous occupant had left a pile of wood and some kindling next to the door. The iron hinges squeaked as he opened the stove door. Dan smiled when he noticed that it was loaded with kindling, ready to have a match put to it. Whoever had used the cabin last had planned to return and wanted the task of starting his fire to be simple.

He lit the kindling and shut the stove door. He opened the draft door to allow more air to be fed to the flames. When Dan went to stand up, pains shot through his back and he slumped back to his knees. Gripping the edge of the stove, he waited for them to subside. Using the rapidly warming stove for support, he stood up.

Dan poured water from his canteen into the coffee pot and place it on the stove. While the water was heating, he went out and stripped the saddle from the black. He watered it at the creek nearby and then picketed the horse a short distance from the cabin.

He chewed on some jerky while waiting for the coffee to finish brewing. Everything in the cabin was covered with dust. The floor had been packed dirt and was now soft under foot. Most of the caulking between the logs had fallen out and constant wind blew in through the gaps.

Dan pulled the three-legged table closer to the stove to take advantage of the warmth. A nail keg had been used for a stool. He took the letter from his coat pocket. Using the candlelight, he inspected the envelope. The hand writing was smooth and flowing.

Opening it and removing a folded note, he read:

> Light two fires at night on the rise
> south of town. The next morning
> stay in plain sight and someone will
> come and get you. Have the
> money or the boy dies.

He sniffed the note. It had the smell of soap. The envelope and paper would have been part of a stationary set. The request to stay in sight bothered Dan. *Do I stay in plain sight so a rifleman can shoot me?* He decided that it did not matter. By now they probably knew that he had picked up the letter. They would be expecting the fires.

He carefully placed the note back into his coat pocket. It was too late and he was too tired to light the fires tonight. After drinking a tin cup filled with coffee, he added more wood to the stove and spread out his bedroll. *Damn waste of wood,* he thought. *What heat isn't blown through the walls will go up out the hole in the roof.*

Once in his blankets, the exhausted traveler was asleep in minutes. The moon slowly floated across the night sky, casting irregular shadows on the grassy plain. A fox wandered past the cabin while hunting a plump rodent for a meal. It stopped and sniffed the air, smelling the scent of the sleeping man and his horse. Uncomfortable being close to man, it trotted out onto the plain, with its nose to the ground.

CHAPTER SIX

The sound of mourning doves woke Dan. The eastern sky was just beginning to get light. He lay on his back, with his head resting on his saddle. His blanket was tucked under his chin and his coat lay over the top of him to ward off the cold morning air.

He glanced at the six-plate stove. "Now I wish that thing was loaded for lighting."

Tossing aside his covers, he moved quickly and then collapsed back onto the bed as pain coursed through his back. "Son-of-a-bitch, think before you move," he muttered.

Rolling to his side, he pushed himself up and slipped into the sheepskin coat. Unable to straighten up at that moment, he picked up what was needed to start the fire, then hobbled over to the stove. Kneeling carefully, he placed tinder and kindling into the firebox. It was too bad that he hadn't done this last night. He decided that a wiser man than he had last lived in the cabin. Shivering from the cold, his back began to spasm. He struck a match to light the dried grass. The flames grew, snapping as the pine kindling caught. Smoke rolled into the cabin due to the downdraft from the chimney. Slamming the stove door, he waved his arms to disperse the cloud.

He grabbed the edge of the table for support and stood up. He went outside with his canteen and coffee pot. Fetching the horse, he led it to the creek for water. Kneeling on one knee, he rinsed out the coffee pot and then filled it and his canteen with the icy water. Dan then took a long drink and refilled the canteen.

Picketing the black on a fresh area of grass, he stood for a moment, looking at the hillside around him. Other than the cabin, he did not see an area for a rifleman to shoot at him. He thought about the slope into Ardmore. There were old structures on the hillside that would offer cover. He would have to light the fires well clear of them.

Dan put the coffee pot on the stove to heat and then added more wood to the fire. He put his frying pan on the rusty stovetop and sliced side meat into it. He went to the table and took the letter out and read it again. After breakfast he would collect wood for the two fires.

With the meal done, Dan sat on a sandstone ledge on the hillside above the town. He was enjoying the morning sun on his back. Dan had counted a dozen or more places a marksman could hide while he was lighting the fires at the top of the ridge. As a precaution he had hidden the money belt in the cabin, burying it in the floor.

He remembered hearing that his grandfather

had done the same thing with his gold. It was in a cabin below the Six Grandfathers Mountains, now called Mount Rushmore. Dan looked to the north. That cabin his Grandfather Oli had wintered in was only two or three days' ride from Ardmore. A cold gust of wind brought him back to the task of collecting wood for the fires.

By noon he had two stacks of wood that should burn for over an hour. Whoever was watching would most likely be in the town. Dan planned to light them right after sundown. He returned to the ledge and sat, looking at the town. He took some hard bread out of his coat pocket and chewed it slowly while letting the sun warm him. Collecting the wood and the warmth of the sun had loosened his back muscles.

After taking a drink from the canteen and wiping his mouth with the back of his hand, Dan caught sight of an old man leading a mule. The man looked every bit a prospector. A pick and shovel were tied to the pack on the mule. The old miner was heading for Ardmore. From there he would probably head into the Black Hills to search for gold.

The old timer stopped when he noticed Dan sitting on the ledge. Waving, he headed toward him. Arriving at the ledge, the old man took a seat and reached into his pocket for chewing tobacco. He tore off a generous piece with his stained teeth and began to chew. He offered some to Dan. The rancher shook his head no and continued to eat the hard bread.

"The name is Amos Mudd," the old timer said. "I been chasing the dream of gold most of my life."

"Pleased to meet you, Mr. Mudd. I'm Dan August. I have been living my dream, ranching in a green valley in Wyoming."

"A rancher, hey. Cows or horses?"

Dan looked at the old man. His gray eyes were surrounded by bushy brows and wrinkled skin. His beard was tobacco-stained and he was wearing dirty, threadbare clothing. A wolfskin coat was tied to the pack on the mule.

"Cows or horses?" the miner repeated.

"I'm sorry, I . . . uh, cows." Dan had never met a man who looked more like his vision of a prospector. "Are you coming to Ardmore to spend the winter?"

"Well, Mr. August, that would depend on you," Amos replied.

Dan stiffened. "Why is that?"

The old man spat a stream of tobacco juice. "Did you bring the money?"

Revealed in the old man's waistband while he put the tobacco away was the butt of a shiny, new Colt .45. Dan's rifle was in the scabbard on the black, and his Colt .44 was in his holster with the loop over the hammer.

"Yes I did, but if you shoot me, you will never find it," Dan warned.

"Oh hell, man," Amos exclaimed. "The last thing I plan to do is shoot you. I am here to bring you to the exchange."

"You were supposed to come the morning after I lit the fires. How do I know you're not planning to shoot me in the back and steal the money like the last one?" Dan challenged.

"I don't know nothing about somebody that

was shot in the back. What I do know is someone offered me enough money to winter here in Ardmore, and all I had to do is take you to meet them. Oh, and about the fires. I was camping west of here and noticed you dragging wood to the top of the hill. It wasn't hard to figure you were the one I was waiting for."

Dan looked at the man. His old, wrinkled face was impossible to read. What he said sounded about right, but any good poker player can convince someone that their hand is beat and then rake in the pot without them ever seeing his cards.

"I am going to take the loop off my Colt, if you don't mind. Then we can go and get the money. And we will travel side-by-side," Dan said, setting the rules.

"Don't make no never mind to me. Wave your damn gun in the air if it makes you feel any better. Now we got a way to go, so we best get to it." With that said, the old miner grabbed the lead rope of the mule and started up the hill.

"Where are you going?" Dan asked.

Amos turned and sighed, "You spent last night in the cabin after picking up the letter. You didn't go anywhere else. The cabin is where the money has to be."

The black was grazing just above the sandstone ledge. Dan got it and joined Amos as they headed for the cabin. The two men entered the building. Amos looked around. "When I come back, I may fix this up a bit and winter here."

Dan pointed to the corner near the hole in the roof. "Get the shovel off your pack. It's buried right there."

Amos dug up the money belt and handed it to Dan. He then went outside and stripped the prospecting gear off the mule and brought it inside the cabin. "I may as well leave this stuff here. It kind of makes the place feel homey."

Dan packed his gear on the horse while Amos readied what he needed on the mule. With several hours of daylight left, the two men rode east. Dan sat on the black, ready for anything. Amos rode using a blanket for a saddle and a short switch to slap the mule on the rump to keep it moving. He seemed to be a harmless old man, but money can turn a good man bad. The money belt was stuffed in Dan's saddle bag. Whether it was around his waist or on the saddle made little difference now. If the miner decided to try to take it, Dan would be less restricted not having the bulky belt around his waist.

"Tell me about Mexican Bob," Dan requested, trying to see if the two were tied together.

Amos spat. "Don't know the name. Ain't too many Mexicans up here. It's too damn cold for them."

"Are we going to see Kid Jonny?"

"If you mean, Jon Kidman, the answer is yes," the prospector said. "He's the one that promised me the money. He said that he was trying to help some snot-nose kid."

"That could be, Amos, but I think your Jon Kidman is the one that took the kid."

"That may be so, but it ain't none of my concern. I am being paid to bring you to him."

Dan had to make sure that the black didn't take the lead. The horse liked to be first and choose the trail. "How far do we have to go?"

"Tonight we will camp at Horsehead Creek. We should meet Kidman by noon tomorrow."

Riding in silence, he watched the old man. Could Amos be skilled at keeping him off guard like a cow being led to slaughter? Dan wouldn't be getting much sleep tonight. Kid Jonny could be planning to come in and take the money tonight while they were supposed to be sleeping.

The land around them was made up of large hills and valleys. The golden grass and sage covering the hills was broken up by the naked limbs of oak and maple trees. Clusters of pine were dark against the grass. The wind was getting cold again. Amos had donned his wolfskin coat. Dan rode with his collar turned up.

They had just crested a hill when Amos held up his hand for Dan to stop. He rode a short distance and then drew the Colt .45 and fired. After a brief pause, he fired again. Surprised, Dan pulled his Winchester from the scabbard and had it cocked and ready.

"Got us supper. Danged if after I shot the first rabbit, another hopped out just begging to be next." The old miner slapped the mule forward a little before he got off to retrieve the two rabbits.

The sun was setting when they rode into the valley that Horsehead Creek flowed through. The old prospector pointed the switch at a grove of willow. "There's a good place to camp. The trees stop the wind and there is plenty of wood for the fire."

Amos got the fire going and began to skin the rabbits while Dan put up the horse and mule. Taking the money belt out of the saddle bags, he put it back around his waist. If someone wanted the money, they would have to take it off him.

It turned out that Amos was quite the cook around a campfire. After putting the rabbits over the fire to roast, he whipped up a batch of sourdough biscuits and put them about an inch apart in a frying pan. While the two men watched the meal cooking, they drank coffee with a shot of rye. The old miner said that it was good to keep the chill off.

After the meal was over, Dan spread his bedroll away from the fire. He had a new concern about the old man with him. He had witnessed the smooth, measured draw and firing of the Colt. Both rabbits were killed by head shots. If he ended up between Kid Jonny and Amos, he wouldn't have a chance if the exchange turned to gunplay.

He lay looking at the shadowed outline of the sleeping miner next to the fire. Was Amos that good at masking what he knew, or had he been paid a few dollars to bring him to the exchange and was unaware that Junior had been kidnapped?

Dan lay with his rifle and revolver under his blankets and the money belt around his waist. At his back was a large windfall with lots of dry brush behind it to warn him of anyone coming. His bed was in the deep shadows to prevent a shooter from sighting on him from beyond the camp. He lay fighting sleep. Dan figured that he could catch up on sleep after the money had been delivered and Junior was free.

There was the sound of metal on stone. Dan's eyes opened wide. He had fallen asleep. The sound had come from Amos making breakfast. Searching under his blankets he located his guns and the money belt. Clearing his throat, Dan rolled onto his side and pushed himself up to a sitting position. The back was feeling better.

"Figured you had awaken," Amos said. "You were making quite a racket snoring back there, then you suddenly stopped. Sorry I dropped the frying pan. I planned to surprise you with pancakes."

Who the hell is this guy? Dan wondered. Calling out, he said, "I was ready to get up anyway. Give me a second, and I'll tend to the horses before we eat."

The pancakes were good and the coffee was just how he liked it. With breakfast done, Dan scrubbed the frying pan and plates in the creek. Returning to the fire with the dripping utensils, he set them on a log to dry. Amos was tearing off a new chew. Dan pulled a bag of tobacco from his shirt pocket and rolled a smoke.

"What time will we get to the meeting place?"

Amos was just finishing packing his gear on the mule. Leading it over to a windfall, he used it to climb onto the animal. "You're here. I was told to get you to this spot and leave you."

"When do you get paid?"

"When I let them know you're waiting for them."

With that, Amos on his mule rode up the river, away from Dan.

* * *

For the next hour after the miner had ridden

away, Dan looked over the grove of trees, memorizing the best places where cover could be gained. He dragged some logs and branches to build a makeshift fortress that he could wait behind.

The black was tied within the grove, so he could get to it on a short run if needed. Satisfied that he had done what he could to be prepared, Dan made himself comfortable behind the barrier, then checked and rechecked his Winchester and Colt. The money belt lay on top of the log near the dead fire.

It was late morning when he heard horses crossing the creek somewhere upstream. Leaning the rifle against the barrier close at hand, he stood waiting, the loop off his Colt. He caught a glimpse of the riders coming toward him through the trees.

"Hello, the camp!" one of the riders called out.

"Come on in with your hands empty," he called back. "Have the boy ride in, in front of you."

Three riders approached the camp. He did not recognize any of them. Dan assumed that the young man in the lead was Junior. They stopped near the cook fire.

Junior had dark brown hair. He had a woolen coat and a drooping leather hat. The man to his left sported a week-old beard and was blind in one eye. The one to his right had a broken nose that left it bent to one side.

Broken nose spoke, his eyes fixed on the belt. "Is that the money?"

"It is," Dan replied, allowing his coat to hang open for access to his Colt.

"Sully, git down and bring me the money,"

broken nose ordered.

"You watch him, Hank," Sully said, climbing off his horse.

"Hold on there," Dan cautioned the men. "Send the kid over to me before you touch the money."

Hank rubbed his whiskered chin, "Well, we would, but the boy will be staying with us."

"I got to stay." Junior blurted.

Dan's gun hand involuntarily twitched as he fought the urge to draw. He knew the ransom exchange was rapidly deteriorating. He was expected to return with Junior Wallace. If the boy stayed in Cheyenne or not after that, it was not his concern.

"You listen to me, Junior," Dan said. "Your father sent me to get you. He is worried about you and if you stay here, you will be hurting him."

"I can't go back. My father will blame me," Junior said, his voice barely audible.

"I don't know what's going on between you and your father, but I am taking you back. Now get down from the horse and lead it over here. Hank and Sully can take the money back to Kid Jonny."

"I don't much like that name," a voice behind him said. Dan froze. Kid Jonny was behind him, no doubt with a gun aimed at his back.

"I was asked to deliver the money and bring Junior back. You don't need him anymore, Kid . . . Jon. Jonas has lived up to his part of the deal and keeping the boy will just be a burden on you," Dan said, trying to reason with the killer.

"That's where you are wrong. Every so often

I need a little extra cash. I am sure Junior's father will be happy to send it to keep the boy healthy."

In the next few seconds Dan expected a bullet, ending his part of this deal. The brush behind him was supposed to warn him of someone trying to get close. It would do little good stopping a bullet.

"Run out of things to say?" Kid Jonny taunted. "Just toss your guns toward the boys there so they can collect them. If you don't do something stupid, I just might let you live."

Taking care, Dan tossed the Colt and Winchester over the barrier. In spite of the cold, he was sweating. He watched as Sully grabbed the belt and then picked up his guns, looking admiringly at the rifle.

The voice behind him continued. "I'll be taking the horse. A mile south of here, I'll leave your saddle. You can carry that back to Ardmore. When you get back to Cheyenne, let Mr. Wallace know what a reasonable man I am. He will be contacted about the next payment."

"I think it's safe to say, Jonas Wallace will send someone else to get the boy. He doesn't seem like the type to keep sending money," Dan warned.

"Well, your job will be to convince him that that would be the wrong thing to do."

"Did you kill the girl because the money never came?"

There was no answer from the man behind him. The three riders in front of him turned their horses to leave. At the same time, Dan heard the man behind him ride away, leading the black. They all rode downstream. He stood listening to the sound of the horses' hooves fade away. Helpless to stop them, he stood wondering what else he could have done.

The money was gone, the boy was gone, and his damn horse and gear were gone. Dan felt like a rookie. After all his careful planning, he had let them draw his attention to the front while Kid Jonny walked right up behind him and took it all.

He was suddenly thirsty. Walking down to the creek, he scooped up several handfuls, drinking his fill. He looked to the south. "I might as well get started walking. It will be dark before I get to Ardmore. How could I be so dumb?"

There was nobody to hear his complaints. Accepting the unexpected developments of the ransom exchange, he headed southwest, down Horsehead Creek. The stretch of the creek he was walking along was lined with bare trees. He kicked at the fallen brown leaves as he walked. Dan knew that he should be watching the horizons around him as he walked, but failure weighed heavily on him and at the moment it didn't matter.

The walk was good. It kept him warm against the cold west wind and it helped to relieve the frustration he was feeling. He planned to send a message to Sheriff Kent when he got to Ardmore, letting him know what had happened. He would then take a train back. Nothing went directly to Cheyenne. Dan would welcome the additional time going back.

As Kid Jonny had promised, he found his saddle next to the trail. It included all his gear, less his guns. The total weight was all of 100 pounds. He carried it for an hour before stopping to have something to eat. Taking jerky out of the saddle bags, he sat near the creek, chewing the meat and scooping cups of water to drink.

"Did you lose your horse?" someone on his back trail called out. It was Amos Mudd.

CHAPTER SEVEN

The old prospector was a sight for sore eyes. Carrying the saddle and gear was exhausting Dan. The strain had his back throbbing again. Amos slid off the mule and looked the ransom carrier over.

"Why, hell! Not only did you lose your horse, but I see your rifle and revolver are gone," the old miner said with genuine surprise on his face.

"As you can see, the ransom for Junior's exchange didn't go well," Dan admitted. "Turns out the bastard wasn't ready to give up the boy. I almost think that Junior didn't want to come."

Chuckling, Amos pushed back his hat. "I have been there. My pa raised potatoes in Maine. He worked me hard and I saw no future staying, so one evening after harvest was done, I just packed my things and told him I was going to California."

His face became sad. "I left to chase the mother lode. I never made it to California, but there were always other strikes. The next place would be the one that had gold. That was near 40 years ago. Along the way, I learned my pa had died. They found him in the potato field. I had promised, but never went back, never thanked him for what he sacrificed while raising me."

"Well, I am through with this business. The only things that bothers me are the boy is under Kid Jonny's control and the plan to continue demanding money from the boy's father to keep his son safe," Dan told Amos.

"That ain't right," the prospector retorted, "and it ain't right for you walk away from this. Jon Kidman can take the boy under his wing if he wants to, but using him to get money from the boy's old man is just wrong."

"I agree with you on that, but I got no gun or horse," Dan pointed out. "Kidman got the drop on me and would have shot me in the back if it wasn't that he needed me to carry a message back to Jonas Wallace. If I was to go back there now, someone is going to die. Maybe that someone would be me. I got a wife and child that depend on me."

"Okay, it isn't our duty to right the wrongs that people commit," the old prospector agreed. "Load your gear on the mule and we can make the cabin at Ardmore before midnight."

"I want you to know it's not because I'm scared of Kidman or his gunslingers. But if I was killed doing it, my wife Mary would be left to fend for herself. That would be a tough road for a woman here in the west," Dan said, defending his decision.

The two men arrived at the cabin two hours after dark. The cold west wind had blown in clouds that covered the stars and moon. They got a fire going in the stove and put on some coffee. While they waited for the hot brew they sat in the flickering candlelight, and Amos poured some rye into their coffee cups.

The rye warmed Dan's stomach. He finished the drink and held it out for a second. Taking his time with the second drink, he rolled a cigarette and lit it from the candle. Amos retrieved a pipe and tobacco.

The old miner had dug into his pack for day-old biscuits and handed one to Dan. Once the coffee was done, they added the steaming liquid to their cups and chewed the sourdough biscuits after dunking them in the coffee.

Tired from the long day, the two men spread out their bed rolls next to the stove and turned in. Using the saddle for a pillow, Dan was soon drifting off. He heard Amos say, "One thing I didn't tell you. I saw a young woman in their camp. Looked like she belonged to Kidman. If someone goes back to get the boy, she could get hurt."

The sound of rain on the roof and dripping inside the cabin awoke the men. The prospector was up first and started to light a fire in the stove. "Once I caulk the logs and fix the hole in the roof, this stove will be just fine for heating the place."

Rolling up his blankest, Dan kidded, "That is if it doesn't burn it down first. I don't know if I'd trust that old stove pipe."

While Amos started their breakfast, Dan went out and tended to the mule. The heavy, dark clouds hung over the plain. The cold, damp wind made doing anything outside miserable. The wood in the cabin was just about gone. He looked around, hoping to see a wood pile. There was none. He remembered the wood for the two fires. That could be brought to the cabin.

Hurrying back into the cabin, the warmth from the stove was welcome. Coffee water was on and Amos was mixing batter for pancakes. "This will be the last of the pancakes unless I get down to the general store."

"I appreciate you sharing the last of them with me. After today, your grocery bill will be less," Dan kidded.

"I like to cook, and like watching people enjoy my food even better."

"Last night you said something while I was falling asleep. At the time I thought it was important, but now I don't remember what it was."

Amos furled his brow, thinking of what he might have said. "I told you a bunch of things before I realized you were sleeping. None were all that important, as I recall. I do remember mentioning that Jon Kidman would be heading into the Badlands, maybe even swing down toward St. Louis for the winter."

Dan shook his head. "I don't think that was it. It is good to know though. I'll tell Wallace."

"I talked about the place he was at now. Looked like an abandoned ranch house. The place needs work. All sign said he had been there a while, though."

"Nope, not it."

"Damned if I remember. I think I mentioned Jon paid me before he went to meet you. He hadn't gotten back when I left. I expected you and the boy would be on the way back to Ardmore."

"Nah," Dan said. "I remember it being a warning about something."

Amos grinned from ear-to-ear. "I remember. There was a gal there. Looked to be Kidman's woman. I wanted you to tell them back in Cheyenne so they don't send somebody in there, guns a blazing, and kill the woman."

"That's it!" Dan exclaimed. "I am willing to bet that gal is the one taken the year before. They demanded a ransom, but best I can figure, Mexican Bob got to him first and stole the money."

The old miner poured the coffee and fried some side meat to make grease for the pancakes. The two men sat drinking the coffee while the fat snapped in the frying pan. "That might be interesting, Mr. August, but why is it important?"

"It is, Mr. Mudd, because that means I have to go back and get her. She might be Kid Jonny's woman, but I doubt she is staying willingly."

"Damn, I can just see you walking in there with a stick and taking her from Jon Kidman. Have you forgotten you don't have a horse and, more important, they took your guns?"

Fishing the crisp side meat from the pan, Amos began to ladle the batter in, making two oval pancakes at a time. He had a jug of molasses to sweeten the cakes. While they ate, Dan told Amos the story about the railroad man's daughter being taken, about the money being sent, and the messenger being shot in the back.

"You see, Amos, they think she is dead. Shortly, Kidman is going to disappear for a long time. She may not be with him anymore when they come back in the area. That is, if they ever do."

"I figure they will be back. Jon will want to get more money for the boy. Can't say if the woman will still be there. Maybe, though. She was carrying a brat."

"I will go into Ardmore this morning and send a telegram to Sheriff Kent. He can arrange to send money so I can rearm myself, and buy a horse. Maybe Doc Middleton will get up a posse to go after them."

"I wouldn't depend on Doc Middleton," Amos informed Dan. "He may be the law in Ardmore, but he keeps the peace in town. What happens out of town is not his problem."

"I can't stand by and let him take her away from here. I need to go there and find out if she was the girl taken from Medicine Bow. If she is not, then I will make another try to get the boy, before going back to my Mary in Cheyenne, knowing I did the right thing."

"You don't even know where Jon Kidman's camp is," Amos reminded Dan.

Stopping in mid-bite, Dan set the fork full of pancake back on his plate. He looked at the old man opposite him. "I was hoping you would provide that bit of information."

"I could," Amos said, "but he did pay me to bring the money to him. And that suggests that I would not give away his location."

"What!" Dan snapped, glaring at the prospector.

"I believe you heard me," the old miner said firmly. Softening his tone, he continued, "Of course, I was led to believe that Kidman was helping the boy."

Dan stared at the old man, trying in vain to read his face, waiting for him to say if he would help or not.

Amos looked at the half-eaten pancakes in front of Dan and then at his disappointed eyes. He shrugged his shoulders and said, "What the hell, it looks like you are going to hold me hostage by not eating my cooking. That I can't stand. I guess I will lead you to Jon Kidman."

For a moment, Dan didn't comprehend what the old man had said. When he realized that Amos would help him, he picked up the fork and shoved the pancake into his mouth. He mumbled a thank you around the mouthful of food.

While Dan cleaned up the morning dishes, Amos checked on the mule and worked with his packs. Returning from the gear, the old man said, "If we are going after the young woman, you will need a gun, just in case things get rough."

He handed Dan a Smith & Wesson Model 3. It used a .44 caliber cartridge. "When I got the newer Colt .45, I kept this as a backup. You're welcome to use this on our trip to Kidman's camp."

Dan took the revolver. The wooden grips were scarred from use, while the mechanical workings of the gun were in excellent shape. The balance of the Model 3 was good. He got his holster that was lying with his gear. Once the gun belt was back around his hips, he felt fully dressed.

Turning to the old prospector, he said, "I heard you say 'we'. I don't expect you to risk your life riding into Kid Jonny's camp."

"Risk my life, hell fire," Amos said. "I will be there to protect the horse I'm going to let you use. And, I don't appreciate the fact that Kidman lied to me about the boy."

The old prospector had a sorrel he kept in Ardmore. He told Dan that while hunting for gold he liked taking the mule. It demanded less attention than his horse, and as far as Amos was concerned it was better company.

By late morning the two men rode out of Ardmore. Dan had offered to ride the mule and let Amos have the sorrel, but the old prospector said he preferred the mule. With extra ammunition for the Model 3 and some extra supplies in his saddle bags, Dan felt like he was ready to meet Kid Jonny.

They spent the night at the same grove of trees on Horsehead Creek where the exchange had been made. Amos said that Kidman's camp was less than two hours from the grove. With an early start, they could go to the camp, get the girl, the boy if he would come, and be back in Ardmore just after dark.

Before turning in Dan walked beyond the grove, in the direction where Kidman had gotten the drop on him. It didn't take long to see why Amos had been directed to take him here for the exchange. A wash behind the grove had given Kid Jonny plenty of cover to sneak up on him.

The air was crisp and a few snowflakes were falling when they awoke the next morning. After a quick meal, Dan put his saddle on the sorrel. He checked the Smith & Wesson, adding an extra cartridge under the hammer. He decided that the risk of the gun firing accidently was worth having an extra shot when facing Kidman.

Amos led the way with the mule. He was in a good mood, telling stories of his search for gold and an old-timer named Doo who had showed him the ropes years ago. Dan pulled alongside the prospector and asked, "We are riding into an armed camp and you seem to be having the time of your life. Why is that?"

"We are doing something good," Amos said. "Most of the time our efforts are for ourselves. Not often is it for another. It just makes me feel good."

"We'll see if you feel as good when we're dodging bullets."

Dan's stomach was tight. Odds were that they would ride into Kidman's camp and find out that the woman Amos had seen was not the missing Honey. He had no intention of risking his life for the Wallace boy. If Junior wanted to come with them, Dan would do what he could to make that happen.

If Kidman and his men wanted a fight, he was ready. Dan had had his share of facing others with guns. The difference this time was Mary and the child. If he was killed, that would leave her a widow with a youngster to raise alone.

He knew that if he went into the confrontation with his wife and child on his mind, it could cause him to make mistakes. Mistakes that could get him killed. Dan looked at the old miner riding with him. He would have to depend on Amos to do his part at the camp.

As they rode over the rolling grasslands toward the Kidman camp, Dan placed his hand on the gun loaned to him by the prospector. The butt was smooth from use. His mind drifted back to the time when he and his cousins had faced the Elder gang. Hoss Elder had gone to the gallows, speaking of the quickness of Dan's draw on them.

From his youth, Dan had been gifted with fast reflexes. When it came to handguns, he had a smooth, fluid draw. It had saved him when confronted by the Elders. Being known as a fast gun bothered him. The fear of being forced to live by the gun to survive had been one of the reasons that he had settled in the remote green valley.

Dan's thoughts were interrupted by Amos. "The camp is just over the next rise. We will come up behind the barn. The house is just beyond, on the left near a stream. An old carriage shed and outhouse are on the right."

The sagging roof of the barn became visible first. The men stopped and double-checked their weapons. The sky was thick with heavy clouds. Wind-driven sleet hit the backs of the riders. Dan removed the leather gloves from his hands and flexed his cold fingers.

The smile had left the miner's face, replaced by a cold, expressionless stare. The icy precipitation was sticking to the men and their animals as they rode into the camp. Smoke rose from a rusty stove pipe protruding from the shingled farmhouse roof.

The sound of horses came from the barn as they passed it. Dan glanced toward the open door, trying to see if any of Kidman's men were in there. In the gloom of the day, it was impossible to tell. Amos fell back as the men rode into the yard.

Keeping the blowing sleet at his back, Dan

stopped in front of the house. The stillness of the moment was almost alarming. Were the men he was looking for just behind the dust and ice-covered windows, guns drawn, ready to open fire without warning?

A gust of wind sent the frozen rain rattling against the building. Swinging off the horse, he stepped away from it. He opened his sheepskin coat, exposing the deputy badge pinned to his shirt. It was time. "Jon Kidman, I am Deputy August, from Cheyenne. I am here looking for a young woman named Honey Kent."

The freezing precipitation numbed his exposed hands as he waited for a response. Slowly, the door opened on noisy hinges. A man came out, his hat pulled down against the sleet, one hand holding his coat closed. The other hand was out of sight, slightly behind him.

"You are a long way from Cheyenne, deputy. You have no authority in this area." As the man spoke he edged around, trying to shift the precipitation to his back. Dan move with the man, keeping it in his face.

"Are you Jon Kidman, also known as Kid Jonny?" Dan demanded.

"I killed the last man that called me Kid Jonny. I overlooked your slip when picking up the money. You best be careful, deputy."

"Fair enough, Mr. Kidman. I have no interest in you. As I said, I am here for the Kent woman."

The outlaw quit moving, the sleet hitting the side of his face. Tilting his head back, he looked at Dan. "There ain't no one named Kent here. I would recommend you go now and take the message I gave you to Wallace."

"If you have a gun in the hand I can't see, it will get you killed if you try and move it," the deputy warned.

The wind-driven sleet was covering everything and everyone with an icy coating. Dan knew the Colt at his side would be slippery, and the longer Kidman kept him talking the more advantage it would give the outlaw.

"If you would step back, I would like to check with the woman Amos saw here the other day. If she says she isn't Honey Kent, then I will leave. I expect you will give me my guns and horse. The black was on loan and I have to return it."

Kidman snorted, "You are a pretty cocky son-of-a-bitch, considering I do have a gun in my hand. Right now yours is frozen in your holster . . ."

Without hesitation, Dan grasped the Colt as he saw the outlaw's arm start to move. The revolver cleared leather and bucked in the deputy's hand as he fired. The outlaw's gun caught the edge of his coat, delaying him the split second that gave Dan the edge.

The first bullet struck Kidman low on the left side, turning him and causing his shot to go wide. The second bullet went through the hand holding the coat and deep into his chest. Jon Kidman stood on wobbly legs. His gun had fallen from his hand and his coat hung open, blood running down the long john top. He coughed as he tried to speak and then fell into a twisted heap, his blood spreading on the sleet-covered ground.

Hearing other gunshots, Dan moved, putting the sorrel between himself and the other buildings. The sound of a wounded man came from the direction of the outhouse. The sleet had changed to driven snow. It made it impossible for Dan to see the other buildings. A shadowy figure was coming through the snow.

"You okay?" It was Amos leading the mule.

"I am," Dan answered. "I fear my damn hand is frozen to the gun."

"When you fired, a hombre came running out of the barn with a rifle. He's lying dead just outside the door. The other poor bastard came rushing out of the little house, pulling up his trousers. I didn't have the heart to kill a man with nothing but a hand full of pants, so I just put one through his leg."

"Was either one of them the Wallace boy?"

"Pretty sure they was Hank and Sully," Amos said. "Hold my mule for a minute and I'll go drag the crying bastard over here."

Dan stood in front of the house with his back to the storm. He kept the sorrel and mule between himself and the building. The Colt was stuck in his waistband and he warmed his aching hand under his coat. The body of Kid Jonny was quickly being covered by the blowing snow.

Over the wind, he heard the grunts of Amos as he dragged the complaining Sully from the outhouse. "It ain't right shooting a man with his pants down. I think the bone is broke. I could lose the damn leg."

"Shut up or I will put a bullet in the other leg," the prospector threatened.

"Stand him up, Amos. We'll let him go into the house first." Grabbing the collar of the man, Dan warned, "You best hope they don't shoot without seeing who it is."

Forcing the wounded Sully in front of them, Dan kicked the door open. Shoving the outlaw into the room, he followed, ducking low to the side. He heard Amos crash into a stool as he rushed into the house.

Dan stopped, the Colt leveled in front of him. The brightness of the snow had left him blind in the dim light of the room. If anyone intended to shoot him, he would be helpless to defend himself. He fought the urge to leap back out the door.

There was the crying of a youngster. "Don't hurt me, I haven't a weapon," a frightened feminine voice said.

"Light a lamp!" he ordered.

Blinking rapidly, Dan was able to see a woman moving across the room. As she moved, he saw that she was holding a crying baby. There was the flash of a lighted match and then the glow from the lamp.

The wounded Sully lay on the floor in the middle of the room. Amos was sitting near him, rubbing a banged shin. He kicked the stool he had fallen over out of his way. The young, hollow-eyed woman stood near the table, fear etched into her face. She held the baby close to her, as though trying to protect it from the sight of the intruders in her home. Crouched in a corner near the stove was Junior Wallace.

The prospector stood up and lifted the wounded man onto a stool near the wall. Dan closed the door. Then, turning to the young woman, he asked, "Are you Honey Kent?"

"I am Mrs. Jon Kidman," she stated with pride in her voice. "He just stepped outside, you might have seen him."

Shock raced through Dan. Riding to the camp, he had worried about Mary being left a widow. In front of him was a woman whom he had just made a widow. "Mrs. Kidman, I am sorry. Your husband is dead. He tried to shoot . . ."

He stopped talking. What he was about to say sounded lame. How could he tell the wife that he had just shot her husband? Would any excuse bring her comfort?

Tears began to stream down her face as she cried silently. Amos watched as his brave partner wilted under the knowledge of what had happened. Unable to continue facing the woman, Dan went over to Junior to make sure that he was not armed.

Dan felt angry for not being able to explain to the woman that he had only shot because he was defending himself. The rancher knew that he hadn't done anything wrong. He jerked the Wallace boy to his feet in frustration.

"You can help me bury Kidman," he growled.

From across the room he heard the woman speak. "I am the one you were looking for. I am, or was Honey Kent. Jon and I were married right after we left Medicine Bow. The baby is his son."

Regaining his composure, Dan promised, "Junior and I will bury him and say words over him. It wouldn't be right to leave your husband lying out front."

"Would you bring him in here tonight?" she

asked. "I want to be with him a little longer."

With the snow swirling around them, Dan and Junior went out to bring Kidman in. They tried to brush some of the frozen precipitation off him before carrying the body into the house. Honey pointed to the small bed in the corner of the room. They laid the lifeless Jon Kidman on the brightly colored bed covering.

For the first time, Dan felt the warmth of the room as the heat hit his raw red cheeks. Sully sat on the stool, leaning against the wall. There was a bandage on the wounded leg. Amos was checking out the stove and pantry.

He began to put something together for their meal and called out to Dan, "They had some coffee on the stove. Pour yourself a cup while I make our supper."

After filling a tin mug, he sat at the table with Junior. "Unless you want to spend the winter here alone, I plan to take you back to Cheyenne."

"I'll go with you. There's nothing left here for me," the boy said. "We was going to St. Louis for the winter. Jon said we could live high on the money."

After a bit, Amos brought a pot of steaming beans and some fried ham, placing them on the table. Dan watched as the old miner went back to the cupboard and got plates. Honey was sitting on the edge of the bed with her dead husband. The baby lay next to her. He asked Honey if she wanted anything to eat and she shook her head no.

The four men sat in silence around the table, eating. Dan ran the confrontation in front of the house over and over in his mind, trying to think if there had been any way things could have gone differently. He had clearly seen Kid Jonny's arm move as he'd attempted to bring the gun around. His only other option would have been to let the outlaw kill him.

While watching the young woman grieve for her husband, he knew that he had had no choice. Dan had no appetite and ate little. The old prospector noticed, but said nothing. With the meal finished, Amos checked the house for any other weapons. He found the rifle and Colt taken at the ransom exchange. Dan returned the borrowed revolver to Amos and slipped his into its holster.

Dan went out to water the animals and take them to the barn. It felt good to get out of the house. In the sagging building he found his black along with the rest of Kidman's horses. He put the sorrel and mule into stalls next to the black. He then brushed the snow-covered animals, taking his time. After giving them some hay, he stood in the doorway and watched the blowing snow.

The rifle barrel stuck out of the drift of snow covering Hank's body. Ducking his head, Dan went out into the wind and kicked the snow off the dead man's feet. Grabbing hold of them, he dragged the body into the barn.

The house was quiet when he returned. Honey sat, head bowed, praying, maybe dozing. Amos sat alone at the table with a cup of coffee.

"I tucked the two buggers into bed in the other room. I told them if I saw them before morning, I would dump their bodies in the same hole as Kidman."

"Thanks," Dan said. "I dragged Hank into the barn. Be easier than having to dig him out of a drift in the morning."

"Kidman is worth $500 in Medicine Bow. You should bring the body back with you and claim the reward," Amos advised him.

"I am a deputy," Dan said. "They should take my word that he's dead."

"I kind of looked around the place and didn't see the money anywhere."

"We can look again in the morning. Maybe the woman knows where it is." After a moment he added, "If we don't find it, we'll burn all the buildings. No one will be able to come back after it."

He heard movement from the small bed. Honey was feeding the baby.

The two men took turns standing watch during the night. One of the bed rolls was laid out near the stove. It would have been careless to assume that the woman or the two remaining gang members wouldn't try something during the night. There could be a hidden gun. The ransom was still here and that was a lot of money to ignore.

CHAPTER EIGHT

Dan awoke to the sounds of Amos making breakfast. He had been relieved four hours earlier and had had no trouble going to sleep. Looking toward the small bed, he was surprised to see that Honey had sewn the colorful bed cover around her husband. She had moved over to the table and sat with the baby in her lap and a cup of coffee in front of her.

There were no more tears. She combed the fine, blond hair of the baby with her fingers. Honey was softly humming a lullaby to the child. Dan put up the bedroll before donning his coat.

"I'll be right back, Amos," he told his partner.

Once outside, he squinted from the glare off the snow. The sky was clear, giving promise of a much better day. He walked across the yard and stopped behind the carriage building to relieve himself. Dan then found a couple of shovels.

Returning to the house, he leaned the shovels next to the door and went inside. The smell of fried meat, potatoes, and onions greeted him. "Grab a cup of coffee, this will be done in a couple minutes," Amos called out.

"Potatoes? Where the heck did you come up with potatoes?" Dan inquired.

"I like to eat well. I bought them while you were getting your bullets," the prospector replied, smiling.

Filling his cup with the dark brew, Dan sat at the table across from Honey. Without looking up she said, "I imagine you will be wanting the ransom."

"Yes, we will."

Handing the baby to him, she climbed the ladder to a sleeping loft and disappeared. Dan held the warm bundle in his arms. The child looked up at him and yawned. *As though I couldn't feel worse about shooting your father,* he thought.

Honey returned with the belt still containing the money. She placed it on the table and took the baby back. "Jon was going to take me to St. Louis. He was going to buy me nice dresses and take me to the theater. He wanted to take me away from here. That's why he asked for the ransom."

"I had no choice, but . . ."

Stopping him, she said, "I know. Jon said he was going out and kill you. I was watching from the window."

"I am sorry you were hurt."

"I know what kind of man my husband was. He was mean and had killed many men. But he was good to me and loved his son. That is what I will tell young Jonny as he grows up."

When the breakfast was ready, Amos got Junior and Sully from the back room. After a trip to the outhouse, they were given food. The wounded man was pale, and in pain. "You got to get me to a doctor," he begged.

Showing no sympathy, Dan replied, "We got some burying to do, and then we head back for Ardmore. I saw a wagon near the barn. If we got harnesses, you should be at the doc's by nightfall."

The soil in the area was sandy and had not frozen. Dan and Junior each dug a grave. The boy's face looked sickly as he helped to carry Hank's body to one of the graves. "You best go back to Cheyenne and mend your ways, or someone will be dumping you into an unmarked grave," Dan warned the boy.

More time was taken with Jon Kidman. While he probably didn't deserve more than just being tossed to the coyotes, there was Honey to consider.

By the time the burials were completed, Amos had the wagon hitched and Dan's saddle on the black. As they rode away from the farm, the sun was warming the ground, melting the October snow. The trip was punctuated by Sully's complaining about the leg wound.

It was well after dark when they arrived in Ardmore. Amos drove the wagon right up to a clapboard building with a sign reading *Doctor Kane*. A short, stocky man answered their knock. He had pulled on his trousers over his night shirt, and still had a night cap on unruly gray hair.

"Someone better be dying!" he growled. "Come banging on my door in the middle of the night! What the hell couldn't wait until morning?"

Dan opened his sheepskin coat to expose his deputy badge. "We have a man here that was wounded during the rescue of the young woman."

Putting on his spectacles, the doctor held a lamp up to see the badge. "Cheyenne deputy! You are one hell of a long way from where that there badge means a damn thing."

As though on signal, Sully moaned loudly from the wagon. "Well, bring the man on in here. You have already ruined my sleep," the old doc said, walking back into his office grumbling.

Amos stayed at the doctor's while Dan took Honey and Junior to find a place to sleep. The prospector said that he had heard that the general store had a couple rooms. The memories of Dan's last visit picking up the letter and the question of postage left some doubt as to whether they could afford the rooms at the store or not.

It was late and they were bone-tired, so he headed for the store. Several knocks were finally answered by the merchant. He had a bewildered look on his face. "Can I help you?"

"We need a couple rooms for one, maybe two nights."

"My rooms haven't been used in some time. I can't vouch for the condition they're in."

Dan tilted his hat back. "We can't be too fussy. We'll take what you got."

"Well, let me see. How many in each room?"

"The woman and her baby in one. Myself and two other men in the other."

"That would be . . ." the store owner began

figuring in his head. "I think we can do business. It would be $5 per room per night. So, $10 in advance."

Anger ran through Dan. The merchant was asking a lot for two rooms. Having no bargaining position, Dan dug out two $5 gold pieces, and placed them in the merchant's hand. "We also have horses."

"That will be another $1 for each."

"You will get the rest tomorrow."

The two locked eyes for a moment. The merchant tossed the coins in his hand. "Have the rest first thing."

The rooms were small, dusty, and each had a curtain-less window. The leather strappings on the beds were loose, causing sagging in the middle. They were instructed to use the stairs at the back of the building for access to their rooms. There was a barn just beyond the stairs, and an outhouse. He would owe the merchant an additional $2 in the morning for keeping his and Junior's horses in the barn.

They had just finished putting up the horses and heading back to the room when Amos came down the alley by the store. "The doc let me keep the mule and sorrel in his barn for the night. Sully may lose the leg. The next couple of days will decide that."

Trudging up the narrow stairs, the three men entered their room. "You take the bed, Amos. The boy and I will spread our bedrolls on the floor."

Dan put the money belt under his blankets with his Colt next to it. Those sharing the room with him had given him no reason to think that they had plans for taking it, but the ransom was a fortune in any man's eyes and could be a great temptation.

The next two days were busy. Amos offered to take Honey and the baby back to Medicine Bow. They could catch a train from Ardmore. Dan had the feeling that she was looking forward to going home but was worried about how her father would feel about the baby.

Doc Middleton, the law in Ardmore, summoned Dan to his office. He spent hours threatening the deputy with everything from kidnapping to murder. He demanded to know where the ransom was. After lengthy interrogation, Dan was finally able to convince the lawman that he was working on behalf of the sheriff in Cheyenne and was just doing what he was told.

The killing of Jon Kidman had happened only because the man had tried to shoot him. Both Honey and Junior had been lured away by Kidman. The ransom demand and the letter left at the general store were proof that they might be in trouble.

With a final threat that if he heard of Dan being in the area without checking in first, he would be arrested immediately, Middleton gave him one day to get out of town and stay out. The demand to see the ransom money had been forgotten and Dan headed for the store to collect his stuff. He was glad to head out of town with the Wallace boy.

It was early afternoon before they finally departed, and their first stop on the way back to Cheyenne would be Harrison. Dan had put off buying supplies for the trip from the greedy merchant. They would rest another night at the Harrison Hotel, get what they needed in town, and then strike out for Cheyenne.

As they rode toward Harrison, Dan thought about his good fortune in having run into Amos Mudd. Without the old prospector's help, the outcome of this trip might have ended much worse. When he had wished the old miner goodbye at the train station, Amos had had a broad smile on his face. No doubt Amos was happy because, again, he was doing something good.

They followed Hat Creek, which cut through sagebrush-covered hills. It had been just over a week since Dan had followed the creek north. A cold wind blew, chilling their backs while the sun kept their fronts warm. It was not unlike a roaring campfire on a crisp winter night, only while riding they didn't have the opportunity to turn and warm both sides.

Just short of some sandy cliffs, Junior pointed out antelope grazing on the dry, brown grass. He asked to use the Winchester to try and shoot one. Dan pulled the rifle from the scabbard and handed it to the boy. The young Wallace's eyes were filled with excitement.

He dismounted and lay on his stomach. Using his left arm to support the Winchester, the boy carefully took aim. Dan sat on the black, holding the boy's roan. He was pleased to see that Junior took his time. The rifle shot startled the roan, causing it to pull on its reins. For a second the antelopes appeared unaffected, then suddenly bounded away over a small rise.

Junior jumped up. "Damn, I missed them."

Dan watched the antelopes appear over the next rise, still running wide-open. "You know, Junior, there were seven grazing when you shot. I just saw six run over the next rise. We best go and find out what happened to the seventh one."

The eager boy handed back the rifle and swung up onto the roan. Spurring the horse, he galloped toward the trail of the antelope. Close behind, Dan followed the anxious lad over the rise. Just beyond the crest lay the dead animal.

Junior jumped off his horse and ran up to the kill. Holding its head up, he beamed. "I got it! Can we have some for supper?"

Pulling the knife from his belt, Dan tossed it down to the boy. "Here you go. Gut the antelope and we'll stop short of Harrison and skin it for our supper."

Dan stopped the boy as he began to hack at the animal. "That isn't the way to gut it. Haven't you ever done this before?"

Kneeling at the animal with the knife in one hand and the antelope's hind leg in the other, Junior looked up, expecting to be reprimanded. His face fell. "I'm sorry. I've never hunted before."

"Your father or his crew never took you shooting?"

"Oh, my father had the men show me how to shoot. In fact, after shooting, I always had to clean the guns. He wouldn't let me hunt. He would say we raise beef and we should eat beef."

Swinging down from the black, Dan walked over to the boy. "Let me help you do this. Now, I am going to tell you what to do, and then you gut it. Okay?"

Suddenly eager again, Junior paid close attention to the older man's instruction. Soon the two of them were riding again. They cut over to Sowbelly

Creek, which would take them into Harrison. Short of town, Dan stopped in a grove of cottonwood.

He hung the antelope from a branch and explained the best way to skin the animal. Handing his knife to the boy, Dan began gathering wood for the fire. While picking up the dead branches, he told the boy that the sprouts from the cottonwood trees were often planted by settlers to mark the boundaries of their land.

With the animal skinned and the hide neatly folded to take with them, Junior stood proudly holding the knife out for Dan. "I got it skinned. I ended up making a few button holes while doing it."

Laughing, Dan took the knife. "When I skinned my first deer, the hide was full of holes and the meat was covered with hair. It looks like you did a clean job on the animal."

After showing the boy how to locate the tender loins and cut the animal up, they were soon roasting the meat over the fire. Junior kept up a constant chatter about his dreams. The prevailing theme was doing things that would take him away from Cheyenne and his father.

As the young Wallace took a bite of the sizzling meat, he looked surprised. "This meat tastes funny. Maybe I cooked it wrong."

"What you're tasting is sagebrush," Dan informed him. "This animal ate a lot of it."

Rather than continue into Harrison, the two men made camp in the cottonwoods. Dan planned to pick up what they would need at the mercantile while passing through. Even though Junior Wallace was man-sized and 17, he acted much younger. The trip back to Cheyenne would give Dan a chance to know the boy better.

They hunted and fished their way back to Cheyenne. Dan showed the boy how to find items necessary to live off the land. One night they enjoyed roasted raccoon and baked cattail roots. He told the boy that the key to skinning raccoon was to remove all the fat. If left on, it gave the meat an unpleasant flavor.

The last night, while a rabbit roasted on the fire and beans steamed on the pot, Dan told the boy that they would be in Cheyenne by tomorrow afternoon. Junior became quiet. The smile from the past few days was gone. They ate in silence and turned into their bedrolls as soon as the meal was done.

The boy's mood seemed to improve the next morning. After finishing the beans from the night before and washing them down with the last of their coffee, they put their gear onto the horses. Junior held them while Dan made sure that the breakfast fire was out. He had cautioned the boy more than once about the danger of a grass fire being pushed by the constant wind on the plain.

Turning back to the horses, he stopped. The young Wallace boy was holding the Winchester, leveled at Dan. "What are you doing, Junior?"

"I can't go back to my father. He will blame me for the trouble, because I hung around Jon. He don't want me staying with him. I am not enough of a man in his eyes. He sends me off to toughen me up. I want the money, and I will go to St. Louis like Jon planned."

"And after St. Louis, Junior? After the money is spent, or stolen from you? How do you think a young man gets by in a city like St. Louis? You will find yourself running with a gang, no money, and little future other than spending time in jail, or worse yet, killed."

Shaking his head vigorously, Junior blurted, "It can't be worse than what waits for me at my father's."

"I am not going to give you the money. With or without you, I am going back to see your father. I will tell him anything you want me to. If you shoot me, you best kill me dead with the first shot, because I will draw and fire, if for no other reason than to stop you from going down the trail you're wanting to go."

"I have been impressed with the way you have handled yourself on the trip back. You were a great help and made the trip easier for me. I want you to go back home and do whatever your father asks. I want you to do it well. Next summer, if you want, you are welcome to come to my ranch in the green valley and work for me. I will suggest it to your father when we get back."

Junior stood looking at the broad-shouldered man in front of him. Slowly, he lowered the rifle. He stared at the ground, at his feet. Dan walked to him and took the rifle. "One more thing. I expect you to look me in the eye, and the same with your father."

Little was said the rest of the way to Cheyenne. Junior looked straight ahead, unhappy to be going home. They rode up the paved street to the Wallace house. Swinging down and tying their horses, the two headed for the door.

"I want you to think about one thing, Junior. Your father loves you. He sent me to get you back. He misses your mother, and as long as he has you, he has part of her."

Dan felt awkward to be talking like this, but he felt something more had to be said before the boy saw his father. He stood back while Junior knocked on the door. Jonas Wallace opened the door and a look of relief washed over his face. He looked at Dan, then waved for the two of them to come in.

The giggle of his daughter, Joanie, shifted Dan's attention away from the Wallaces as he rushed past them to find Mary and the child.

* * *

It was well after daylight the next day before Dan arrived at the sheriff's office. The sky was threatening more snow. He didn't notice the gloom of the day. After an evening with his family, he had a bounce in his step. Sheriff Kent was sitting behind his desk, his pipe clenched in his teeth, shuffling through some papers.

"Damn paperwork," he complained. "You'd think I had nothing better to do than sit at my desk and read."

Smiling, Dan said, "It's all part of being in charge."

"I saw Carlos this morning. He told me you came back with the Wallace boy and the money," Sheriff Kent said. "He also said you found my niece and sent her back to Medicine Bow. I was pleased to learn this, but would like to know why the hell I am getting reports on what you have done from the man at the livery?"

"I'm sorry I didn't wake you and let you know, but after dropping the boy off and seeing Mary, I hurried to bring the horses to the livery. Carlos was there, and I guess I mentioned it to him. I was kind of in a hurry to get back to Mary and my little one," Dan explained.

"Well, I guess I can't be too upset at you. You did one hell of a job, and finding Honey was damn unexpected. You say she had a baby by Kidman?"

"She did. Turns out she went with him, they were in love. Got married and everything."

The sheriff went over to the potbelly stove and poured two mugs of coffee. Handing one to Dan, he sat back behind the desk and blew on the hot brew.

Smiling, Dan tasted the coffee, then his face turned serious. "Are Topper or Peck around?"

The sheriff leaned back in his chair and relit the pipe before answering, "Peck is sending a telegram for me. I sent Topper to Lilly's to get breakfast for my prisoner. Why do you ask?"

"I take it the prisoner is the fellow that shot the dealer."

"He is. He will be in front of the judge next week and should be hung by the end of the month," the sheriff replied. "Now, why the interest in the deputies' whereabouts?"

"I hope I'm wrong, but someone here in Cheyenne knew I was carrying the ransom, and sent a man to take it from me."

Kent furled his brow. "The only ones that knew you was going were me, Jonas Wallace, and I *did* tell Topper and Peck. Maybe someone else could have heard us, but I don't know."

The broad-shouldered rancher watched the sheriff. "Had you ever seen either of them with Mexican Bob?"

Sheriff Kent snorted and swept the stack of paper off his scarred oak desk. "Damn that Topper! A year ago he was spending some time with that crooked bastard and I put a stop to it. Told him if he wanted to hang out with his kind, he could hand me back his badge."

"I killed Bob in Harrison when he tried to back-shoot me. My guess is he killed the man carrying the ransom for your niece."

"Damn his hide!" the sheriff exploded, slamming his fist on the desk. "After my niece disappeared, folks noticed that Topper was spending pretty freely. He said he had an uncle die and left him some money."

The sound of footsteps out on the walk silenced the conversation between the two men. The door opened and a lean deputy carrying a steaming pot of porridge entered. "Damn, it is cold out there. Looks like we might get some more snow."

Topper stopped when he noticed the two men staring at him. "I got the prisoner's breakfast here. Sheriff, are you mad about something?"

"Put the porridge on the stove there," the lawman instructed his deputy.

Placing the pot next to the coffee pot, he opened his coat and turned to his boss. "Did something bad happen, Sheriff?"

"I am afraid so, Topper. I got some bad news

for you. Your friend Mexican Bob is dead."

A look of shock swept across the deputy's face. Then he forced a smile. "It makes no never mind to me. I quit hanging with him when you asked me to."

"Topper," the sheriff said. "I want to know who the uncle was that you got the money from a year ago. He best be dead and left paper saying you get the money."

Like a trapped rat, the deputy glanced around for a way out. In desperation, he reached for his gun. He hadn't even cleared leather when he froze, looking into the barrel of Dan's Colt.

Disgusted, Sheriff Kent said, "Take his gun and badge, Dan. Put him in with the bastard in the back. Maybe they will kill each other and save the cost of a trial."

Dan relieved the disgraced deputy of his hardware and pushed him toward the cell. "I didn't mean for anyone to die. It was the Mexican. He done it."

"Save it for the judge, Topper," Dan said. "With luck, you will be out of jail before you're an old man."

With the new prisoner locked away, Dan came out and refilled his coffee. Sitting across from the sheriff, he thought for a moment. "I will be leaving soon. Mary will soon be strong enough to travel. I have to get back to the ranch."

The lawman looked vacantly across the room. "Why the hell would Topper do it? Hell. The way I'm losing deputies, I will never be able to retire."

"Did you hear what I said, Bernard?"

His face reddened a bit, and he answered, "Yes, yes I did. I also noticed you were damn fast to get the drop on Topper. I didn't even get my hand on my gun. Cheyenne could use a man like you."

"It wouldn't be for me, sheriff. Like you said, it's becoming more and more paperwork. The days of a fast draw to enforce the laws are ending. I have a ranch in a beautiful valley, a place where my family will be safe and can grow. I even offered the Wallace boy a job next summer."

"Well, Deputy August, I can understand your wanting to go. You'll have to see the city attorney before you leave and give statements about everything, including Topper."

Dan turned to leave. It was time to make the rounds and show the badge. He left a tired-looking Sheriff Kent staring at his cold cup of coffee. The west wind drove small flakes of snow against Dan as he closed the door. The cold, fresh air was a relief after the tension in the stuffy office. He looked up and down the streets of Cheyenne. He missed the openness of the plains.

CHAPTER NINE

In the sitting room at Jonas Wallace's home, Dan sat watching the bedroom door. Inside that room was Dr. Walsh with his wife. He prayed that the good doctor would emerge and tell him that Mary was strong enough to travel.

It was late October, and soon the winter snows would be covering the plains, making travel difficult. The sheriff had seemed to lose the desire to do the job after Topper's arrest. Most business had been left up to Dan and Peck. Even the letter from his brother thanking him for the safe return of his daughter and grandson had not cheered him up.

Peck walked proudly beside Dan on the rounds. The word was out of how fast the rancher had drawn on Topper. Dan had become quite the hero in Cheyenne. In his youth, he had enjoyed the attention given when he had won a shooting contest back in Elkader. When the attention came from his ability to draw and kill another man, it was not welcomed.

Dan had spoken at length with Jonas about his son. The boy had been sent to a line camp with the crew to watch the herd. The only hope he had been given was when Junior beamed and said, "Father promised me if I worked hard this winter I could come to the green valley in the spring to work for you."

The bedroom door started to open and then stopped. Dan sat up in anticipation. He could hear the muffled voice of the doctor telling Mary something. Then there was her acknowledgement and Dr. Walsh stepped into the room.

"Dr. Walsh, how is my wife? Can she go home?"

"Mrs. August is doing very well. Her temperature has finally stayed normal for the past week. Her color is good. In fact, the opening is completely closed."

"That's good news, right, doctor?" Dan asked expectantly.

"Yes, Mr. August, that is good news. My only concern is that her system is still weak. The stress of going back to your ranch may lower her resistance and it may be a setback for her."

Dan's face showed his disappointment. His mind raced, searching for a solution. "What if we took the train back to Casper? She could stay with the Hartwicks while I go back to check on things at the ranch. Dr. Morgan is there to check on her, and if anything happens, it is only a train ride away for her to come back here."

Dr. Walsh shook his head. "I don't know. If the trip, or anything, causes her to turn, there may be nothing I can do to bring her back to health. Here I can control things and give her body time to recover completely."

"What if I let you ask her and let Mary make the decision?" Dan suggested.

"Wouldn't you want to do that?" Dr. Walsh asked.

"If I ask her, she will say yes no matter what the risk. If you talk to her and make her aware of the problems that could arise, then if she is willing, we will go."

"Then, Mr. August, you will be going to Casper. I just spent the past half-hour trying to convince your wife to stay here in Cheyenne. She posed the same argument you just made about going to the Hartwicks'. I think her mind is made up."

"I will make sure she doesn't overdo things. The rest will be in God's hands," Dan promised the doctor.

It took two days to ready everything for the trip to Casper. A telegram had been sent to Bert Hartwick requesting lodging for Mary and the youngster. Jonas Wallace gave Dan a sum of money for bringing his son back, and Sheriff Kent wished him well after attempting to convince Dan to stay and run for sheriff.

There was a light snow the day they departed from Cheyenne. The passenger car had a small coal stove for warmth. It had little effect against the drafty windows of the car. The rhythmic sound of the wheels hitting the rail seams lulled the occupants into a trance. Each was with their own thoughts.

Mary had taken a seat near the stove and huddled under a blanket from Dan's bedroll. She held

Joanie under the blanket so they could share each other's warmth. The snow-covered plain raced by as the train labored toward Casper. The passengers' breath soon covered the glass with a layer of frost, shutting the outside world out.

A husky rider sporting a thick moustache whispered to a young boy next to him while nodding toward Dan. Noticing them staring at him, Dan smiled at the boy. The gesture was enough to bolster the nerve of the man. Leaning across the aisle, he asked, "Were you a deputy in Cheyenne?"

"Yes, I was," the broad-shouldered man replied. "I resigned last night to go back to my ranch."

"Are you really as fast with your guns as they say?" the excited man asked. "I heard you had killed many men in the line of duty and you always let them draw first."

"I hate to disappoint you, sir," Dan responded. "I didn't kill anyone in the line of duty. I can draw a gun, but I doubt it is as fast as they say."

Taken back by the answer, the man's face reddened. "I'm sorry. I didn't mean to offend. The boy was curious."

It would have been the right thing to do to let the man down gracefully but at the moment Dan felt the frustration of being known as a fast gun. All he knew was that the sooner he got back to the green valley, the better it would be.

He suddenly realized that Mary was looking at him. She had heard the man's question. He shuddered to think what she must be feeling. She had never questioned him about the men he had fought and killed. When he had tried to tell her how he had changed since leaving Elkader, she had called him a sweet, brave, and honest man.

How long could a wife keep believing in her husband when those around him continually reminded her that he had killed men? Dan sat back, thinking about their life in the green valley. Things were simple there. They worked hard, but in the evenings, when sitting on the ranch house porch, the beauty of where they lived was all a person could want.

The first sign that they were approaching Casper was in the foothills of the mountains to the south. On the north side of the train, the tree-lined route of the North Platte River cut the snow-covered plain. A water tower, stock pens and loading ramp went by.

The blast of the steam whistle announced the train's arrival at the Casper station. The sound startled Joanie, and Mary spoke softly to her, trying to comfort her. After the train lurched to a stop, Dan stood, stretching his legs. The snow had stopped and the sun was low in the western sky.

The stocky man pushed by on his way to depart. The look he gave Dan indicated that he was still upset at the answer he had received earlier. Mary handed the child to Dan and then gathered up the blankets. As they stepped down from the train, Angie Hartwick called out from the platform.

The Hartwick's mercantile was housed in a single story. Behind the store was a two-story addition that was their living quarters. The sleeping quarters were above a large kitchen and sitting room. There was a second bedroom that had been planned for children. This room would be used for Mary and Joanie.

After his family was made comfortable, Dan accepted Bert Hartwick's offer to join him for a drink at the Casper Saloon. It was frequented by loggers, derrick hands, and cattle men. Most of the time the patrons enjoyed tossing back a few drinks and playing a few hands of cards. Once in a while, one group would get into a brawl with another and then the local sheriff would quickly put a stop to it.

Sheriff Ben Winslow was a large, powerful man who had worked in the woods, the oil fields, and ranch. His revolver seldom came out of his holster. His ham-sized fists had enforced the law in Casper for the past four years. He was respected by all three groups, and any fights were quickly abandoned when he came onto the scene.

Bert and Dan joined the lawman at a table near the bar. The dim room smelled of tobacco smoke, sweat, and rye. The crowd was small on the frigid November evening. Most of the cowboys were wintering in the line shacks and the loggers were in the camps cutting timber. Only the derrick hands had idle time. Two tables of card players with tar-covered boots were near the potbelly stove.

"This is the best time of year for me," the sheriff commented. "The winter is quiet. Come the spring thaw, the cowhands and loggers come into town, with their pockets full of winter wages. The damn town is busting loose until they have wasted away their pay."

The men toasted to the quiet times. Dan rolled a cigarette and lit a match on the heel of his boot. Taking a deep drag, he coughed before saying, "With luck, my herd will be big enough to add to your troubles this spring when Curly and Lars drive them into the stock pens."

"A fellow came in with a few cattle last week. He was looking to make a few dollars for some nights on the town. Two were unbranded, but the third one had your Circle A brand on it," Sheriff Winslow informed Dan. "He claimed he had found the cattle out on the plain. For all I know, all three were yours, but the only one I could stop him from selling was the branded animal. It is still down at the stock pens. When you head back for the ranch, you can take it with you."

"It ain't right," Bert objected. "It the cows were taken off Dan's range, they should be his. You should have sent the bum out of Casper with empty pockets."

"I appreciate you sticking up for me, Bert. I want you to have the animal for helping Mary and me. The other animals could have wandered in from someone else's range. Anyone could legally . . ."

Dan's comment was cut off when the saloon door banged open, bringing in a blast of cold air. It was J.P. Burdick. There was the look of surprise on the cattle dealer's face when he saw Dan sitting in at the table.

"Damn, I thought you were spending the winter in Cheyenne, Dan. I heard you had a position as a deputy for Kent. You even rescued some folks up in the Dakotas."

J.P. had a way of filling a room with his presence. He was wearing a top coat with a fur collar, kidskin gloves, and a black wool bowler. His face was framed by a broad smile displaying perfect teeth, but

Dan knew the man bought cattle low and sold them high for a living, and the smile was just a tool of his trade.

"Mary was feeling strong enough to travel, J.P., and I thought it best to get back to the ranch and help Curly and Lars. They should be running out of supplies by now," Dan replied.

The cattle dealer ordered a bottle of expensive brandy to be brought to the table and sat down. "It's a cold one out there. There is nothing like warming the insides with brandy."

The three men watched as J.P. poured glasses of the brandy. The man's coat opened briefly, exposing a revolver worn in a special holster high on his side. Sheriff Winslow excused himself before taking the drink. "I got some rounds to make. Maybe another time, Burdick."

Ignoring the actions of the lawman, J.P. held up his brandy and said, "To a short winter, gentlemen. May 1887 not be repeated."

Both of his companions said, "Amen," aware of the losses of the cattlemen during that harsh winter.

After finishing their drinks, Dan and Bert excused themselves and left J.P. alone at the table. Trudging back toward the mercantile against the wind, they had to agree that the brandy did warm the insides nicely.

* * *

Dan lay under the heavy comforter, dreading the thought of getting up. He could feel the warmth of Mary next to him. The sounds of the business owners could be heard coming from the street. Someone was chopping wood for the morning fire, another was scraping snow from a front porch. A freight wagon rumbled by, and the call of the driver's "good morning" greeting to a fellow early riser.

The smell of wood smoke told him that the Hartwicks had the fire going downstairs and soon the heat would rise through the floor vent. Dan planned to leave for the ranch right after the morning meal. His wagon sat alongside the mercantile, loaded with supplies. The team was still in the barn behind the mercantile.

He quietly slipped out of bed, wanting to let his wife sleep a little longer. She had been exhausted by the train trip. Dan stood over the vent while dressing. The warm air coming from below stopped his shivering. He carried his boots and tip toed out of the room. The warm air rising up the stairs filled the hall. He left the bedroom door ajar to let more heat into the room.

Mrs. Hartwick had the coffee on and was cooking porridge. She poured him the dark brew and set it down on the table for him. "Bert is in the barn. He wanted to harness your team for you."

"How will we ever be able to repay you and Bert for all your kindness?" Dan asked.

"It is no more than you would do in return if you found us in trouble on the plain," she said, smiling. "Folks do for folks."

The coffee was strong and satisfying. He heard the merchant coming in from the barn. From the back porch he called, "After milking, I got your team ready.

They're in the wagon bay. It sure as hell is cold out this morning."

"Don't track into my kitchen, and watch your language around company," Angie scolded.

The broad-shouldered man smiled at the red-faced Bert. "I thank you for getting the team ready."

"Set that milk on the sideboard. Breakfast is ready," the robust woman instructed.

The conversation remained light around the kitchen table. Shortly after they sat down to eat, Mary came down with the child. Joanie came running in ahead of her mother and jumped into her father's arms. Mrs. Hartwick served up bowls of the steaming cereal for everyone. She set a pitcher of fresh milk on the table to pour over the porridge.

Dan was surrounded by family and friends, but his mind was on the ranch. He needed to get back to help Curly and Lars. They could use the supplies he was bringing. There could be issues with some of the cattle. It would feel good to ride his chestnut across the valley and look over the herd.

Mary would have to stay in Casper until spring. He planned to spend a month or two at the ranch and then come back into town. Bert had a winter project he wanted to do and Dan had promised to help him. He would then go back in March and April to move the herd back on the plain. By May, he could bring his family back to the ranch.

They were just finishing breakfast when the slamming of the front door alerted them that a customer had entered the store. "Give me a minute and I'll be right out," Bert called to the visitor.

"Take your time. The fellow at the sheriff's office told me Dan August was staying here," the man in the store answered.

Dan looked up in surprise, recognizing the voice. "Amos! Amos Mudd, is that you?"

The old prospector's frame filled the doorway to the kitchen. "I thought you'd be in that valley of yours by now."

The surprise on Dan face was only surpassed by the confusion on everyone else's. He quickly let Mary and the Hartwicks know about his meeting the old miner in Ardmore. Not wanting to discuss the gunplay at the Kidman camp, he just told them that Amos had helped him with the ransom.

With everyone satisfied with who Mr. Mudd was, Angie brought Amos a mug of coffee and offered him some porridge. While Dan was happy to see the old prospector again, he felt pressure to be off for the ranch.

"What happened to wintering in the cabin in Ardmore?" Dan asked.

Between mouthfuls of porridge, Amos answered, "After dropping off the gal in Medicine Bow, I planned to head for Ardmore. The train stopped in Cheyenne, and I saw Sheriff Kent on the platform. He told me you had gone back to Casper. I figured what the heck and come to see your valley."

"I was just about to leave. All I have here is the wagon and team. You are welcome to ride along."

With the breakfast dishes taken care of, the Hartwicks went to work in the store. Mary took Joanie back to their room. Dan and Amos headed to the barn to get the team. Their breath trailed behind them in the brisk morning air.

After hitching the team, Dan brushed the light snow from the wagon seat. Amos tossed his blanket roll and pack into the wagon. "I'll be right back," the rancher said. "I want to say goodbye to Mary."

Amos climbed onto the wagon and pulled it to the front of the store. He then went in to purchase some tobacco, jerky and bullets, while waiting for Dan. A few minutes later the two men were heading out of town, the horses welcoming the chance to be out of the barn.

While the temperatures were cold, there wasn't much snow in Casper. The mountains to the west were already covered. Many of the higher passes were blocked. His valley was surrounded by mountains that protected it from the most severe storms that ravaged the plains.

The morning sky was clear, assuring that their first day of travel would be without snow. Amos was smiling. "This is great weather. It's been too many years since I traveled this area. I just might do some prospecting come spring."

"I was thinking you might want to work some cows," Dan kidded him.

"Me and cows don't get along so good. When I weren't digging potatoes for my father, I was milking his cows."

"You wouldn't be milking these cows, you'd be working them on horseback."

Amos chuckled and shook his head no. Then, rubbing his bearded chin, his face got serious. "I wish you could have been with me when I took the young gal and her baby to Medicine Bow. I sent a telegram to her father before we left Ardmore. When we got there on the train, he was waiting, with tears running down his face. Turns out she had her head turned by Kidman and saw no way to come back home. Honey was sure her father would never want to see her again."

"Like you said when we were riding to their camp, we were doing a good thing." Dan replied.

Rather than stop, they ate their midday meal of jerky and water while bumping along on the plain. The team was kept at a comfortable pace to prevent tiring them. While Amos took over the driving, Dan rolled a cigarette. The bouncing wagon made keeping the tobacco on the paper difficult. Finally, he licked the edge and rolled the smoke.

The November sun set early on the plain. They camped along the edge of a small lake in a grove of willows. The men stood along the shore and watched a dozen mallards set their wings and light on the open water.

Amos smiled and said, "If any fly within range, they would make a mighty tasty meal." A few moments later two took off, heading past the men. Amos knocked his down with one shot. It took Dan two to bring his bird down.

While cleaning the ducks, the men kidded back and forth about Dan requiring a second shot. While Dan left the prospector to roast the birds, he rigged a tarp off the side of the wagon to cut the frigid wind. The stars had disappeared from the night sky as clouds rolled in. He brought the horses in closer and fed them grain from a bag in the wagon.

Amos surprised him with potatoes. They were covered with clay and baked in the coals of the fire. He looked up as Dan approached. "I remember hating every potato my father made me dig, but I sure enjoyed eating them. I was happy when the Hartwicks had some for sale. Kept them in my coat so they wouldn't freeze."

While the men ate, they sat in the protection of the wagon. Their tin mugs of steaming coffee quickly cooled in the chilly night air. "We will be at the ranch by noon tomorrow," the rancher told his guest. "It will feel good to sleep in the warm ranch house."

"Oh, I don't mind the cold," Amos said. "Many a winter night I spent sleeping under a spruce tree shelter when trapping. The brisk fresh air clears the mind. When I'm curled up under the blankets, I sleep like a baby."

"So, you were a mountain man too. Well, you'll sure as heck like this night. It will be damn brisk."

Dan washed their dishes in the lake. The water numbed his hands. There was ice forming in the sheltered areas along the shore. With his chores done, he crawled under the wagon and rolled out his bed roll. Then, sitting near the fire with his collar turned up on the sheepskin coat, he rolled a smoke. After lighting it with a brand, he sat staring into the dark.

The old prospector had produced a pipe and was smoking a bowl before turning in. "We got snow coming," Amos informed Dan. "It will make tomorrow's travel more difficult."

"The wagon tongue is pointed toward the valley. If the blowing snow makes it hard to see, we will keep the wind from the same direction as we drive," Dan told him.

Amos looked at the rancher with approval. The fire was burnt down to coals when the two men crawled into the bedrolls. The wind and the horses cropping the grass were the only sounds they heard as they dozed off.

CHAPTER TEN

Blowing snow covered the plain when the men awoke. Dan shook the snow off his bedroll cover. Lying on his back under the wagon, he pulled his boots on. Then, pulling his coat out from under his blankets, he crawled out and squinted against the stinging snow.

"You still working on clearing your mind, Amos?" Dan called out as he dug under the wagon tarp for the kindling they had stored the night before.

Sheltering their fire pit with his body, Dan brushed the snow aside before placing the tinder and stacking the kindling. On many a morning, he had felt the warmth of the previous night's fire still in the ashes, but this morning there was nothing but the cold. Cupping a match in his hands, he struck it and touched the flame to the tinder.

The waving willow trees and the wagon helped to cut the wind a little, protecting the struggling fire. Grabbing some wood, they had stacked, Dan knocked them together to remove the clinging snow. He stacked the wood, creating a chimney effect for the fire, and a wind break on the windward side. Soon the flames were climbing the firewood and snapping as they hit drops of dried sap.

Amos had gotten up to tend to the stock. Dan broke through the ice on the edge of the lake and filled the coffee pot. Setting it next to the fire, he went back under the wagon and rolled up the bedrolls.

The coffee water was steaming when he finished. Amos came back covered from head to toe with snow. "Damn it, man! This stuff sticks to everything. A few degrees cooler and it would blow right off."

"When I was young, my cousins and I used to look forward to the sticky snow. We had some great snowball fights," Dan said, reminiscing.

"Fun enough when you have a warm house to go into when you get soaked to the skin," the old prospector replied.

Agreeing, Dan said, "We will have a warm house to go into in a few hours. With luck, Curly will have a pot a coffee on the potbelly in the bunkhouse."

With the fire spitting and sputtering from the snow, the men sat against the wagon wheels while the snow blew over the top of them. Dan dunked his hard bread into his coffee to soften it.

Allowing the fire to burn down, the two men hitched the team, keeping the direction of the tongue in mind. Kicking snow over the coals before they left, the men began their last leg of the trip to the valley. The blowing snow made it impossible to pick out any landmarks. The wind was blowing from the front right corner of the wagon. With their hats pulled tight on their heads and their chins buried on the tops of their coats, they rode in silence.

Once, the team came to a sudden stop. Dan was about to slap them with the ends of the reins, but then thought better of it. Climbing down, he found that the horses had stopped at the bank of a three-foot deep wash. Amos got off the wagon and braced himself against a wheel. Dan held the reins close to their heads, forcing the horses to back up. Together, they managed to back the team and wagon enough to swing clear of the obstacle.

The men led the team along the wash until it played out. Brushing the snow from around the head of the horses, Dan said, "I best let you be our eyes in this storm. From what I can see from back there, I could drive right off a cliff."

Amos nodded. "You got to trust your animals when darkness or blinding snow make it difficult to see. Had an old teamster once tell me that the animals could sense the danger. I figure they just see better than we do."

Once under way again, Dan lost confidence that they were still headed in the right direction. The wind was still coming in from the front right, but he well knew that the wind often changed direction during the day. Not only were landmarks obscured, but he couldn't tell the location of the sun.

While it seemed longer, Amos' pocket watch told them that they had only been underway for two hours. They rode into some rougher country strewn with boulders and washes. Dan was sure that they had drifted too far south. The men decided to stop and let the horses have a breather. After an hour, the snow stopped. They were able to pick out some of the higher peaks, confirming that they had added at least another hour to their trip.

There was a dense, six-inch layer of snow on the ground. Amos had put together a small fire and made coffee to warm themselves before getting back on the road. Dan got out some more grain for the horses. Soon they were on their way to the valley.

With a great deal of pride, Dan described the ranch and valley to Amos. He told about his grandfather Oli coming upon it and writing about it in his ledger. He explained that he and his cousins had stopped there to rest after they had finished a cattle drive. Once he had seen it, he'd known that it was the place where he wanted to build a ranch.

The wagon left a long, winding track on the fresh snow. Dan talked about his future plans in the valley. He pointed at a snow-covered peak and told Amos that a trapper and his wife lived near it. The only movement around them was the swirling snow driven by the wind. Finally, the opening to the valley was in sight.

Dan was tempted to push the team and hurry to the ranch, but he resisted the urge. The wagon was loaded with supplies and the team had slowed, laboring under their burden. He stopped them and let them have a breather for a few minutes.

After a brief rest, they continue toward the opening. The heads of the team came up as they recognized the familiar surroundings. They seemed to step out a little more quickly. As they entered the valley, they were welcomed by a vast expanse of white snow rather than the lush green of summer.

The peak of the barn was in view first, and then the back of the ranch house. Beyond the house would be the bunkhouse. Dan had expected to see smoke rising from that direction, from the potbelly stove. A moment later he knew why there wasn't. As they rounded the end of the ranch house, he saw the bunkhouse. It had burnt! The charred remains poked out of the snow.

There was a stillness around the ranch. The snow-covered yard was devoid of any tracks. The only sound was the clucking of chickens in the barn. Climbing off the wagon, Dan hurried over and stood near the burnt ruins. The only explanation was that the bunkhouse had caught fire, forcing Curly and Lars to move to the line shack in the valley.

He heard Amos walking up behind him. Without turning, he asked, "Why wouldn't the boys move into the ranch house if the bunkhouse burnt?"

Amos stopped beside Dan. "Maybe it's because the windows have been shot out!"

"What!" the rancher exclaimed.

"Dan, I just looked at the house. Something happened here. There was some shooting."

Dan hurried to the ranch house. The front windows were shattered. He saw that the door had bullet holes. Trying the knob, the door was locked. Taking the skeleton key from behind a bench, he unlocked and opened it. The floor was littered with glass and broken dishes. It didn't appear that anyone had come into the house, but rather this damage was from bullets shot from the outside.

Rushing back outside, Dan headed toward the barn. The poles of the corral had been pulled down.

The main door was open, which was often done. He stopped just outside the door and caught his breath. Lying on the dirt floor was a body! He was sure that it was Lars.

Walking into the barn, he knelt near the ranch hand. There was dried blood on the back of his vest from a bullet wound. There was another in the back of his head that had blown much of his face away when exiting.

Nausea came over Dan. *Who would have done this?* he wondered. Looking around the barn, he saw that, other than the chickens, the rest of the stock was gone. By the looks of the barn and Lars, whatever happened had occurred some time ago.

He stood up and turned. Amos stood just inside the door. "What the hell happened here, Dan?"

"This here is Lars, Amos. He was back shot. Curly is not around. His body is probably in the ashes of the bunkhouse."

Stepping back out into the yard, Dan saw a mound of snow. Kicking some off with his boot revealed a dead mustang. It was the one Curly liked to ride. Amos looked at the rancher. His friend was pale, clenching and unclenching his fists.

"Dan, we have to take a minute and try and get a picture of what happened here. Once we figure that out, we might get an idea where to start."

"Amos, I should have come back sooner. As soon as Mary was out of danger, I should have come."

"What we're seeing here happened some time ago. You couldn't have stopped it."

Anger was clear in Dan's voice. "There would

have been tracks to follow. With the damn snow we have nothing!"

"You are right, Dan. Any sign left by them is covered with snow. When you are ready, we will learn what we can and bring those that done this to justice," the prospector said, speaking as gently as he could. "I am going to make the house livable and clean up the mess. Then I will bring the supplies into the house. We will then look as much information as we can to help us find the bastards. Tomorrow, we will find a pick and dig a proper grave for your man there."

Dan hesitated a moment before following Amos. He knew that his friend was right. Standing in the middle of the ranch yard and shouting at the mountains about the injustice done here would solve nothing. There were things that had to be done first to survive in this wild country.

After the windows were covered and the glass cleaned up, Amos started a fire in the stove. Dan went out and took the tarp off the wagon. He went to the barn and laid it over Lars body. Dan took a moment to say a prayer over the cowhand ending with, "I am sorry I wasn't here for you." After tossing some grain to the chickens, he returned to the wagon to help empty the supplies.

"I'll unhitch the team and put them in the barn," Dan said.

"Before we do that, let's drag the dead horse out of the yard. It is a reminder we do not need. And then we will check all the sign in the barn before we bring the team in," The prospector suggested.

Again, Amos was right. He was thinking things through logically. Until Dan got over the shock of finding his world destroyed, he decided that he was going to let his friend take the lead. Putting the horses into the barn would have ruined what little sign that could be found on the dirt floor.

They dragged the dead mustang beyond the pond. Before winter was over the wildlife would find it and make short work of the carcass. The men rode back on the team horses, stopping near an upright post of the corral. Tying them there, they went to the barn.

The late afternoon light filled the barn with deep shadows. Dan stood near the door, looking away from the body. He felt strong guilt over Lar's death. In the ruins of the bunkhouse he was sure they would find Curly's bones.

The men lit lamps and slowly worked their way around the barn. There was an abundance of tracks. Amos had a tally book and was sketching various boot prints. "My memory isn't what it once was. These here drawings will help keep me straight."

Slowly, a picture developed in Dan's mind. There were prints from a running Lars, deep and distinct. Another man had walked up to the wounded man and shot him again. He found the boot tracks of three men and one horse. The horse had new shoes, with an X on each side. That was the trademark of the blacksmith in Casper.

One of the men wore boots with a small heel and stepped on the outside of his right leg. Another wore boots with a wide heel and, by the depth of his steps, was probably heavy. The third was typical of dozens of men in the area, but had a worn area on the inside of the sole, probably from the stirrup, which told him the man rode for a living. He was the one who had walked up to Lars. It was dark when the two men completed the search.

After putting the horses into the stalls they walked toward the ranch house, holding the lanterns high. The fire in the stove was down to coals, so Amos added some wood. The room had warmed up from the fire. Both men shed their coats and hung them on pegs near the door.

Dan sat thinking about what they had found so far. In the corner of the kitchen leaned his shotgun. On the shelf in the sitting area were boxes of shells for the shotgun and bullets for the Colt and Winchester. Other than the horses in the corral and a couple of young stock in the barn, nothing had been taken. Why would they kill the cowhands for so little?

Looking up at Amos, who was putting together a meal, he said, "Tomorrow we ride down the valley and check on the cattle, but first we bury Lars."

Supper that night consisted of biscuits and beans. The beans could have used a little more time on the stove. The satisfying flavor made up for the crunchiness.

Amos finished his meal and filled the bowl of his pipe. Lighting it, he took a deep drag and slowly blew out the smoke. "Pipe smoking is much more civilized than chewing. Took it up from an old friend I use to run with. I tend to like both, though."

After a moment, he continued. "I counted three men in the barn. We can't know how many more may have been outside. One of the men led his horse into the barn. The shoes have X's on them."

Dan interrupted, "They would be shoes from the smithy in Casper."

"Good," Amos said. "If one was local, we can figure some of the others may be from Casper also. The horse was a gray mare."

"How would you know that?"

"There was a damaged saddle tossed in a stall in the barn. The horse we dragged out of here had no saddle. I figure the man pulled that saddle off the dead horse and put it on his horse. The broken saddle had gray hair on it. Oh, and the horse took a piss while tied to the stall. It was a mare."

A sudden realization came to Dan. "That's right! Curly's horse had a bit in its mouth, but no saddle."

Tired from the long day, it was time to sleep. Dan offered his bed to his guest. Amos shook his head, "You got a fine loft in the main room. I will sleep well up there. I slept in a loft back in Maine."

The rancher found sleep slow in coming. The double bed felt lonely without Mary. The deaths of his cowhands had left him shaken. Finding the tracks in the barn gave him hope that they would find the men who'd killed Lars and Curly. He also knew that sometime he would have to go through the charred ruins of the bunkhouse and find Curly's remains to give him a proper burial.

Dan awoke to the sounds of the stove being lit. For a moment he thought it was Mary and all that had happened was a bad dream. Suddenly wide awake, the memories came back to him. Dressing quickly, Dan went into the kitchen.

"Pancakes and side meat will be ready in a bit. There will be coffee as soon as the water boils."

Amos looked right at home in the kitchen. Dan wondered about the long life of the prospector. He'd gone through the barn like a Pinkerton detective, cooked like a chef, and shot like an expert. He was a fascinating man and an asset to ride with.

With breakfast finished, the two men stood on the front porch. The sky was threatening more snow. Dan prayed that it would hold off. Amos tore a piece of chewing tobacco from his plug. He offered the rancher a chew, but Dan declined.

They went to the tool shed and got a pick and shovel. The ground was only frozen a couple inches deep, and the digging of the grave was completed quickly. The grave site was on a rise overlooking the pond and valley. They returned to the barn and wrapped Lars in a piece of tarp. Securing the tarp with light line, they carried his body to the grave. After filling the hole, both men stood holding their hats, heads bowed.

The men returned to the barn. Taking the shovel, Dan scraped up the dirt where Lars had lain and tossed it out the back of the barn. He then went to the tack room and came out with his saddle, and another for Amos. They saddled the team horses in silence.

The two men rode down the valley. The unspoiled snow stretching in front of them was breathtaking. Amos pointed out several rock formations that might have minerals. By noon they had reached the pasture of the one and two year olds. There were no tracks in the snow, nor an animal to be seen. After riding a mile circle and finding nothing, they sat on their horses.

"Damn them anyway!" the rancher growled. "It had to be the cattle they were after. The only way to get them out was past the ranch buildings. That could not be done as long as the hands were alive."

"One other thing to think about," Amos said. "Why didn't they burn the house and barn?"

After chewing some jerky and washing it down with water, the men continued through red cliffs to the second part of the valley to look for the older stock. It was mid-afternoon when they saw the first tracks of grazing stock. Soon afterward, they started seeing grazing cattle. It appeared that the killers had rustled only the younger cattle. It could have been the split between the valleys that had saved these cattle.

"It looks like they missed some of your cows. These ones would have been ready for market in the spring," Amos said.

Dan took a drink from his canteen before answering. "Could be they weren't looking for cattle to sell, or maybe the men that were sent to get the cattle were just plain lazy and didn't ride deep enough into the valley. This older stock are 40 percent of my herd. Most were to be sold after fattening up in the spring. Without the younger ones, I won't have any to sell this year."

"Well then," Amos concluded, "we best get the others back. All we have to do is figure where the hell they drove them."

The old prospector could see some relief on his friend's face after finding this bunch of cows. More than likely the rustlers had overlooked these in their haste to get clear of the valley. They had killed the cowhands before rounding up the younger stock. The longer they stayed in the valley, the more risk they'd been taking.

The two men rode back to the valley line shack to spend the night. It began snowing right about dark. The drafty shack offered minimal protection against the storm. They sat at the table with their coats on, drinking evening coffee. The heat provided by the small stove quickly blew out through the walls.

They discussed the various scenarios of why the older stock had been left. One thing that did come up was the possibility that they planned to come back in early spring and rustle the rest of the herd, therefore allowing them to graze in the valley this winter.

"If they planned to come back again," Dan concluded, "I will be waiting for them." The rancher knew he would offer no mercy.

"Well, we got one hell of a lot to figure here," Amos said. "I suggest we hit the sack and sleep on it."

Smiling for the first time, Dan kidded, "This here cold air will surely clear your mind."

* * *

Once back at the ranch house, Dan sat at the table and listed the things they knew about the killers. He figured what they would need to make an extended search for the rustled cattle. This would be difficult, because they could only bring what a rider's horse could carry.

He wished that there was a way to send word to Sheriff Winslow, so he could watch for the men with the characteristics they had found. He suddenly remembered the animal he had given to the Hartwicks. It was a two-year-old. Could it be from the ones that were stolen? Dan would have liked to know exactly where the animal had been found.

To ride back to Casper and back would take four days. He didn't want to lose that much more time. How long ago had the cattle been stolen? Was it a week, two weeks, or did it happen right after he and Mary had left? Dan didn't want to accept the fact that the herd might have been driven out of the territory already.

He began to write a letter to the sheriff. It told him what they had found here and that they were going to pursue the rustlers. Dan's plan was to give the letter to anyone they met heading for Casper. If he was killed and later found, it would be on his person and hopefully get to a lawman somewhere. At least they would know why he was killed.

Amos came to the table with a golden-brown chicken pie. "Put that paper away and sink your teeth into some of this pie. One of your chickens gave its all for this here meal."

The chicken pie was wonderful. Dan filled his fork with tender meat and crust, dripping with tasty gravy, and placed it into his mouth. Closing his eyes, he slowly pulled the fork from his mouth. Around the mouthful of food, he said, "Damn, Amos. You do know how to make a meal special."

"I told you when we met that I liked cooking," the old prospector reminded him. "Truth is, what I really enjoy is eating."

Dan helped himself to a second helping, much to the joy of his friend. "I am glad to see you have your appetite back. For what we have to do, you will need some fat on your bones."

Finishing cleaning his plate, Dan pushed it away. "If I want to be able to move, I best stop there. I'll go down to the tack room and get us a couple sets of saddlebags."

Walking back into the barn gave Dan an uncomfortable feeling. He could still visualize where Lars had lain, the thought of his friend lying there, ignored by those who'd shot him. Walking into the tack room, he ducked due to the low ceiling. He took ropes, saddlebags, a rifle scabbard, and some pigging strings.

He stopped a moment when his eyes gazed upon a leather riata hanging on the wall. Lars had braided it last winter. He had meant to use it during roundup. He hadn't, maybe because it was more a work of art than something to be used and broken.

Coming out of the tack room with his arms full of gear, Dan looked at the chickens. There was no way they could eat all of them before leaving. Maybe they could kill some to take along. The cold weather would prevent them from rotting. Grain could be spread around for the remaining chickens. If they survived the winter, so be it.

Amos had items to take with them stacked on the table. A quick look over the selection told Dan that the old prospector had done this before. Picking up the shotgun, he offered it to Amos to take with him.

"I thank you, Dan, but I won't be needing that." Patting the .45 in his belt, he said, "If the Colt won't do it, I best move out of the firefight."

Setting it back in the corner, the rancher said,

"I figure we should take some chickens with us. We can clean them and hang them from our saddles. The cold will keep them good."

"Roasted chicken on the trail. I like that idea."

That night they finished the rest of the pie, washing it down with coffee. After cleaning their guns and sharpening their knives they turned in, wanting to be on the way by first light. Dan hoped that the weather wouldn't be against them.

Porridge sweetened with honey was their breakfast. Amos held up the tin of honey, smiled and then stuck it in his bedroll. "This will make our morning coffee worth waking up for."

Before leaving the ranch house, Dan picked up a flint and steel from the shelf and stuck it into his coat pocket. "My father told me to never leave for the wilds without taking a flint. He told me stories of my grandfather eating raw meat because he couldn't make a fire."

The sky was clear and filled with stars when they left the house. In about an hour the sun would be coming up. They looked a little odd with two chickens hanging from each saddle. With the reins in their gloved hands, they rode out of the valley. The men had no idea where they were heading. Scattered around the plains were a few settlers. With luck, one of them might have seen the herd being driven by. Dan was sure they wouldn't have gone in the direction of Casper. Too many people would recognize the Circle A brand.

If by chance they were looking to sell the cattle, they would have to go to Medicine Bow or another town along a railroad. Even then, questions would be asked why they had only younger animals. Keeping them another year would add several pounds to the cattle.

Amos had taken a chaw of his tobacco plug. He rode beside the rancher. Dan had never asked him to help. It was just something you did. The miner was sure the rancher would do the same for him. He was glad to see that Dan had become focused on the challenge facing them. He had accepted what had happened and was now on a mission to correct the wrongs.

The men headed for the line shack used during roundup. The plan was to spend a day or two searching the area for anything that might tell them that the herd had been driven that way, like another stray animal with the Circle A brand or some type of long-term camp used while the rustlers did their planning.

Dan intended to stop and see Juan Torres. He and his family might have seen the cattle, or strange riders. After the two stops, he wasn't sure what to do after that. He could make a couple of sweeps around the plain and hope to stumble onto something.

The sun made the snow blinding. The men squinted as they rode. They both had heard stories of men wandering the plain until they froze, blinded by the brightness of the snow. Slowly, the two riders traveled across the wide expanse of white, without an animal track or human to be seen.

It was almost noon when Dan pointed to at an outcrop of rock rising on the plain. "The line shack is just beyond those rocks. We'll have something to eat and leave some of the gear to lighten the burden on these horses. We can then make a couple circles to the north and east to see if we can find anything."

"Sounds like a good plan," Amos agreed. "I will put on a pot of beans. They will be nice and tender by the time we get back."

As they rode around the rock formation, Dan hissed, "Stop!" There was smoke coming from the chimney of the shack.

Without another word, the two men rode slowly toward the blind side of the line shack. Stopping short of the building, they dismounted. There were the sounds of a horse in the corral. There weren't any tracks around the back or sides of the building, so whoever was inside didn't move around much. The small outhouse to the right of the building had not been used since the snow had fallen.

Dan pulled the Winchester from the scabbard. Amos opened his heavy wolf skin coat to expose the grip of the .45. Moving closer to the building, the snow crunched under their feet. Dan went to the right while Amos moved to the left. Peering around the corner, Dan stepped back quickly. The men moved closer together behind the building. Amos was shaking his head. "Nothing on that side."

"The horse in the corral is the dun Lars liked to ride. I think we have one of the rustlers in the shack," Dan whispered.

Both men jumped when they heard the clanking of the wood stove, sending smoke and ash up the chimney pipe. They stepped back from the shack. Dan spoke in hushed tones, "The window in front is on my side. Let's go around your side. I will kick the door open and go in first. You follow me."

"You got to remember, Dan, we don't want to

kill the man. We need him alive to find out where the rest of the rustlers are, and what they did with the cattle," the miner cautioned his friend.

"Well, maybe I will shoot him just enough to hurt real bad."

"Another thing, Dan, we can't rule out there being more than one in the shack."

The rancher led the way. He slipped off his hat and looked around the front. He stepped back, shaking his head. "The lazy bastard is pissing right out the door. I guess walking a few steps from the door or using the outhouse is too much work."

Crouching, the rancher went around the corner, followed closely by Amos. They stood in front of the door, listening to the man move around inside. It sounded like he was making a meal. Dan nodded to his friend and in one motion kicked in the door, then went forward with the Winchester leveled for action.

The surprised occupant made a jump toward a rifle near the bunk. He then cried out in pain and went down. Dan stopped and raised the barrel of the rifle. Amos ran into the shack and they both stumbled forward.

"It's Curly!" Dan shouted. "Don't shoot him!"

Lying on the floor moaning was the sandy-haired cowhand. He had a splint on his leg. Dan hurried to the injured man.

Gasping for air, Curly said, "Thank God it was you, boss. I was sure that the rustlers had found me."

"Let me help you up," the rancher offered.

"While you're taking care of your man, I'll go get the horses."

While lifting the injured cowhand up, Dan said, "That was Amos. He's offered to help me find the rustlers."

Curly moaned at he was helped onto the cot. The rancher checked the splints on the leg. They were tight around the swollen leg. Other than the shock to the leg caused by the sudden movement, it didn't appear that any additional damage was done.

"I see it is your good leg that is broken."

Forcing a smile, the cowhand replied, "Ain't that the way it is. It couldn't be the short leg."

Amos came back into the line shack with the saddle bags and bedrolls. "I put the horses in with the dun. I pitched them some hay." Setting them near the door, he walking up to the cowhand and reached down. "Mr. Curly, my name is Amos Mudd. I've had the good fortune of meeting up with your boss here."

"The name's Curly Wells. Dan says you offered to help find the cattle."

"Your boss is a good man and he was wronged by some bad people. I see you have a meal started. I'll finish it for you." Amos went to the stove and looked over what Curly had started.

Dan pulled up a stool near the cot. "Tell me what happened."

The cowhand looked up at his boss with sad eyes. "Lars is dead, ain't he?"

"Yes, he is. We buried him on the rise above the pond."

"I couldn't help him. They came . . . It, it was early in the morning."

Dan placed his hand on the cowboy's shoulder.

"Take your time. I need to know everything that happened."

"It was just after breakfast. I was taking the kinks out of the mustang. Lars was just finishing shoeing the dun. They must have been waiting behind the ranch house, they come on us so fast. My gun was still in the bunkhouse. I spurred the horse and yelled to Lars. I heard a rifle shot and my horse went out from under me. I managed to kick myself free of the mustang, but broke the leg when I landed."

"Lars had his gun on his saddle in the barn. He made a run for it and they shot him as he went in the door. I don't know how I did it, but I got up and made it to the bunkhouse. I slid a cot in front of the door and went to get my rifle. Bullets were smashing through the windows and walls. I ducked down to avoid being hit."

"They stopped shooting into the bunkhouse for a bit and I looked over the window sill again. A man with a revolver walked into the barn and I heard a shot. I knew it had to be a finishing bullet in my friend."

Curly's voice was cracking and he stopped talking for a moment. Dan waited for his cowhand to continue. Amos stood near the stove holding a large spoon, fixed on what Curly was saying.

Clearing his throat, the injured man continued. "I heard them putting something against the door. I shot a couple times though it, hoping to hit them. I heard some cussing and they started peppering the building again. Then I started to smell coal oil and smoke. I realized they planned to pin me down and burn me alive. Every time I moved, the leg hurt like hell. I broke a walking stick near the stove and tried to use the two pieces to make up a splint. It helped a little."

"The smoke was awful thick in the bunkhouse. I slid along the floor to the back. I fired some more shots through the front wall. They began firing again. Using their gunfire to cover the noise, I used a block of wood and began knocking the bottom board off the wall. By the time I got it loose, flames were coming through the windows. I sucked in some air from the opening and then dragged myself out. I knew they might be back there waiting for me, but being shot would be better than burning alive."

Amos brought two cups of coffee to them. Dan helped Curly sit up so he could drink it. After taking a couple sips, the cowhand started talking again. "No bullets came, so I dragged myself away from the building, using what little brush there was for cover. Then I saw Lars horse standing near the cedar grove. It must have run there when the shooting started. Praying every inch of the way, I worked my way toward the horse, worrying that I would spook it."

"It was standing with the lead rope hanging to the ground in front of it. I got to believe the Lord was with me, because that horse just stood there until I got my hand on the rope. The smoke from the bunkhouse was giving me cover from the shooters. I pulled myself up and grabbed a hand full of mane and let the horse help me get into the cedars. I hid with the dun and listened to the men in the ranch yard."

"They stayed until the roof of the bunkhouse caved in. Then, with a cheer, they rode by the ranch house, shooting into the building. That's when it dawned on me they hadn't even checked the house. They probably had been watching the ranch for a while and knew you had gone."

"I got a glimpse of the riders as they galloped into the valley. I figured they were after the cattle. There was movement near the barn. Three men were rounding up the horses and were driving the young ones you had in the barn. I can't be sure, but I think one of them was Hurley. I didn't get a good look, but it might have been him that went into the barn and put the second bullet in Lars."

Dan felt a jolt go through him. They now had a name of one of the rustlers. He remembered that John and Lars had fought during the roundup. Hurley had been upset when he was not kept for the winter. Could he have been taking revenge for being let go?

"What happened next, Curly?" Dan asked.

"Let's see. I hid in the cedars with the horse, listening to the men near the barn. The smoke was blowing over them. One suggested they move the horses near the pond and wait for the cattle. After they went, I climbed on the dun and guided it through the trees. I went behind the ranch house and then worked my way towards the opening, using trees and brush for cover. Before riding out, I could see the men looking down the valley, waiting for the cows."

"I knew there was nothing I could do for Lars, so I walked the horse out of the opening and headed for the line shack. I figured I would stay there for a couple days until the leg hurt less and then head for Casper. The leg is worse than I thought. It has been just over two weeks since they hit the ranch, and the damn thing ain't any better."

Dan asked the cowhand if he could describe any of the other men, but between the pain from the broken leg and the desperation to avoid being shot, Curly hadn't seen much. He did remember that one of the three men rode a black and white piebald and he had seen a Bar H brand on the shoulder of one horse.

The injured man was exhausted and dozed off. Dan and Amos sat at the table with steaming cups of coffee. "Curly cleared up some of our guesses and gave us some more to go on." Amos said.

Nodding, Dan replied, "We do have a better picture. I was thinking about the piebald. That horse would stand out. I didn't see anything like that around Casper."

"Do you know of anyone with the Bar H brand?" Amos asked.

"I don't know of the brand," Dan said. "Maybe he was mistaken, a lot was happening."

The rancher rubbed his chin, frowning. "I hate to say it, but we got to go back to Casper. Curly needs a doctor, and we might be able to find a couple of the rustlers in town."

"He'll never be able to ride a horse with that leg. After two days of hard riding, he will be more dead than alive," Amos warned.

"There is a Mexican family about four hours from here. They will have a wagon and stock to pull it. If I leave now, I should be back by mid-day tomorrow. Using our extra team, and driving straight through, we'll have Curly at the doc's by the end of the second day," Dan proposed. "And while I'm there, I can find out if they saw any riders or cattle being driven."

Both men knew that with the information they had learned from Curly, they had to go to Casper and talk with Sheriff Winslow. The livery or blacksmith might be able to tell them about the piebald, maybe even the horse with the new shoes.

There were three more hours of daylight when Dan left the line shack on the dun. He kept the horse at a trot, snow spraying out with each step. He was riding toward the southeast and the sun was more toward his back. It made the strain on his eyes much less.

He was sure that Juan Torres would loan him the use of a wagon and team. It was near full moon and he would be able to head back well before daylight. All he would need was a few hours of sleep. All of a sudden, he saw something on the plain in front of him. It was a set of tracks coming from the south and disappearing over a rise to his left. It could be an elk, or maybe even a lone cow. He ruled these out in his mind because the trail ran on a straight line. Most animals would meander one way or another unless being chased.

As he crossed the trail, he confirmed that it was a horse and that it was being pushed by the rider. Dan would have liked to follow them for a while, but he had to get back with the wagon and couldn't afford the time. He also knew that it wasn't that unusual to run across an occasional trail. It could be a trapper or hunter.

The rancher was wondering what Juan's wife Teresa was making for their supper. She was a fine cook and he might be lucky enough to join them for supper. He smiled when he thought about Juan's children, Ricardo, Karla, and Diana.

As he rode up a hill he saw a flash of light from the direction of a red rock ridge. He pulled up the dun to take another look. Unexpectedly, the dun threw its head back, falling back on its haunches. Dan was thrown, rolling into the snow. As he fell, there was the sound of a shot.

Dan landed with the thrashing horse between him and the rock wall. There was a whack against the dun and then the sound of another shot. The horse lay still. The trapped rancher lay hugging the snow-covered ground behind the dead horse. Someone was shooting at him from the ridge. They must have been leading him for the shot, and when Dan had pulled the dun up, the horse had taken the shot in the neck. Now the shooter was trying to finish the job.

The butt of his Winchester was sticking above the snow from under the horse. The red ridge was well out of the range of his Colt. Every little while a bullet would hit the horse or ricochet off the saddle. If he showed any part of his body above the horse it would invite a bullet. Sliding toward the rump, he got his hand on the rifle.

Dan gave a jerk, trying to pull the rifle free. The shooter must have seen movement, because the next bullet clipped the horse just above him. Reaching under the snow as close as he could get to the scabbard, he pulled again. It moved a bit. A couple more pulls and the Winchester came free. As this happened a bullet clipped the top of his hat.

Removing the hat, Dan lay still, clutching the rifle. He was still an hour away from the Torres farm. The sun was low in the western sky. The shooter would become desperate soon. Once the sun set, Dan might be able to get away.

Lying in the snow, the rancher looked around. When the horse had gone down it was on the top of the rise. He had landed in a slight hollow, offering him more protection from the man on the wall. Time slowly went by, occasional bullets whining above him.

Dan adjusted his position and felt something tug his coat and sting his buttocks. He hugged the snow, muttering, "You best keep your ass down or the man will shoot it off."

One of the front legs of the dun was in the air above the animal's neck. This could give him a way to try and spot the shooter without being seen. Dan squirmed to the front of the horse. Reaching back, he raised his hat above the animal. The action immediately invited a shot that clipped the crown. *The son-of-a-bitch has good eyes,* he thought.

Then, slowly, he moved ahead until he could peek around and see the wall. At first, Dan saw nothing. There was the occasional shot that hit the horse. The rancher just prayed that he wouldn't put a shot toward the head. The sun was on the horizon and soon it would be too dark to see anything on the ridge. Finally, there was movement. The shooter was working his way down an indention in the red wall.

Dan knew that the man couldn't shoot while climbing down. He checked to make sure that his rifle mechanism wasn't hampered by dirt or snow. Then, taking a deep breath, Dan sat up and steadied himself on the body of the horse. The shooter was about 100 yards away. He aimed dead center on the body.

The rancher squeezed the trigger. The

Winchester bucked. Without waiting to see the results, Dan levered another shell in the chamber and fired again at the man. The shooter had stopped climbing down and was hanging on to a small aspen. Taking his time, Dan shot again. The man lost his grip and tumbled 30 feet to the base of the red ridge. There was the sound of a rifle clattering as it struck the rocks below.

Crouching, Dan ran forward, his attention on the base of the ridge. He had lost sight of the shooter. Having heard the rifle fall meant that the most the shooter had was a handgun. Hurrying toward the ridge, the rancher gasped for breath, ready to throw himself onto the ground if he caught sight of any movement.

Slowing short of the red rocks, Dan continued forward with his rifle at the ready. The first thing he saw was the man's legs sticking up from the rubble at the bottom. The shooter was lying face down. Before he reached the man he knew that it was Hurley.

Grabbing the shoulder, Dan turned him over. Hurley lay there, his sightless eyes wide-open. A quick search of his pockets provided some coins, a few folding bills, tobacco and fixings, matches, and a couple folded pieces of paper. Stuffing them into his coat pocket, he stepped back, wondering if John Hurley was the leader of the rustlers.

Along the wall of red rock, Dan saw boot tracks leading from a stand of aspens. He followed them back and found Hurley's horse. It was the chestnut. Pulling the reins loose from a sapling, he led the horse out to the downed dun.

Taking the saddlebags and bedroll off the dead

horse, he put them on the chestnut and swung into the saddle. Dan looked toward the ridge. Hurley could wait until he returned with the wagon. It was dark. Soon the moon would be coming up, helping him see his way better.

The icy night wind cut through the tear in the back of his sheepskin coat. The chestnut was well-rested from its time under the aspens while John had waited for Dan. He wondered how Hurley would have known that his prey would pass near the ridge. It was possible that he had followed their tracks from the ranch and his plan had been to kill him there.

The horse had been ridden hard, to get ahead so Hurley could get into position. With the rolling plain, it wouldn't be too hard to stay out of sight. The chestnut was carrying a thick bedroll, and saddlebags with several days of food and lots of shells for the rifle.

For the first time, Dan had a hope that the herd was being held within a day's ride of the ranch. Hurley was part of the gang that had stolen the cattle and wouldn't just ride off while the animals were driven out of the territory. Dan had to get Curly to Casper, then get back on the plain and start checking the numerous canyons the cattle could be kept in. With renewed urgency he rode toward the Torres farm.

The moonlight reflected off the snow, giving the plains a ghostly appearance. He passed the ridge where he had first seen the smoke of the Torres farm. He had unrolled his blanket and had it draped over his shoulders for warmth. It hung down and protected the chestnut also.

Before he saw the dark shadows of the Torres buildings, he caught the glimpse of light. As he drew closer, he saw that it came from beyond the house. Dan rode into the yard and tied the horse to the donkey corral. The crunch of the snow under his boots alerted the occupants in the barn before he entered. Juan appeared in the doorway, a rifle casually held in his arms.

"It is a cold night, Señor. Can I help you with something?"

"Señor Torres, it is me, Dan August," the rancher replied.

Turning, he called out, "Teresa, it is Señor August. Quick, go to the house and make something to warm him."

Juan's wife stepped out of the barn and flashed a quick smile at Dan before hurrying to the house. "Come into the barn, it is warmer. We have an animal giving birth."

Dan followed Juan into the barn. The smell of hay and manure reminded him of the barn in Elkader. He and his cousins would rush to the barn and hug the cows for warmth on frigid winter days. Ricardo was kneeling behind the expectant mother and pulling on the legs of the newborn. Soon, the head appeared, followed by the rest of the foal.

Ricardo looked up, smiling. "It's a jack." He used clean straw to wipe down the newborn. The mother was up and dutifully licking the foal, which was trying its best to stand on wobbly legs.

"The jenny will take care of the young one now," Juan said. "Let's go to the house and drink to the successful birth."

Ricardo offered to take care of the chestnut.

Diana ran up and gave Dan a hug when he entered the house. "Ricardo heard that your wife was ill the last time he went to Casper. We prayed she would be okay."

"She is, and thank you for your prayers," he replied.

"I have made a special dessert for us," Karla announced as she worked over the stove. "With you here to share it will make it even more special."

Juan and Dan sat at the table, sharing a glass of wine made from plums. The rancher explained why he was here. He told about finding one of his hands murdered in the barn and the other with a broken leg. He explained that they needed a wagon to carry the injured cowhand to Casper.

"I would recommend you take the buckboard," Juan suggested. "It is lighter, and the horses will travel longer before tiring."

"Have you seen any riders or a herd of cattle in the last few weeks?"

"I am sorry to say I have not," the farmer said. "It will be spring before they can move the herd to market. If we see any, I will have Ricardo come and tell you."

Shortly, the table was set with tamales wrapped in corn husks and a mix of vegetables canned from this year's harvest. After thanking the Lord for the food, they dug in. When the main course was done, the special dessert was served. It was a tender crust filled with dried wild strawberries and cheese sweetened with honey.

The meal was topped off with cups of strong

coffee with honey and goat milk. Dan sat back from the table smoking a slender cigar and sipping his coffee. He felt a twinge of guilt knowing that Amos and Curly were probably eating soup made from chicken and beans.

Dan wondered if he would be able to sleep after the robust drink. Juan offered Ricardo's bed for the night, but the rancher declined. "I will unroll my bedroll in here. I have to be up early, and don't want to be too comfortable and oversleep."

The rancher lay in the darkness in the main room off the kitchen. The family had gone to bed. For a short time, he could hear the whispers of the girls talking. It was a comfortable home. He wondered how long it would be before his and Mary's home would be back to normal. Tired from the meal and long day, Dan was soon asleep.

Teresa had barbecued goat and corn tortillas for breakfast. Dan looked at his pocket watch when she woke him. It was 4 a.m. He was pulling his boots on when the door opened. It was Juan and Ricardo.

"The team is all hitched to the buckboard. Your chestnut it tied to the back and the gear you brought is packed," the senior Torres said. "When you get to Casper, ask for Jose Sanchez. He will keep the team until Ricardo makes a trip in the spring."

"I will pay Jose for keeping the team over the winter," Dan offered.

"It is not necessary. We are honored to help you. If you need anything else, just ask."

After more strong coffee and some well-seasoned barbecue-filled tortillas, the rancher was ready to go. Karla and Diana awoke just before he left and wished him a safe trip. Teresa made up some extra tortillas for him to take along.

Standing next to the buckboard, the men said their goodbyes. Before leaving, Dan pulled the saddle and bridle that Hurley had used. He turned to Ricardo and handed them to him. "I have no use for this extra saddle. I would be pleased if you would accept it. When you are ready, stop by my ranch and I will have a horse for you."

Juan snorted, "Now he will be riding the meat off my work horses." Then, smiling, he added, "It is probably time he started riding to Casper. He will get back faster and I can get more work out of him."

The men laughed at the humor. Ricardo held the saddle, grinning broadly.

Well before daylight, Dan was on his way back to the line shack. The well-rested team stepped out eagerly into the cold night air. The moon still lit the plain, making the earlier tracks easy to follow. He reached to the back of his coat to close the bullet tear. His finger found that the rip had been sewn closed.

The form of the dead dun came into view. Stopping, he removed the saddle from the animal. He then turned the buckboard towards the wall. He pulled up near Hurley's body and tossed the dead man onto the back of the buckboard.

"I should leave you here to rot, but they will only have to send someone from Casper to pick your sorry ass up. From here to the line shack you can ride on the buckboard. After that you ride slung over a horse," he muttered.

CHAPTER ELEVEN

Amos had everything ready to go when Dan arrived back at the line shack. The miner looked at the dead man in the buckboard. "Where the hell did you find him?"

"This is John Hurley, the rustler Curly spoke of. He tried to bushwhack me. As you can see, it didn't work out well for him."

"We ain't got anything to bury him with." Amos pointed out.

"Just roll him onto the ground. We got to bring him back to Casper. I'll tie him over the chestnut for the ride there," Dan replied. "In the meantime, Juan's wife put something in the back for us."

In the gear on the wagon was a package of cheese and a dozen filled tortillas. The old prospector warmed them on the stove before leaving. The three men made short work of the meal.

Amos beamed at the sight of the cheese. "I will make you some tasty meals with this," he promised.

A bed made of the men's blankets was made up in the back of the buckboard for Curly. Dan's team was hitched for the first part of the trip. With Hurley secure on the back of the chestnut, it was tied with the extra team to the back of the buckboard. They were on their way to Casper. Amos drove while the rancher watched the plain for danger. Shortly after they left the line shack, they passed the spot where Hurley had watched. He could have shot Dan from there, but then there would have been the others in the shack to deal with.

The wind had change to the south. There was the smell of rain in the air. The cloud cover was thick, reducing the glare from the snow. Dan moved several times, trying to get comfortable on the buckboard seat.

"Are you having a problem with my driving?" Amos asked.

"Nope," the rancher answered. "I got shot in the butt by Hurley. More of a bruise than a wound, but it sure is tender."

"Couldn't keep your rear down?" Curly kidded from the back.

Dan told the others about Hurley's ambush. The dun had been killed and the rustler had had his chestnut. "The damn rustlers will make me horse-poor if they keep killing my animals."

He told them he thought the cattle were being held closer than they'd first thought.

"If we find the cattle, I am sure we will find the rest of your horses," Amos concluded.

Two hours later, the rancher sat dozing while the buckboard bumped across the plain. Curly slept in the back, moaning when he tried to move. Sleet was beginning to come down, covering the travelers with a thin layer of ice.

The injured cowhand pulled the blanket over his head. Dan was jostled awake on a small wash. "Damn this sleet," he complained. "We'll slide right off our seat on the next bump."

"It could be worse," Amos advised. "We could be dealing with a blizzard."

Glancing at his watch, the rancher said, "We will switch the team in another hour. Keep an eye out for a stream to water them."

The damp cold was cutting through their clothes, and the men shivered as they rode. The old prospector pulled the team to a stop. "I got to get down and lead them for a while before I freeze right where I sit."

Dan took the reins of one of the horses and Amos the other as they set up a brisk pace walking. It wasn't long before the chill left them. They passed a creek that had a pool of water. The rancher kicked a hole in the ice so the animals could drink.

They had nose bags and grain on the buckboard for the team, which were each given a portion to help keep their strength up. Curly slid to the edge of the wagon and hung his legs over. They all chewed some jerky, along with a hunk of cheese.

"Doesn't it hurt to hang your leg like that?" Dan asked.

"The damn thing is aching no matter how I have it. My back and butt started competing with the leg, so I had to move around."

The teams were switched and they checked on Hurley's bonds. With everything finished, they continued toward Casper with Dan handling the team. The weather cleared toward late afternoon. The wind switched to the north, bringing back the cold temperatures. It created a crust on the remaining snow. The buckboard slid back and forth on the uneven terrain.

Throughout the night, the sound of the horses' hooves breaking through the snow kept up a constant rhythm. The changing of the team was the only relief from the rough-riding buckboard. The moonlight made traveling across the plain easier.

They stopped shortly after daylight to make a hot breakfast and some coffee. The chestnut was beginning to tire carrying the dead rustler, so the decision was made to load him onto the wagon with Curly.

Muttering, the injured cowhand said, "It's damn poor company I have to keep on this here buckboard. You should loop some rope around his legs and drag him behind us."

"Hell, Curly," Amos said "he is as stiff as a log. You can rest your bad leg on him, maybe use him as a pillow."

"Go to hell!" the grouchy cowhand growled as he moved as far away to the back as he could.

Six hours later, the exhausted party arrived in Casper. They pulled up in front of Doc Morgan's. The two men carried Curly between them into the medical man's office. The doc looked up as they came through the door.

"What have we here?"

"Curly here broke his leg when his horse was shot out from under him," Dan explained.

"Who the hell is shooting horses?" the doctor inquired.

"The dead man on the wagon outside," the rancher explained.

"I don't know what the hell you are talking about. Bring Curly back here and let me take a look at the leg."

When Dan got back to the buckboard, Sheriff Winslow was looking at the dead rustler. Amos was tying the extra horses to the hitching rail.

"What happened to Hurley?" the sheriff asked.

"I have a lot to tell you," Dan said. "Let me run into Hartwick's and see Mary. Then I'll come over to your office. Don't feel too bad about him. He was a killer and rustler."

With that, the rancher went in to visit his wife. Amos stayed behind and started filling in the sheriff. Mary was sitting near the stove in the family quarters, brushing Joanie's hair. A look of joy and surprise crossed her face when she saw her husband.

"Dan! You're back early!" she cried. She picked up the child and rushed into his open arms.

"I can only stay a minute, Mary. There was some trouble at the ranch. Lars is dead and Curly is up at doc's with a broken leg. Some of our cattle are missing."

The joy on her face turned to shock. "Lars is dead?"

For the first time Dan choked up, thinking of the cowhand. He found it impossible to continue and just buried his face in his wife's hair. They stood holding each other while their child squirmed to get free, not understanding the tragedy they were experiencing.

Dan took Joanie while Mary sat back in the chair. Tears were streaming down her face. "Who would . . . who would kill Lars? He had no enemies."

"It was the rustlers, honey. He just got in the way. Don't try and make any sense out of it," Dan said, trying to console his wife. "Amos and I buried him on the rise above the pond. We gave him a proper burial and said words at the grave. I have to go over to Sheriff Winslow's office. He will make sure the rustlers are caught."

"Catching or killing them won't bring Lars back," she said, staring straight ahead.

Dan didn't tell her about the bunkhouse or the ranch house. He didn't want to create any additional stress that would hamper her recovery. He handed the child back to her mother and left the room, wishing that there was more he could say to stop Mary from worrying.

Amos and the sheriff were sitting drinking coffee when Dan entered the office. Sheriff Winslow motioned to the potbelly stove. "Got fresh coffee and the cups are on the shelf."

After pouring himself a cup of the strong brew, Dan roll himself a smoke. "I told Mary about Lars and the missing cows. She took it pretty bad. If it's okay with you, sheriff, I would just as soon not bring up the killing of Hurley if at all possible."

"We're a small town, Dan," the law man advised him. "She is staying at the store. Word will get to her." He took a deep breath and continued. "I will do what I can. She will not learn anything from me."

"Thank you, sheriff."

"Amos here brought me up to date on most of what happened at the ranch," Sheriff Winslow informed the rancher. "I have some questions for you. We should start with the body outside."

Dan reached into his pocket and withdrew a folded paper. "I have listed all that we knew at the time we were still at the ranch. At that point we didn't think Curly was alive, and didn't know about John Hurley."

The sheriff took the paper and opened it. After looking it over, he nodded. "Pretty much agrees with the information that Amos gave me. He said after you found Curly you learned that one man rode a piebald. Earlier this month, there was a cowboy that put up a horse like that at the livery. He spent freely at the saloon and I figured he was spending his summer wages. He left town, let's see, about the same time you took Mary to Cheyenne."

"None of your horses have shown up in town to the best of my knowledge. I will wire the sheriff in Medicine Bow and the rest of the towns along the railroad to have them watch for any of your cattle being sold. Amos here said they were one and two-year-olds. My guess is they will alter that brand and keep them another year or two before selling them. But it doesn't make sense to steal cattle you can't sell."

The sheriff leaned back in his chair. "Maybe they plan to sell them to someone stocking their range."

"Curly thought he saw a Bar H brand on one

of the horse's shoulders," Dan added. "Is there anyone in the territory with that brand?"

"I can check with the registry, but I haven't heard of the brand. I do want to talk to the smithy and the hostler at the livery. Maybe they will remember something," Sheriff Winslow said. "I do need to know how you ended up shooting John Hurley."

"After he killed the horse I was riding and shot the hell out of it trying to drill me, I finally had to shoot back," the rancher said, his dander rising a bit.

"Easy, Dan, I am not saying you didn't have just cause shooting the man, but there will be an inquest, and they need to understand and have clear answers."

"He was watching the line shack when I left. He got ahead of me and found a high vantage to shoot me. As you know, he got the horse instead. After pinning me down until almost dark, he gave up and started to climb down. I took advantage of the fact he couldn't climb and shoot, and I sent a few his way. I hit him and down he came."

"Did you check to see if he had any money on him to help with the burial?" Winslow asked.

Reaching into his coat pocket, Dan placed the money and notes on the sheriff's desk. "This is all I found on him, except some tobacco. That I am smoking in return for bringing his carcass to Casper."

"Well, I appreciate you coming in. You would make a good lawman. You pay attention to details. I have to ask you not to go hunting for these men. Let the law take care of finding the rustlers and bringing them to justice. Stay around, in case I have any more questions." Then, turning to Amos, he said, "You are welcome to stay or leave. Both yours and Dan's statements pretty much tell the same story."

Expecting more out of the meeting with the sheriff, Dan took the last sip of his coffee and got up. "I can't promise you what will happen if I meet one of the rustlers on the street. If a man comes into town riding one of my horses and leading one of my cows, I will give him the opportunity to give up, but if he reaches for his gun, I will send him straight to Hades."

Smiling, the sheriff replied, "Fair enough. Just make sure he is shot from the front and the cow isn't a three-year old."

Dan and Amos walked out of the office and went to bring the team and buckboard to Juan's friend. The old prospector was thoughtful. "The sheriff back there is worried that you will make yourself judge and executioner."

"He is not the only one. Every time I think about Lars' face blown away, I want to hurt those that did it."

Amos looked at his friend's determined face. "Thirty, even 20 years ago, you could have gone out and hung them all and no one would have said a word. Today, we have laws that say we can't do that. They want us to sit back and let the law go after them. I would heed the sheriff's advice, but if you run into one of them, make sure they're shot dead, and I would make sure there was a gun in the dead bastard's hand."

Dan's face softened. "I know you are right. It's just hard to sit by and wait for someone else to act. There is lots of stuff we found that needs someone looking at."

The buckboard and team were still in front of

the doc's. John Hurley had been picked up by the undertaker. Amos took his gear from the wagon. "I will be staying above the saloon. I'll keep my eyes and ears open."

Dan led the chestnut and his team to the barn behind the mercantile. He brushed the animals and gave them grain and hay. He then returned for Juan's buckboard and team. Jose Sanchez was glad to take care of the team and keep the buckboard for Juan. It turned out that Teresa was his sister.

The rancher stopped short of the mercantile when returning from Jose's. He looked at the lamp that was burning on the front porch. He couldn't believe that it had gotten dark already. Inside, he had a wife who needed consoling. He feared that he wouldn't be able to make her feel secure or assure her that the pieces of their lives could be put back together.

He spotted a chair on the porch and sat down. The night was cold, but he didn't feel it. He knew that he needed to make plans. The ranch needed repair, and the cattle that were still there had to be protected. Mary needed him here for support. He could not take care of everything. As he sat there he worried about others, not himself.

The door of the mercantile opened and Bert stepped out. "What are you doing sitting out here in the cold? Supper will be ready in a minute. Angie baked a roast from the beef that you gave us."

Following the store owner inside, Dan apologized. "I am sorry. I was just trying to figure out what had to be done next. You know, I am darn hungry. I think I could eat the whole cow about now."

The meal was a grand affair. Angie had made

it special to welcome Dan back. As hungry as he was, the worry did not let him do justice to the meal. When the custard pie came for dessert, he had to force himself to eat it. Mary picked at her meal. The Hartwicks did their best to keep the conversation pleasant, but most of it went over Dan's head. He struggled to answer appropriately to questions he hardly heard.

When Bert brought out brandy and cigars, they were the first items that the rancher welcomed. He sipped the comforting brandy and was soon fighting the need to get some sleep. Mary had taken Joanie upstairs to bed and had not come back down.

Bert stared at his friend, who was fighting to stay awake. "After you get some sleep, we will sit down and you can let me know how I can help you."

"I wish I could be better company, but guess the trip from the line shack took more out of me than I thought. Please tell Angie that the supper was wonderful. I truly appreciate her going to all the trouble."

"Now, you go on up. I have kept you too long," Bert conceded. "Mary is waiting for you."

Dan thanked him again and started up the stairs. He paused for a moment, wanting to say something more to Bert, but his mind couldn't come up with the words to express how important their friendship had been.

Mary lay in their bed, with her back to his side. On a small cot Joanie lay sleeping. Dan bent down and gave his child a kiss. Then sitting on a chair next to the bed, he quietly undressed. Sliding into the bed, he lay on his back staring at the ceiling. He was beyond tired, but could not fall asleep. His mind kept racing. The scene of Lars lying on the barn floor kept flashing through his mind.

"You are not alone in this," his wife whispered.

The sound of her voice startled him. "I have to do something, Mary. But I just don't know where to start."

There was the sound of her crying beside him. They lay inches apart in the small bed, but tonight there was miles between them.

* * *

The next day, Dan checked in with the sheriff, hoping that more information had emerged. Sheriff Winslow had just come back from the undertaker. "Digger said that Hurley didn't die from a bullet. He broke his neck in the fall. Your shot went through the elbow, causing him to lose his grip, but like I said, it was the fall."

The rancher hadn't known that the first two shots he had taken at John Hurley had been near misses, just spraying the man with shards of rock. The last shot had hit the man's arm, causing him to fall.

"Well, dead is dead, and John Hurley certainly deserved it," the rancher replied, defending himself.

"I am not questioning your actions, Dan," the sheriff assured him. "Later today is the inquest, and I just wanted to let you know what the undertaker had found. I will need you to come to the office around 3 p.m. Judge Kearny will be here."

Walking to the door, Dan opened it, looking

back at the sheriff and growling, "He shot at me and left me no choice but to shoot back." With his voice rising, he continued. "For Christ sake, he was the bad guy!"

"Three o'clock, Dan. Be here!" the sheriff said sternly before the rancher slammed the door.

Dan walked up the street. He was steaming. The trouble was, he did not know why. The sheriff had not said that he was in the wrong. "But, damn it. He didn't need to keep asking me about it," he muttered. "I need a drink."

Walking into the saloon, he called to the bartender, "Lem, pour me one and leave the bottle."

He tossed a coin onto the bar and took the drink and bottle. Setting the bottle onto the table, he tossed his hat onto the chair next to him and then sat heavily. His elbow bumped the table and the whiskey sloshed out of the shot glass, running across the table. Snorting, he looked at the spilt liquor and said, "Perfect."

The shadow of a man loomed over him as Dan sat holding the whiskey. "You look like a man that is ready to drink that whole bottle," the prospector said.

"Thinking about it, Amos. Grab a glass and have a seat. You can help me."

Seating himself across from the rancher, his friend poured a drink and took a sip. "Not the best I have tasted, but it should do the job for *you*."

Sitting back, Dan looked at the old prospector. "I don't understand what the hell is going on. I am madder than hell inside and don't know why."

"I can tell you this," Amos assured him.

"Getting drunk and yelling at everyone won't help. I tried it once. Had me an Ojibwa woman. Gosh, she was beautiful. I wanted to take her to California, but she wanted me to stay in Michigan near her family. My dreams of gold were more important and I left her. I stayed drunk for a month. Almost killed a fellow I was playing cards with."

"So drinking didn't help?" the rancher asked.

"Well, you see, it don't last. Come morning you wake up with a sore head and sick stomach. For a long time, I blamed her for not coming with me. Now, I know I should have stayed." the prospector replied. "No matter how much I drink, it don't go back and fix my mistake."

Dan poured another drink and pushed the bottle away. "All I need is to show up at the inquest drunk. They will have me sitting in a cell before the judge finishes asking me if I will tell the truth."

Seeing the humor in the statement, Amos laughed, slapping the table. After a moment his face became serious. "I did find out a couple things last night before turning in."

"Tell me, my friend. I can use the news."

Amos wiped his mouth and leaned forward. Speaking in hushed tone, he started. "I mentioned having seen a piebald and how I liked the looks of the black and white horse. A man drinking down the bar piped up that he had seen one in Casper. Acting surprised, I told him that I'd like to talk to the man about selling. That was when the man said that I'd have to ask Hurley who the man was."

"Next, I bought the fellow a drink and said that I wasn't sure who Hurley was. I asked him if this

Hurley had a partner that rode a gray. He replied that there was a fellow that ran with him that had a mare that was kind of mouse color, and then agreed that it might be gray."

"Did you ask him the names of either of the men?" Dan asked.

"I did, and he told me the fellow with the piebald was out of Texas. He guessed they called him Tex. Said he was a mean-looking cuss. Wore a tied-down gun and liked to make lesser men nervous. The other fellow with the gray talked like he was from the south, could be Texas also."

Amos poured himself another drink and offered to fill Dan's glass. The rancher shook his head no. "I had best stay sober for the inquest. I want to thank you for helping me come to my senses. Maybe the smithy can help us with a name. He had just shoed the horse."

Then, placing his hat on his head, he said, "First, I have to go apologize to Mary."

Walking along the slippery street toward the mercantile he thought about how he had acted toward Mary since he'd gotten back to Casper. He hoped that he would know what to say before he got there.

Entering the store, he pulled his coat off and hung it on a nail near the door. Bert was behind the counter. "It got a little heated with the sheriff by the sounds of it."

"It wasn't my finest moment," Dan said. Not seeing his wife, he asked, "Is Mary upstairs?"

The merchant started unloading a box of canned goods. "I believe she brought Joanie up for a nap. When you see her, let her know that Angie has sliced roast beef and fresh baked bread for lunch."

He thanked Bert and headed up the stairs. Pausing just a moment at the door, he turned the knob and entered. Mary was sitting on the bed with her back to the door, brushing her hair. Next to her was the sleeping child. At the sound of the door opening, she raised her head.

"Don't turn, Mary. If I look into your eyes, I won't be able to finish what I have to say." Dan closed the door quietly behind him. "I have no excuse for the way I have acted since getting back from the ranch. At first, I convinced myself that it was from the lack of sleep and by the morning I would feel okay. It wasn't okay. I have been charging around like a bull, seeing red all morning."

"I felt that I was responsible for what happened at the ranch. I blamed myself for Lars' death and Curly being hurt. We lost cattle and horses, the bunkhouse was burnt, and the men shot up the house. I felt that I was personally wronged and I needed to strike out at those that did this. I set myself apart from everyone else, fearing that if I gave them my attention those that did this would slip away."

"I love you and would rather die than hurt you. When I told you about Lars, I saw the pain in your face and didn't know how to take it away from you. I was afraid to let you close, because if I did, all I could do is share more painful information with you. I was wrong to see you as being weak and unable to handle the truth."

"I forgot that our strength was facing challenges together, helping and supporting each other as we raise our family. Together we can get through hardships and . . ."

Mary stood up, throwing herself into his arms, holding him close. "I was afraid that what had happened would drive you away from me," she said. "That you blamed me being ill for our troubles."

"No, Mary. I could never blame you. We are family and we protect each other. Like you said last night, I wasn't alone. I think I had forgotten that."

"The food is on the table," Angie called from the kitchen.

Dan softly kissed his wife and whispered, "You are my strength."

Arm in arm, they closed the bedroom door and went downstairs to break bread with the Hartwicks.

CHAPTER TWELVE

While the inquest was going on, J.P. Burdick stopped in at the mercantile. Bert always liked seeing the man. He was a big spender. J.P. asked, "What's going on at the sheriff's office?"

"They're having an inquest. Dan August shot John Hurley," the merchant informed him.

"Hurley? When did this happen?"

"I don't know too much, but I guess it was out on the plain, somewhere near the ranch. Word from Digger is that Hurley tried to ambush Dan," Bert replied. "Now what can I get you, Mr. Burdick?"

J.P. dug into his pockets and then smiled and shook his head. "Sorry, I had a list, but I must have left it at my place. Let me bring it in tomorrow."

As he left the mercantile, he saw the judge leaving the sheriff's office. He walked across the street and stopped just short of the door. He could hear voices beyond. Dan August was apologizing for the way he had acted earlier in the day. Then he heard the sheriff say something about checking out a gray having shoes put on at the blacksmith's, and about sending inquiries to Texas on the Bar H brand.

Burdick was just about to go in when Dan and Amos came out of the sheriff's office. He stepped back as the old prospector hurried by.

"I am going to the mercantile and see if I can get Mrs. Hartwick to rustle up some of that beef and bread you said you had for lunch," Amos said as hurried across the street.

Seeing J.P., Dan smiled. "I was just coming to see you."

"How can I help you?" the cattle buyer inquired.

"You recommended Hurley for the roundup. I was hoping you knew more about where the man came from," the rancher said.

"Hey, Dan." It was the sheriff. "Can you come back in here for a minute?"

"I'll be at the office when you're done with the sheriff," J.P. said, smiling. "Stop in and we'll talk."

The sheriff had two cups of coffee poured and placed them on his desk. He was fingering the two notes that Dan had given him. "Did you read these?"

"No, I didn't," the rancher replied. "I had just stuck them in my pocket and then gave them to you when we dropped off Hurley. I was so tired I hardly remember giving them to you."

The sheriff opened them up. The first one said: "Get the boys together."

The second one said: "$100 for you when it's done."

Dan looked at the notes and his brow furled. "Who were the notes from?"

"I can't tell you that, but the one about the 'boys' is more worn, so it was probably written first," the sheriff said. "The second, my guess, is about killing you."

"The notes are written on packaging paper, like the stuff Bert uses," Dan noted.

"Most people save the wrappings for writing on. That could be any of them," Sheriff Winslow said. Then he took a large swallow of his coffee and drained his cup. Setting it down, he looked at Dan. "Why don't we visit Ebert at the blacksmith shop and see if he remembers the gray."

The sound of iron being shaped on an anvil rang in their ears as the men entered the blacksmith shop. Dan had always liked the stocky blacksmith. His muscular forearms were scarred from contact with red hot metal. His heavy, stained leather apron protected him from the spray of sparks when he struck the iron.

The smithy plunged the hot metal into a tub of water, sending up a plume of steam. Setting the shoe and tongs on the edge of the forge, he smiled at the sheriff and rancher. "What can I do for you?"

Getting right to the point, the sheriff said, "You put shoes on a gray two weeks ago, maybe more. The owner might have been from out of town, maybe Texas."

"You talking about Cal Duncan?" Ebert queried.

"We didn't know the man's name. Did he say where he was from?"

"Didn't have to, sheriff," the smithy replied. "I recognized him as a fellow Texan. Turns out we both grew up in Clay County."

Dan stood watching the sheriff as he listened to the smithy talk about growing up in Texas. He wanted to interrupt, but respected the sheriff being in charge of the interview.

Once Ebert finished talking, Sheriff Winslow asked the next question. "Did this Cal have anyone riding with him?"

"A fellow he called Tex was riding a piebald. He came by with him once. The horse had a loose shoe. Cal said they had driven a herd up from Texas. That Tex fellow didn't look too much like a cowboy. He looked more like a hired gun."

The smithy picked up the stub of a cigar and held it against the smoldering coals in his forge. Taking a couple drags, he blew some smoke rings. "Come to think of it," he continued, "the fellow Dan killed paid for putting the shoes on the gray."

The sheriff appeared to be finished asking questions of the smithy. Dan had a question. "Ebert, did you ever see anyone else from outside of Casper with Cal, Tex, or Hurley?"

"Oh, I would see others riding through town with them on occasion, usually picking up supplies at the mercantile. More than once I saw them ride out with a wagon loaded. There was a heavyset driver that looked every part a freighter. I fixed a wheel for him last summer. He sat under that oak tree over yonder waiting for me to fix it. Didn't hardly say two words to me. Come to think of it, Hurley came by and paid for that repair also."

As they were walking away, the sheriff told Dan that he would check if anyone knew about the men at the saloon. The smithy called to them, "These men didn't drink in Casper. I remember the gunman was in a hurry to get the shoe fixed, because he was headed back to the Rooster Saloon to meet some gal. My guess is that was the watering hole for the whole bunch of them."

Dan was familiar with the saloon named after the small town of Rooster. It was about 10 miles away, in a cluster of buildings left over from the building of the railroad. The place sold cheap, watered-down rye and had women of the night who would spend time with a cowboy for a reasonable price.

Then another thought came to him. "Did you ever see the Bar H brand on any of the horses?"

The smithy chuckled and walked toward the men. "Up here, no, but back in Texas there was a mean cuss that used that brand. Most folks said he rustled more cattle than a man could count. His favorite method was as a herd cutter. It was said that some smaller ranchers just up and disappeared along with their cattle. It was suspected that he killed them and took their herds. He took care of the local law, and they turned their heads to what he was doing."

"Could he be up in this area now?" the sheriff asked.

"Only as a ghost. A vigilante group hung him right in front of the court house. Yes, sir, old man Prince had his bad doings catch up with him."

The wind started blowing waves of snow across the town. The sheriff thanked the smithy and headed for his office, turning his collar up to the cold wind. Dan followed the lawman. He felt excitement run through his body. Rooster was the key to finding the gang. There was the look of a storm coming. He dreaded the thought that they might have to wait it out.

Sitting in the sheriff's office, Dan drank coffee with a shot of whiskey. Sheriff Winslow said that it would warm him. Dan picked the notes up from the desk and looked at them. After studying them for a bit, he returned them.

"What you looking for, Dan?"

"Someone else has to be running the gang," the rancher surmised. "If it was someone in Rooster, or even John Hurley, there would have been no need for the notes."

The sheriff nodded. "I been thinking that since you gave me the notes. I have been racking my brain about who might have moved to Casper in the past year. Of course, they might be out of Medicine Bow or another town. I plan to send some telegrams checking on Cal and Tex to see if they might be wanted. Maybe I can get the names and descriptions of men they hung out with."

The wind rattled the shutters on the office. Dan glanced out and saw the snow blowing by the window. "I guess I better be heading out. I wanted to see if J.P. knew anything about Hurley."

Getting up and stretching, the rancher left the sheriff's office, tilting his head against the wind. There wasn't much accumulation on the streets. Clumps of frozen mud made walking difficult. Dan found the door of the Cattle Exchange locked. The time spent at the livery had taken too long and J.P. had gone home for the night.

Walking against the wind, Dan decided to stop and see if Amos was at the saloon. Grabbing the corner post, he pulled himself up onto the porch and kicked the snow and dirt off his boots.

The air was filled with wood smoke when he entered the drinking establishment. Lem was adding wood and poking at the fire in the stove. Slamming the iron door shut, he hung the poker on a nail and headed back behind the bar.

"Damn it, Lem," Dan kidded, "I thought the place was on fire when I come in."

"Ah hell, that old stove don't draw worth a darn when the wind blows. Trouble is, that's most of the time. If I get it good and stoked up, it works a bit better. Now, what can I get you, Mr. August?"

"Shot and a beer, please," the rancher replied. Looking around, he asked, "Have you seen Amos?"

"I sure did," the bartender snorted. "He come in here chewing on a thick roast beef sandwich and ordered up a beer. He ate the whole damn thing without offering me any. After a couple more beers, he headed for his room to take a nap."

Dan tossed down the shot and chased it with the glass of beer. Wiping his mouth with the back of his hand, he told Lem, "When he comes down, tell him I'll be at Hartwick's."

Pulling his gloves back on, he stepped back outside. The wind almost pulled the door from his hand as he shut it. The hills beyond Casper were hidden behind the blowing snow. Checking on Rooster would have to wait until the storm pushed through.

It was two days before the snow quit. Most businesses had remained closed in Casper out of fear the storm could turn into a blizzard. Dan was shoveling off the porch in front of Hartwick's Mercantile. The sun was rising in a clear sky. Today he would ride to Rooster to learn what he could. He saw Amos coming up the street. The old prospector had started to take meals with them. Angie loved cooking and Amos loved eating. On a couple meals they'd worked together and made a wonderful spread.

After breakfast was done, the two friends sat bundled up on the front porch, smoking. "Another storm is building in the mountains," Amos predicted.

"As long as it holds off today. It is a three-hour ride to Rooster on a good day. I plan to leave in a short bit."

"I'll ride along with you. I hear tell they got some fine young ladies at the saloon. Maybe I'll parley for one of their favors," Amos said, laughing at his own joke.

The sheriff came by and Dan told him where they were riding. The lawman warned him, "If you do, remember, you're just there to get information. Once you get it, bring it back to me. Keep your guns in their holsters. I don't need you to bring back any more bodies."

The old miner left after finishing his smoke. Dan went back into the mercantile to spend some time with his family. Mary's color looked good and her strength had come back. Mrs. Hartwick offered to let her help in the store when she felt up to it.

Dan placed a penny on the counter and took two peppermint sticks from the jar. Going to the sitting room, he handed one to Joanie. The other he stuck into his coat pocket.

Sitting next to his wife he said, "I'm heading for Rooster. I will be back by tomorrow afternoon. The smithy told us that the men we think stole the cattle hung out there. Maybe someone knows where they took the herd."

"Is Amos going with you?" she asked.

"Yes, he is."

"Well, make sure you take care of him. He has a biscuit recipe he hasn't given me yet."

They both laughed over her humor, while realizing that the trip he was making could be dangerous.

Dan went to the barn and saddled the chestnut. He saw that Amos hadn't gotten one of the team horses ready. He felt a twinge of impatience. He wanted to get going. He led the chestnut out of the barn and walked through the knee-deep snow in the alley next to the mercantile. Rounding the corner to the front of the building, he stopped. There stood the old prospector with a long-legged mule, saddled and ready to go.

"Where did you get that cantankerous animal?"

"Not so loud," Amos cautioned his friend. "I call her Jenny. She's very sensitive. I bought her from the hostler at the livery. He gave me a very good price and even threw in the saddle."

"I'm sure you got a wonderful deal, now let's go." Dan said as he swung into the saddle.

The men rode out of Casper, following the railroad east. The rancher noticed that Amos was smiling, in spite of Dan being a little short with his friend, when they left. He couldn't ask for a more reliable person to ride beside him. The problem Dan was having with the ranch was not Amos', yet his friend didn't hesitate to step forward.

They kept the animals at a walk. The knee-deep snow caused them to struggle, and there was the danger of a misstep by a hidden obstacle. After three hours, they were still a few miles from the saloon. There was the sound of a steam whistle in the distance. The train was coming and it had given a blast as it went past Rooster.

They pulled their animals clear of the track. The locomotive went by, sending the snow from the tracks flying several feet to either side. As the train disappeared down the track it left a trail of swirling snow. Dan led the way with his chestnut, lunging through the snowbank left by the train. The long-legged mule followed the horse onto the railroad bed. Being clear of the snow, the men trotted their animals toward Rooster.

The Rooster Saloon was one of the buildings that had been built at the railhead when the railroad had come here. Most of the buildings had been pulled up as the railroad had continued to lay rails west. All that remained in the shabby town of Rooster were the saloon and brothel, a rundown livery, and a small general store. The store also offered a few rooms for the night, a telegraph and the post office. The town survived because of its convenient location to local ranches, and a coal mine.

As the men rode toward the saloon, they passed the livery. Next to it was a rail spur, a water tank, and pens with a loading chute that had been used in the past for shipping cattle. The larger pens in Casper and Medicine Bow had made this location unnecessary.

The man from the livery had fastened a rope onto each end of a log and was dragging it up and down what could be called the main street. It packed more than plowed the snow, making travel a bit easier. It was midday and the Rooster Saloon was quiet. The aging clapboards had once been painted yellow, but now the paint was mostly worn away by the constant wind and blowing summer sands of the plains.

Next to the saloon, sharing a common wall, was a two-story wood building that housed the brothel. The first floor had a large sitting room where the men chose their companions before they climbed the stairs to one of five rooms to take their pleasure. A room in the back of the first floor sitting room was for the ladies to rest and get themselves ready for the next customer.

Amos headed into the saloon while Dan was loosening the cinch on the chestnut. He followed his friend into the establishment. The dimly lit room smelled strongly of spilt whiskey, sweat, tobacco smoke, and cheap perfume. A bar ran along the right side of the room, with an opening to a red door for the patrons who wanted to go to the brothel. Bottles of rye lined the back bar, along with boxes of cigars. The bartender was reading a newspaper at the end of the bar. Two men were nursing drinks at one of the tables. By their appearance, it looked like they were out-of-work cowboys and had spent the night sleeping in their clothes.

The bartender looked up and closed the newspaper. "Welcome to Rooster, gentlemen. Name your poison, we have whiskey or beer."

Dan ordered a beer, while Amos ordered a bottle of whiskey and a glass. After placing the prospector's order on the bar, the bartender took a glass mug and drew Dan a draft using an ornate handle to pump the brew from a barrel located in a room below the bar. The rancher tasted the foamy beer and found the drink very satisfying.

The men sat near the door. Looking around the room, the rancher saw a beat-up piano next to the wall, across from the bar. On the back wall there was a doorway that led to an outhouse. The door was framed, with elk horns on one side and a buffalo hide on the other.

The bartender drew himself a beer, walked over to the table and had a seat. "If you men are here to visit with the gals next door, they are mostly sleeping. I would be happy to wake a couple of them to visit with you."

"Maybe later," Amos said with a broad grin on his face.

"I am looking for a fellow named Cal Duncan that I knew in Texas," Dan lied. "I heard he was up in this area and I have a job I'd like him to do."

The bartender gave him a hard look. "Duncan has been here. He hangs around with a gunman named Tex Porter. You got someone you want killed, they would be your men."

Taking a chance, the rancher confessed, "I own a ranch in a valley about two days out of Casper toward the Big Horn Mountains. I had a hand killed and some cattle stolen. I've learned that Cal and Tex were part of the gang that did it."

"Sounds like something they would be involved with," the man replied, his voice low. He began to stand up to move back to the bar, but Dan stopped him.

"If you have another minute, I have a couple more questions," the rancher said.

Sitting back down, with a look of irritation on his face, bartender waited.

"I am trying to find out what happened to the herd and who is heading up the gang. I thought it was John Hurley, but now I am sure it was someone else."

"I suggest you ask Hurley who he's working for."

"He can't do that," Amos chimed in. "The lowlife tried to ambush my friend here and he had to kill him."

"Hurley is dead?" the surprised bartender replied.

Dan stared at the bartender without speaking. The old prospector drained another shot and said, "I am surprised you didn't know. Seems that kind of word travels fast."

"I don't know nothing about any cattle rustling. Men come in here to drink and spend time with the women. They don't talk about what they been doing," the man said, gaining respect for Dan.

"How long has it been since the men have been here?" the rancher asked.

"It's been two, maybe three, weeks since they been here."

"When they were here, did any one man seem in charge?" Dan continued.

"Hurley seemed to be the man. He led the others," the man said, appearing uncomfortable with the conversation. "I got some stocking I have to do"

Dan watched the bartender hurry back behind the bar and make himself busy. He knew that the man wasn't telling him all he knew. Being closed-mouth about the men who came here was an important part of his success.

"I will be back after a bit. When you bring the chestnut to the livery, bring Jenny with you," Amos requested as he stood and picked up his bottle.

The old prospector walked up to the bar and asked, "Who is the oldest gal you got working back there?"

The bartender looked at the roughly dressed miner. "That would be Miss Raye. We got some younger ones that could ride you hard and put you up wet," he suggested.

"No, I kinda got a taste for the more mature woman. Miss Raye would be the one."

The bartender said, taking Amos into his confidence, "I heard she learned everything from Mother Featherlegs in Lusk. After Davis killed Featherlegs, Miss Raye come and started this place."

"Thanks for the history lesson. What I need to know is how much for Miss Raye," Amos asked.

"The girls are $3, but the madam would be $5, in advance."

"It sounds fair to me." Amos agreed. "Do I pay you, or them in there?" he asked, pointing to the red door.

"I got to check if the Madam is available." With that, the bartender hurried through the door.

Leaning with his back to the bar, Amos smiled at his friend. "I may not need a room for the night, Dan. The lady might want to tuck me in."

"I'll wager you'll be back out here before I finish another beer. Then together we can take care of the animals and find a place to sleep," the rancher replied.

The bartender came through the red door, still nodding at whatever the person on the other side was saying. He then smiled at Amos. "Miss Raye will be with you in just a moment. You can pay her."

Dan motioned the bartender to bring him another beer. He saw the red door open. A full-figured woman dressed in an emerald green dress entered. Her lips were red and her eyes were accented with heavy makeup. She had stately grace as she invited Amos to follow her.

The bartender brought another beer to Dan. He whispered, "Don't ask about Cal and Tex. It ain't healthy conversation."

Sitting alone at the table, the rancher wondered about the friendly warning. Why should the man behind the bar be worried about him? The front door banged open and three men dressed like miners entered.

"A bottle and a deck, Hal," the lead man called to the bartender. They went to the back of the room. After pulling off their coats, they sat. None of the miners wore a firearm. Dan noticed that the out of work cowboys were nursing their drinks and talking quietly among themselves.

The dim light through the frost-covered window told the rancher that the sun was going down. The bartender, Hal, walked around the room lighting the extra lamps. The room was still poorly lit. Dan raised the mug of beer to his lips, when it suddenly exploded in his hand. The deafening sound of the gunshot rang in his ears as he threw himself backwards.

Shots continued to ring out as Dan rolled over, drawing his Colt. He had no idea who was shooting at him. His eyes burned from the beer in them. He was unable to open his right one. Not wanting to hit any innocent bystanders, he fired two shots, keeping them high, hoping to worry whoever was firing. There was a flash of a gun and he felt something burn across his bicep.

The rancher fired at the flash, then ducked and crawled behind the table. The shooting stopped. Dan was looking for a target from under the table. "It's over, mister. They're both down," someone called out.

Unsure that the person speaking could be trusted, the rancher lay still, the cocked Colt in front of him. The red door behind the bar burst open. Standing in his long johns, with his .45 leveled for action, stood Amos. Seeing his friend covering the room, Dan slowly stood up.

Two of the miners were on the floor next to the bar, attempting to avoid the flying lead. The third stood near their table, while the two shooters lay on the floor. "You hit one of them and I threw our bottle and knocked out the other," the standing miner said. "The sons-of-bitches just got up and started shooting at you. I don't know how the hell they missed you."

The prospector walked over to Dan. "Damn it man, your face is cut to hell. Did they hit you anywhere else?"

"The cuts on my face are from my beer mug. I think they hit my arm once." While Amos checked his friend over, Hal went to look over the shooters. Dan had put a bullet into one, low on the right side. The other began to come to after the knock on the head from the bottle.

The bartender picked up the shooters' guns, and slid them in Dan's direction. He then grabbed the wounded man by the back of his coat while the helpful miner grabbed the other, and dragged them to the door.

The wounded man whined, "We wanted the $100 for killing him. I'm shot and need a doctor."

Snow and cold air blew in when the bartender opened the door. "You bastards know better than to shoot in here!" he snarled. Hal then tossed each out into the weather and slammed the door shut.

Remembering that their animals were out there, Dan cracked the door opened to make sure that the two men didn't try and take them. He watched as they stumbled toward the livery. They would probably head along the railroad to find a doctor in Casper.

The rancher turned back to see two of the women from the brothel waiting to clean up his cuts. They paid special attention to his right eye. After soaking it several times with a warm damp cloth, he was able to keep it open. Amos had headed back to see Miss Raye. After the women finished with his face and had put a bandage around his arm, they asked him if he planned to visit the brothel. The rancher declined, remaining seated at the table. Hal had placed another beer in front of him. The two women went back through the red door and it seemed to be business as usual, as though the shooting had never happened.

The bartender sat across from Dan. "The two men that tried to shoot you are no-goods that hang around here. They said there was $100 on your head. They knew of it and tried to make some easy money."

Memory of the note flashed through his mind. The rancher asked, "Can you guess who put up the money?"

"I've seen Hurley buying the men drinks," the bartender told him. "Maybe he put out the word. The longer you stay around here, the more danger you will be in."

"I got to take care of the animals. I do appreciate knowing about there being a price on me." Dan got up to leave.

"Take them to the barn behind the saloon. You would be a target for any fool with a gun out there. If you want you can spend the night with your animals," Hal offered.

Dan thanked him and then pointed at the miner that helped him. "Bring my friend another bottle."

Dan stepped out the door quickly and put the animals between himself and the livery. He didn't see any movement. Taking the reins of the animals, he led them around the building to a low structure. He pushed the door open and the warm smell of the stock inside greeted him.

There was a lamp near the door. Striking a match, he lit it. He could see three open stalls. He chose two and led the animals into them. Removing their saddles and bridles, he gave each a rubdown and then some hay. He looked around the barn and decided that he would sleep here.

Dan returned to the Rooster Saloon, using the back door. There were now a half-dozen men scattered around the room. The three miners were back to playing cards and offered to let him sit in their game. The rancher was given the seat with his back to the wall. Thanking them, he sat and let them deal him in.

He sat watching the room more closely than the cards. None of the men paid any attention to him. Most were drinking and working up the courage to go through the red door and visit the women. As the evening went on, the bartender brought Dan a thick cheese sandwich. He sat out a few hands while he ate. He was about even with the men and he found that he was enjoying himself.

Slowly, the saloon continued to fill up. Three of the women had come out and were mingling with the customers, trying to encourage them to buy their favors. A short, fat man in a white shirt and a derby hat sat down at the piano and started playing. The place was getting too busy to watch everyone, so Dan was beginning to feel like a target.

There was another man helping Hal behind the bar. The card game with the miners broke up when one of the men waved to a girl working the room and then joined her behind the red door. The man who had thrown the bottle and knocked out the shooter was called Pepper. The remaining miner was Josh.

Dan toyed with his mug, trying to decide if he should turn in. He had been in the Rooster Saloon for four hours. For all he knew, Amos was settled in for the night upstairs. Hal came from behind the bar to add wood to the potbelly stove in the back corner. On his way back, he stopped at the table. The miners had pretty much finished their bottle.

"Hal, will you bring Pepper and Josh another bottle? I'll have one more beer before heading out back. Would you get word to Amos where I'll be sleeping?" Dan asked

A moment later, the bartender brought another bottle and a beer. The men toasted each other and drank. Josh poured another drink, thanking Dan for the bottle.

"Can you tell me why the two men were shooting at you earlier?" Pepper asked.

Knowing that he probably owed his life to this man, Dan said, "My ranch was raided and one of my hands was killed. They took a good part of my herd. Two of the men that were involved were Cal Duncan and Tex Porter. Another, which I killed, was John Hurley. I learned today that someone put a price on my head. I imagine the rustlers figure if I was killed then the search for them would go away."

"We've seen them in here," Josh said. "They kind of run the roost when they were here."

"I heard Cal and Hurley arguing about what someone named Jack wanted," Pepper added. "Hurley was the one defending this Jack."

There were shouts from down the bar as two

cowboys began to throw haymakers. One lunged at the other and they both went down, wrestling and punching. Hal came around the bar with a short club and rapped both men on the head, stopping the fight immediately. Sitting on the floor, the two men held their throbbing heads.

"You get one chance, boys, and you just used it! Any more fighting and you are out the door!" the bartender threatened.

Dan scanned the room for anyone who might be looking for the $100. Everyone's attention was on the two men with bruised heads as they went back to their drinks.

"I appreciate your stepping in during the shooting and for inviting me to play cards. Hopefully, we will meet each other again." With that, Dan went to the back door and quickly stepped outside. He closed the door and moved to the right, waiting for his eyes to adjust to the darkness. He knew that as long as he was in this area, he was in danger.

After a quick stop in the outhouse, he made his way to the barn and took his bedroll off the saddle. Dan spread it out on some hay and was soon asleep. The creaking of the door brought him wide awake. Gripping the Colt alongside his blankets, the rancher strained his eyes in the dark, trying to see who was coming in.

There was a chuckle and then, "Damn fine hotel you got us here. I left a feather bed to sleep in a smelly barn."

Uncocking the .44, Dan tucked it back under the blankets. "What I am wondering is why you left the feather bed. I reckon you ran out of money to stay there."

The old prospector sat next to Dan, grunting from the effort. He struck a match and began lighting his pipe.

"Be careful with that match," the rancher warned him. "You'll burn the place down around us."

"I'll be most careful," Amos promised. "I come to sleep here because I got news, and a snoot full. I was afraid that if I slept on it, it would be gone when I awoke."

Dan sat up and leaned against a post next to his blankets. "What have you learned?"

"I went with Miss Raye. I want you to know she is quite the lady and a warm person. Anyway . . ."

"Anyway, Amos," the rancher interrupted. "The news first, and then the story."

"Oh yes, the news," the prospector said, remembering why he had come to the barn. "While sitting in the afterglow with the madam, I apologized because I would have to leave on the morrow. While trying to explain why, I told her about the cattle being stolen."

"She commented that there was too much of that going on and it was bad for business. I questioned her about 'there being too much of it'. She told me in the past three years more than one small rancher had lost all his stock and some were found dead. She said it was like the Johnson County War was still going on. When the herds were rustled, the larger ranchers would keep their hands guarding the cattle so they couldn't get away and spend money at the saloon."

"Then she told me it was those damn Texans.

Too many of them come to Wyoming."

The rancher sat listening to his friend, wishing that he would get to the point, and worrying that he had already done so. "Was the news her business had suffered?"

Amos looked at him, the glow of his pipe showing surprise on the old face. "Why no, Dan. The news is what was being done with the stolen cattle."

The rancher's interest was piqued. "What happens to the stock?"

His friend sat in silence in the dark, and Dan began to fear that he had fallen asleep. "Amos, you were talking about the rustled cattle."

"My damn pipe has gone out," he complained. "Oh well, about the cattle. Miss Raye told me in the past two years some smaller herds had been loaded right here at the old chute. A bunch of cattle cars would be left on the side rail and then later cattle were loaded and shipped to who knows where. Nobody local was allowed to help. It was Hurley, and his crew that brung the cows."

The rancher's mind was racing. "They could load the stolen cattle and ship them well out of the territory. With a forged bill-of-sale they could be sold and the evidence could soon be peddled in butcher shops."

Amos nodded. "A steak at a time, it would disappear." Then he chuckled.

His friend had indeed found out some important information. When they got back to Casper, Sheriff Winslow would be interested. Unfortunately, it had him no closer to finding his cattle.

"Your news was interesting, but now I suggest we get some sleep and get an early start back to Casper," Dan said, scooting back under his blankets.

"Wait, wait, there's more," the tipsy prospector insisted. "Miss Raye thinks she knows where they keep the cattle until they can be sold."

Dan sat up with a start. "Where? Where do they keep them?"

"The madam said one of her customers complained about the long ride and the crummy cabin they had to stay in on the way. The man told her he almost froze after getting his ass wet crossing the Little Medicine Bow River. I asked her if it was Hurley's ranch." Yawning, Amos continued. "She said it was the man that Hurley worked for."

"The river is south of here in the Laramie Mountains. It runs toward Medicine Bow. The area is filled with valleys that would be perfect for hiding a herd," the rancher said, waiting for a reply from his friend. The only answer he got was snoring.

Pulling his blanket over his shoulder, Dan muttered, "We'll talk more in the morning."

CHAPTER THIRTEEN

It was barely getting light enough to travel as the men stood outside the barn with the chestnut and mule saddled. Amos handed Jenny's reins to Dan and said that he had to run into the Rooster Saloon for a minute. The rancher looked around the cluster of dwellings. He would be happy when they put distance between this place and his back. He felt he was the game and all around him were hunters.

The old prospector came out the back door, clutching a bag. "You wouldn't believe it, Dan. There are still cowboys and miners drinking, trying to decide on going through the red door."

They climbed onto their steeds and rode away from Rooster. The railroad was clear of snow and it would make traveling faster. Amos pulled a ham sandwich out of the bag and handed it to his friend. The two rode with the sun coming up behind them, eating their breakfast. *It was a good sandwich*, Dan thought.

They saw the smoke before they reached Casper. Dan spurred the chestnut into a gallop, with Amos following closely behind. The smoke was coming from the charred remains of the cattle exchange. The men stopped in front of the ruins. A few posts from the walls and a blackened safe with the door standing open were the only things that remained of J.P.'s office.

A rider came by with a bag of supplies hanging from his saddle horn. He stopped and look at the burnt building with Dan and Amos. "Couldn't believe the son-of-a-bitch would shoot the sheriff."

The rancher exclaimed, "Winslow's dead!"

"No, he's at the doc's. Burdick shot him and lit the place on fire to hide what he had done. Lem from the saloon saw the fire and saved the sheriff."

"I was supposed to see Burdick before leaving for Rooster," Dan said, realizing J.P. may have intended to shoot him when he came to the cattle exchange.

"Has anyone gone after J.P.?" Dan asked.

"A few men talked of getting a posse together, but with the weather being what it is, they haven't gotten too far." Touching the brim of his hat, the man rode away with his supplies.

The two men rode their tired animals to the mercantile barn and took care of them before heading into the store. As they entered, they heard the sound of laughter coming from the sitting room. Bert called out when he heard the bell hanging on the door, "Look around, I'll be right out!"

Dan walked into the sitting room and what he

saw floored him. There sitting at the table with cups of coffee, were his cousins Vic and Zac. "Where the . . . when did you get here?"

Vic replied, smiling, "Mary sent us telegrams, asking if we could come to Casper."

"You sent a telegram?" he asked, looking at his wife.

"Someone had to. There was no reason why you had to go after the rustlers by yourself," she replied. Then she noticed his face. "What happened to you!"

"It was nothing," he assured Mary.

"I'm sorry," she said, seeing Amos. "Amos Mudd, these are Dan's cousins, Vic and Zac."

The old prospector stepped forward and gave each of the cousins a hardy handshake. "It is a pleasure to meet the two of you. Your cousin here can certainly use the help."

"Anyone that wrongs one of the Augusts have the whole bunch of us to deal with," Zac declared.

Amos was a bit confused. "I have to ask. How did it happen that the three of you are cousins?"

The prospector had noticed that Zac had a dark complexion and black hair that he wore in a single braid down the center of his back. Vic was blond and blue-eyed while Dan had brown hair and gray eyes.

Vic spoke up, "Let me explain. The three of us share the same grandfather, Oli August. He met Zac's grandmother first, before Dan's and mine. She was a Ho-Chunk and had been kidnapped by another tribe. After escaping from her captors, she ran from them, not having time to search for food. Grandfather

Oli found her exhausted and starving, about to be attacked by a wild cat."

"He nursed her back to health. She showed him how to survive in the wilderness, with nothing more than a knife. When he found her, he was eating raw meat, unable to make fire. She had taught him fire starting as well as making fish traps. As they traveled through the wilds, they grew close."

Embarrassed, Vic turned red. After a moment, he continued. "Grandfather Oli lost Zac's grandmother when some members of her tribe had found her while she was away picking berries. She feared the braves would kill our grandfather, so she went back to her tribe. Grandfather Oli was unaware that she was carrying his baby, and never saw his wilderness companion again."

"When our grandfather found his way out, he met Grandma Joan. They married and had two sons. They were Dan's and my fathers."

"Years later, Zac's father had come across ours while on a raiding party. They had intended to steal some horses that were being driven. An emblem given by grandfather Oli to Zac's grandmother, and the use of the last name August, had made them realize they had the same father, saving a brother-on-brother fight that could have left any one of them dead."

"We grew up in Elkader, playing, working, and hunting with each other. We then came west together and enjoyed several adventures. We all married and made our homes along the Rocky Mountains. Coming together to help Dan is the first time we've seen one another in five years."

"And it has been too long," Dan said.

Angie had a large pot of bean soup on the stove and loaves of fresh bread. "It's time to eat," she said, turning to Dan and Amos. "Put your coats away and wash up. The soup is ready."

Over the next hour the cousins sat around the table, eating and talking of old times and what they were doing now. Zac was a hunting and fishing guide, working from his trading post on the Boulder River. Vic had a farm in Idaho and was growing potatoes and other vegetables.

Amos exclaimed, "Potatoes! Loved to eat them, hated growing them."

They all laughed at the old prospector's outburst. Dan then brought his cousins up to date on the attack on his ranch. By the time he finished, the men's faces were serious.

"Do you think this Burdick is the leader?" Zac asked.

"It looks like he might be," Dan replied. "I got to get down to Doc Morgan's and see if the sheriff is able to tell me what happened at the cattle exchange."

Mary had finished feeding and cleaning up Joanie. She ran from her mother and climbed onto her father's lap.

"You named her after Grandma Joan," Vic said. "Both Zac and I have daughters also. We have to get the girls together. They should know each other."

Mary excused herself and went into the kitchen to help Angie clean up. She was now putting in a few hours every day in the mercantile. When Dan was ready to go back to the ranch, she would be going with him.

Not wanting to crowd the wounded sheriff, Dan went to see him alone. Amos and the cousins continued to visit. He was telling them about Jon Kidman and the ransom. Slipping on the sheepskin coat, the rancher smelled the pungent odor of the barn they had slept in last night. He would have to air the coat out.

The sky was overcast, with heavy clouds, threatening another storm. Dan kicked the snow off his boots before climbing the stairs to the doctor's office. Doc Morgan was sitting at his roll top desk when he entered.

Looking up, the doc said, "Making up a list of supplies I have to order. The sheriff is in the back. He was awake a minute ago."

Walking around the curtain, Dan looked at the washed-out face of the wounded man. "Where did he shoot you?"

Wincing when he moved to look at the rancher, he replied, "In the chest. The bullet shattered on my badge, cutting the hell out of me. I hit my head when I went down and awoke here in the doc's. I figure with all the blood he saw on my shirt, he figured I was a goner."

"What brought you to J.P.'s?"

"I went back to talk to the smithy. I wanted to know more about the man Prince that they hung. The rustling here sounded a lot like it." Sheriff Winslow tried to stifle a cough. His face was covered with perspiration from the effort. He lay back, catching his breath before continuing.

"He had called the man Prince. It turned out the man's name was Jackson Prince. I thought, J.P. It made sense. Right there I figured he was the son or a close relative of the man they hung and had taken the man's name. Somewhere along the line he had picked up the last name Burdick. Maybe it was his mother's."

The lawman rested for a moment. "The bullet broke a damn rib. Makes breathing kind of hard. I went to see J.P., planning on just doing some nosing around. If my telegrams sent to Texas supported my thinking, then I would arrest him. I walked into his office and he had the safe open and was putting everything into a carpet bag. I asked him if he was planning a trip. He turned to me and fired."

A look of regret crossed the wounded man's face. "I should have waited for you to come back. With Amos and you to back me, he wouldn't have dared to make the move he did."

The rancher shook his head no. "He would have been gone. You caught him getting ready to run. I think Amos and I found out where he is heading. It is also where I will find the cattle."

Dan brought the sheriff up to date on what they had found out at Rooster. "My cousins are here and we will be going after them."

"Go to my office and get badges out of the desk. I will deputize you so you can have the law on your side. If they resist and you have to kill them, we won't have some judge questioning what your motives of going after them was."

The sheriff had closed his eyes and looked exhausted from the effort it took to tell Dan about J.P.. As Dan left, the doc asked him to sit in the chair next to him. "Let me check the cuts on your face before you leave. Some of the cuts look kind of raw."

Taking his time, the doctor found several pieces of glass shards in the cuts. Dabbing some alcohol on them caused Dan to grimace with pain. "Any other areas I should look at?" the doctor asked.

Dan removed his coat and let him look at the arm. "The ladies in Rooster did a good job on the arm. I will just put on a fresh bandage."

Leaving the doctor's office, Dan hurried back toward the mercantile to talk to his cousins. He was grateful to have them here to help, but by doing so he would be putting them in harm's way. What if one or both of them were killed? He would have to live knowing it was his fault for the rest of his life.

The snow had started while he had visited the sheriff. It would cover any trail that J.P. had left. He felt an urgency to start after the bastard. Mary was behind the counter when he walked into the store. She stopped him before he entered the residence.

"How is Sheriff Winslow?"

"He is in pain, but should be okay."

"Did the doctor look at the cuts on your face?"

"He did, Mary, and he also changed the bandage on my arm."

"Your arm?"

He gave his wife a hug and said, "I have to talk with Vic and Zac."

"They won't let you go alone, Dan. The three of you mean too much to each other to let one face a gang like the men who did all this," Mary told him.

"I know, darling, I know only too well."

Dan went into the sitting room and found the others at the table enjoying glasses of brandy and smoking cigars.

"What are we celebrating?" he asked, smiling and taking his place at the table.

With the snow, they wouldn't be leaving today. They could only hope that the storm was a short one. The discussion went to the herd remaining in the valley. Burdick would know about them and know that there wasn't anyone at the ranch. He might have told his men to go and take the rest of the cattle. As far as he was concerned there was only one man who would come after him. In J.P.'s mind, he would be easy enough to kill. Even if Burdick knew about Amos, he had a gang of six or more men. The odds were in his favor.

Amos came up with a suggestion. "Let me go to the ranch and protect the herd. If they come after the cows, it won't be all of the men. You might know of someone else that can join me."

"Ralph and Kelly help with the roundup each year. I can check if they are available for some winter work," the rancher said. "But you have to promise me, if they come after the cattle, you let them take the herd and you follow them. We can take them back as a group."

The old prospector winked and said, "I won't let them kill any more of your hands."

To his cousins, Dan said, "We will be wearing badges when we go after J.P. and his gang. The sheriff is resting right now. Before supper we can go and pick them up from his office, and stop by the doc's to get sworn in."

Zac pulled the "good knife" from the nape of his neck. He fished a whetstone from his pocket and started honing the edge of its blade. Zac's father had taught his son to be an expert with the throwing knife.

Vic reached into his vest pocket and pulled out a two-shot derringer. His father had gotten it years ago when some thugs on the waterfront in St. Louis had attacked him. The thugs had lost and his father had ended up with the compact handgun.

"Amos here found out that there was a ranch on Little Medicine Bow River near the Laramie Mountains. I figure that is where J.P. is headed and the cattle are being held. It is a long, two-day ride from here. There is a cabin about halfway. Burdick will make for the shack and spend the night. He might even have men staying there as forward lookouts."

"If the snow wipes out his trail from here and the snow stops, we should be able to pick it up after he left the cabin. We can spread out as we ride and cover a mile-wide swath," Vic suggested.

Zac added, "If the wind drives the snow, it will fill in the tracks but leave an outline of them. We will be able to see this in places that this storm blew the loose snow off the crust."

"We will need horses. My chestnut should be rested by tomorrow. I will talk to the hostler at the livery and make arrangements for two more animals," the rancher said.

The snow continued to blow past the windows. Amos left to go to the saloon. The cousins headed for the livery to get horses. The hostler was a short, balding man they called Pop. His skin was like tanned leather from a lifetime of wind and sun. He had lost his front upper teeth when a disgruntled horse had kicked out and he had ducked too slowly.

"I need a couple horses for my cousins to go after Burdick. We'll probably have them up to a couple weeks," Dan told the hostler.

"You paying for them or the town?" Pop asked.

"We will be deputized," Dan said.

"The town will be paying, then. I got a dun and a mustang. Will you need saddles?"

Dan started to answer when Vic interrupted, "No, we brought our own."

With arrangements made for the horses, they went to the sheriff's office and picked up three badges from the desk. The sheriff was sleeping when they got to the doctor's. They sat watching Doc Morgan eat a meal brought over from Lilly's Café while they waited for Winslow to wake up.

Finished with his meal, the doctor went to check on his patient. He came from behind the curtain and smiled. "He's awake now."

The cousins went to see the wounded lawman. The sheriff asked them to raise their right hands. He said a few words about upholding the laws of Casper and Wyoming. "You're now deputies tasked with the responsibility of bringing J.P. Burdick and any of his gang to Casper for a proper hanging."

"You mean for trial," Dan said.

"Yes, there will have to be one of those. See Pop about some horses for your cousins. Get one for yourself if you want. You will get $5 a day or $25 a week, whichever is less," the sheriff said.

The cousins left the doctor's office with their badges. Vic said, "I don't think the sheriff wants us to bring any back alive."

"If we have to pack them back, the cold will stop them from stinking," Zac said.

It was dark when the cousins arrived back at the mercantile. They met Bert coming out. "Going over to the saloon for a drink. Will you join me?"

"Good idea," Dan said. "I might run into Ralph or Kelly there."

They stepped into the drinking establishment and leaned against the bar. "Set us up with whiskeys, Lem, and pour one for yourself," Bert said.

While the bartender was pouring, Dan asked, "Have Kelly or Ralph been in?"

"Not yet," Lem told him, "but I am expecting them anytime."

The men raised their glasses to the demise of J.P. Burdick and drank them down. Bert ordered another shot while the cousins ordered beers. They sat down at one of the tables.

Over the next hour the cousins compared what they knew about the Laramie Mountains. There were several streams and rivers that flowed out of the mountains, and scores of canyons where a herd could be hidden.

The door opened and Ralph and Kelly walked in. They saw Dan and came over. "What brings you to Casper? Who's watching the cows?" Kelly asked.

"I am hoping you and Ralph would."

The cowhands ordered a bottle and pulled a couple chairs up to the table. They were filled in with what had happened at the ranch. They were told that a man named Amos would be going with them.

"Will Curly be coming out?" Ralph asked.

"He will be spending the winter with some family while his broken leg heals," Dan explained.

They all looked up as Amos came down the narrow stairs from the second floor. In front of him was a lady known to have a questionable reputation. At the bottom of the stairs she gave him a peck on the cheek and said she hoped to see him again soon.

Amos saw the men at the table and pulled another chair over. "Looks like we are about to run out of table," he kidded. Then he called over to Lem, "We'll need another bottle over here."

Dan introduced Amos to Ralph and Kelly. Amos looked the men over and nodded. "They will do just fine. I don't think you will have to worry about your cows."

"Remember what I told you, just follow the rustlers," the rancher said.

"Oh, I remember."

"By the way, Amos," Dan wondered. "Didn't you spend last night with Miss Raye? Now I see you with Lizzy."

"I am going to be at the ranch for quite some time. I just wanted to take some sweet memories with me," the old prospector explained.

They all laughed at Amos' reply and raised their glasses to memories of women.

* * *

The weather cleared the next day. Dan and Mary came downstairs together. The rancher hadn't gotten as much sleep as he had hoped before heading out. Mary had spent a long time saying goodbye and reminding him why he should hurry back home.

Vic and Zac were already up eating breakfast. Amos came in shortly after Dan sat down. After they had gotten back from the saloon the night before, Bert had opened the store for them so they could stock up on things they would need on an extended trip.

With their meals finished, they strapped on their handguns and knives. They each carried a rifle. Their saddle bags were packed full and they had canteens carried under their coats. The horses from the livery were tied in front of the mercantile. The chestnut was still in the barn behind the store.

Zac chose the mustang, leaving the dun for Vic. Dan brought his horse around front. Mary stood on the porch wrapped in a blanket, drinking coffee. She watched as her husband swung onto the saddle. She was proud of him and his cousins. The three of them sat square and tall, ready to make things right.

Amos had gone back to the saloon to meet with Ralph and Kelly. He would be taking the team back to the ranch with him. He would be riding the mule, and the hands had their own horses. The trip normally took two days by wagon. He planned to make it in one long day of riding. They would rotate the animals, using the team.

The three cousins left Casper, heading south toward the Laramie Mountains. Dan had figured that the rustlers were holding the cattle halfway between Rooster and Medicine Bow. Just outside of town they spread out. Zac was the best tracker, so he took the middle. Dan went to the left and Vic to the right.

An hour out of Casper, they picked up the first tracks that might be J.P.'s. They were in the snow on a rise that had had the new snow blow clear. Zac studied them and the landscape for a few minutes before moving on. The terrain determined the route that a rider would take. They would avoid deep cuts, waterways, mountain ridges, and rough areas. Habit also set the route. The rider would use the same landmarks to keep themselves on the trail. By looking for things that stand out in the distance, a good tracker could often pick the direction in which the rider would go. The trail could be lost for a while if the rider made an unusual change in direction.

The men rode back and forth, looking for areas where the wind had blown the new snow clear. They found the tracks twice more. "Right now, the rider is using the highest mountain peak to keep himself on track," Zac concluded.

A broad basin lay before them, ending at Deer Creek. They sat on their horses chewing jerky and sipping water while they looked across the valley.

"He will have to go south when he hits the Deer," Vic surmised. "The hills beyond would be difficult to drive cattle."

Looking over the basin, Dan suggested, "We should make a sweep across the valley heading further south. If I was traveling and came to this rise, I wouldn't continue to go toward the Deer. I'd start cutting across to save miles."

"If we don't pick up any tracks, we can cut back along the creek to try and pick them up again," Vic suggested. "All we lose is a little time."

The three cousins started in a more southerly direction across the valley. The wind blowing over the hill created little whirlwinds with the loose snow. Zac stood in his stirrups to see as far as possible ahead. They were looking for a small cabin used by the rustlers first. If it was occupied there would be smoke coming from the pipe.

In the middle of the basin there was a clump of pines. Dan rode toward the trees. J.P. had been riding during the snow storm. He may have taken refuge while giving his horse a rest. The trees were tightly clustered. He swung off his horse and led it into the grove.

He stopped short when he saw numerous horse tracks along with boot prints in the protected areas within the trees. There were empty tin cans, bottles, and other refuse on the ground. This was a meeting or resting place for a number of riders.

Dan stepped out of the trees and waved, catching the others attention. They turned their horses in his direction. Zac swung wide, making his way to the trees. He stopped once and swung down to take a closer look at something. Vic and Dan waited until their cousin reached them before moving into the trees.

The three of them slowly worked their way through the pines. Meeting back near their horses, Dan asked, "What do you think?"

Zac pointed to two trees that had bark damage. "Someone tied a rope across the two trees to tie up several horses. I can't be positive, but there may have been five animals at a time. They had a spot used for a fire. Two logs had been pulled near it for resting."

"Based on the rubbish," Vic added, "they had to kill time here. They liked to shoot at a tree on the north side. There was lots of busted glass under the snow at the base of the tree. They didn't fear being seen or heard."

"Much of the sign is before the snow in the past few weeks. There are some more recent than that. Men led three horses in before the last snow," the rancher said. "I didn't find anything that looked like J.P. stopped here."

"I am worried," Zac said. "When I was coming to the trees, I saw where three men had ridden away from here. Which way would you say the ranch is?"

Dan glanced around and pointed to the northwest. The direction he indicated intersected with the tracks Zac had found. The three cousins realized that three riders had headed in the direction of Dan's green valley. The only purpose would be to rustle the rest of the herd. The men would be near the valley by now, and there was nothing that the three of them could do to warn Amos or the hands.

"I told Amos not to confront the rustlers if they showed up at the ranch," Dan reminded the others. "They were to follow the herd at a safe distance and wait to meet up with us, so we could go after the rustlers as a group."

The cousins mounted their horses and continued riding the zigzag pattern across the basin. Vic was the first to see the smoke from the cabin. He rode at a trot to let the others know. They had figured that if there was smoke, it could only be a lookout who would ride to warn the rustlers. Dan had a fleeting thought that it could be J.P. resting up, or thinking that he had gotten away. That would be unlikely.

The cabin sat on the west side of Deer Creek. The foothills of the Laramie Mountains loomed on the other side of the creek. Aspen and oak lined the creek, along with tag alders, choke cherry bushes and other small brambles. The sun would be setting in two hours. Zac figured that cabin was just over five miles away. They would be in plain view approaching the building through the valley. That would give ample warning to the occupant to get away and ride to warn the rest of the gang.

"We should wait until after sundown before we move from here," Dan said. "We just have to hope they didn't already spot us."

"It doesn't make sense," Vic replied. "It would be easy to come up on the cabin after dark. If I was to set this up, I would have a couple men between where we are and the cabin. They would hear us come in the dark. They could then attack us as we passed, or ride through the trees and to warn the others. I wouldn't be surprised if they kept a fire going in the cabin and then ride this way to watch."

"J.P. wouldn't know you were riding with me and Vic," Zac said. "They would be expecting you to be riding alone. The ambush would be the way to finish you off."

"If they were willing to shoot me riding alone, I am sure they would try and take out as many of us as possible when we rode by," Dan reasoned. "That is, if Vic is right."

Zac handed the reins of the mustang to Dan. "I will go and find out if anyone is waiting. Give me a 15-minute start and then move toward the cabin, riding in the open. Anyone watching will have their attention fixed on the two of you."

The buckskin-cladded cousin moved quietly into the trees lining Deer Creek. He had spent his life stalking game as well as men. The calf-high moccasins allowed him to move quietly. He carried a Winchester rifle, a Schofield .45 caliber, and the "good knife" at the nape of his neck.

Dan and Vic took the bedrolls and saddle bags off their horses and tied them over the saddle of Zac's mustang. It would give the appearance of a pack horse, not a rider less horse. They waited, straining their ears for any sound coming from ahead. All they heard were chickadees and jays.

Anyone watching would be on the edge of the trees, giving them a clear view of the basin. Zac moved through the shadows of the trees. His Ho-Chunk heritage gave him the patience and skill needed to come upon this prey unexpectedly.

Zac came within rifle range of the cabin without finding anyone watching in the woods. He could see his cousins slowly coming on the horses. West of the cabin were some snow-covered boulders. Zac caught movement in that direction. It was a rifle barrel!

He swung his Winchester to fire at the shooter behind the boulders when there was the crack of a Sharps .50 caliber. A half-mile away, the mustang stumbled and went down kicking and screaming. Dan and Vic spurred their horses for the trees.

Without hesitation, Zac fired several times into the window of the cabin, trying to shut down the "Big Fifty" and give his cousins time to make for cover. Looking back at the boulders he saw that the rifleman had exposed himself to try a lucky shot at the fleeing riders. Zac fired, spinning the shooter, who disappeared behind the boulders.

Zac shifted his attention to the cabin. Whoever had fired the Sharps had not tried another shot. In an attempt to bring the shooters into the open, he called out, "We are deputies of Casper. Give up and come out or . . ."

He was cut short by a shot that sprayed wood chips next to his head. Stunned for a moment, Zac fell to the ground, blood running from the cuts on his face. Lying still in the snow near the oak, he heard a man swearing and coming toward him.

"I got one of the son-of-a-bitches!" he called out to those in the cabin.

Zac saw a monster of a man, coming toward him, a smoking revolver in his hand. Zac's rifle was buried in the snow under his body. Muscles tense, ready to move, he let the man get just a bit closer. Zac reached for the "good knife" and threw it. Streaking toward the brute, it hit him in the throat. The gun went off harmlessly into the air and the hulk slid to his knees. Grasping the handle, he jerked the knife free.

The wild killer roared, spewing blood and bubbles from the hole in his throat and from his mouth. Zac roll to put the oak between him and the man. A shot from the revolver kicked snow up where he had been seconds ago. Zac scrambled to draw his Colt. From behind him there was a shot and a dark hole appeared in the forehead of the behemoth, who then fell headlong into the snow.

"He was one determined bastard," Dan said as he came up to his cousin. Seeing the blood on Zac's face he said, "You might want to stay back. Looks like you need some work on those cuts."

"I'm okay to fight, I let my guard down," Zac admitted. "My attention on the cabin made me forget they could come from anywhere. When he shot at me, I went down and couldn't keep my guns in play. Without my knife and you, he would have gotten me."

Vic moved through the trees and spotted his cousins. He called in hushed tones, "I will go wide of the cabin and get behind them."

"There is one near the boulders and another in the cabin," Zac told them.

It would soon be dark. They would be unable to see movement around the cabin. Vic and Dan headed around the building while Zac moved up close behind the cabin. All of a sudden, there was the sound of a horse smashing through the brush.

Breaking into the open, the rider was low over the back of the animal, slapping it with the reins to get more speed. Vic and Dan both lifted their rifles and fired. The man jerked, grabbing the neck of the horse to hold on. As the animal ran, he slowly slid to the side, lost his grip on the horse and fell. His left foot remained caught in the stirrup and he dragged beside the plunging horse for a short distance before coming free.

They watched the downed man, half-buried in the snow. The horse ran a short distance beyond and then trotted back toward the barn. Shifting their attention to the cabin, they moved in to join Zac. The darkness of the interior made it impossible to see through the open doorway.

Zac went into the cabin low, his rifle level and ready. Vic followed, ducking to the left. Dan stayed outside, watching the area around the cabin for any other rustlers and making sure the man who was shot off the horse stayed down. Vic called out, "Nobody in here. Whoever it was even left the Sharps."

Dan saw a wash that ran from the cabin to the boulders. There were footprints in the snow. That was how the rustlers could move back and forth without being seen. Cautiously walking up the wash, he stopped when there was movement behind the boulders.

"If you want to get out of this ditch alive, move into the open," Dan threatened.

"Don't shoot. I'm hit, I need help."

A bearded man, with blood covering his chest and his right arm dripping blood on the snow, walked on unsteady legs toward the rancher. Checking to make sure that the man was unarmed, Dan walked behind him as they returned to the cabin. The man collapsed against the hand-hewed log wall, unable to continue standing.

"Don't leave me here to die," the man begged.

Vic and Zac came out of the cabin. "You got a live one," Vic observed.

"It must have been the one I shot at behind the boulders," Zac told them.

Dan knelt down near the man. "If you want us to help you, you best tell us where the cattle are being kept," he demanded.

The man sat looking at the rancher. Worrying that the man might die on him, Dan spoke in a gentler tone. "Tell us, and we will bandage your wounds. If you don't, you will bleed to death."

"South . . . a day's ride," the man said, struggling to speak. "You will see a small butte. The ranch is east, two or three miles."

Dan and Vic carried the man into the cabin and sat him on the edge of a bunk. Zac lit a lamp and put on water to heat. The cabin had two double bunks against one wall, a potbelly stove, a homemade table with four chairs, and a plank sideboard for storing supplies and fixing meals. The floor was packed dirt. The rustlers' evening meal was on the stove.

Vic and Zac went to get their horses and the gear off the downed mustang. Arriving at the downed horse, they saw that it had been hit high, behind the front legs. The snow around the animal was splattered with blood as it had struggled to stay on its feet.

While his cousins were gone, Dan worked on the wounded man, removing his coat and shirt. Zac's bullet had gone through the right bicep and cut across the man's chest. The man's head fell slack as he passed out. Dan laid him back on the bed and cleaned and bandaged the bullet wounds.

After getting the gear, Vic rode to get the rustler who'd tried to run, while Zac looped a rope around the big brute's feet, dragging him toward a three-sided building in the trees. He found the rest of the rustlers' horses tied in the crude barn.

Vic came in leading the dun, with the body of the fleeing man draped over the saddle. The two bodies were laid face down, next to each other. Holding a lantern above the corpses, Zac commented, "The one you and Dan shot at has two holes. That was damn good shooting by both of you."

Turning to take care of their horses, Vic glanced at the large fellow who had attacked Zac. "If he had ever gotten his hands on you, he would have torn you apart."

They stripped the gear off the horses and tied them next to those already in the barn. By the time the cousins headed back to the cabin, it was dark. The smell of fried side meat met them as they entered. Dan glanced over and called to them, "I figured I'd add some crisp bacon to the meal they started."

A short time later they were sitting around a small table, devouring the meal. The man on the bunk began to cough. He groaned and said, "Man, that hurts when I cough. You got any coffee there? I am damn thirsty."

Dan poured a cup of coffee and brought it to the wounded man. "We didn't get your name, and who were the men here with you?"

With shaky hands, the man took the coffee and sipped it. "Ah . . . you make good coffee." Shifting his weight a bit to get more comfortable, he looked up. "Luke Peters, most folks call me Pete. The beans you're eating were made by the big fellow, Bull. He was a freighter down in Texas before coming up with Burdick. The fellow I heard riding away was Cal Turner. He was never one to depend on in a fight. He killed your horse with the Sharps, then run for it."

"He won't run no more," Dan replied.

"You got him, hey." Nodding, the man

seemed pleased.

Finishing the coffee, he handed the cup back to Dan. "You got any of the beans left? Bull sure did make good beans."

Filling a tin plate, the rancher stuck a spoon in them and brought them over. "What brings you to be with Burdick?"

As Dan held the plate for him, the man shoveled a couple spoonfuls into his mouth before speaking. "I was working for J.P.'s old man until they hung him. I just sort of stayed with the younger and followed him up here. I won't say that the men I have worked for were honest men, but they paid regular."

"Sounds like the kind of job that you don't have to worry about old age," Dan commented. "You'll be shot or hung like his pa."

The rancher waited until the man had scraped the last of the beans from the plate before asking the next question. "How many men does J.P. have on the ranch?"

Pete looked at Dan for a moment, as though trying to decide what he was going to say next. "First off, there are three men after the rest of your cattle. One of them is Tex Porter. I never much liked him. On the ranch there are five hands and Mr. Burdick."

"Any of them gun hands?" Dan asked.

"All of them can shoot, but none were hired for their gun. They are mostly cowboys looking for a place to spend the winter," the wounded man said. "Seven of us come up from Texas with the Bar H cattle. It included the men headed to your ranch and Hurley, Bull, Cal and me."

The rancher set the plate on the sideboard and filled two cups of coffee. He handed one to Pete and then returned to the table. "Three of us against the five men and Burdick, maybe more at the ranch."

"More than likely the cowhands won't be willing to shoot it out with us," Zac figured.

"If they ride for the brand, they will protect it," Vic reminded them.

"We were deputized by Winslow to bring J.P. in and stop their killing and rustling in Wyoming," Dan said. "My first concern was to get the cattle back. Now our plan should be to get Burdick and bring him back to Casper for a proper hanging."

The wounded man cleared his throat. "When the boss stopped by here, he told us we were moving the cattle to Colorado. He wasn't waiting until spring. We was to leave as soon as Tex got back with the rest of the cows."

The rancher looked at his cousins. "Looks like our job is to ruin his plans to run."

CHAPTER FOURTEEN

The cousins decided to leave the dead men in the barn until they returned with J.P. and the cattle. Tossing a ground cloth over the bodies, Vic and Zac saddled the horses and led them to the front of the cabin. Dan was inside, talking to Luke Peters.

"We're leaving you here, Pete," the rancher said. "We're taking the horses. You got wood and your cabin has enough supplies."

The wounded man shook his head vigorously, "No! No, you can't leave me here with the bodies. I don't like them. What if it don't work out for you going after Brudick? I would never make it out. I want to go with you."

"We can't take you now. First off, while you did give us some information, you also tried to shoot me and Vic," the rancher reminded him. "I guess you better hope we take Burdick and come back this way."

"I am weak from the blood I lost and won't be able to keep a fire going and cook for myself. I got

234

only one good arm, and I think the bullet that clipped my chest broke a rib," the rustler pleaded. "I beg you to take me with you. I told you what you wanted to know. You can trust me."

Dan came out of the cabin. Zac asked him, "So, Mr. Peters is waiting here for us to come back?"

"Nope," Dan said flatly. "He getting a coat on and will be coming with us. It was the only damn way to stop him from whining. We need to saddle a horse for him."

Chuckling, Vic headed for the barn. "I will get his horse."

Pete came out with a big smile on his face. His coat was unbuttoned and a long leather belt hung over his shoulder. "I'll need help closing the coat and getting on the horse. My saddle bags are in the cabin."

Zac went to him and pulled the coat open wider, checking for a hand gun in his waist band. Pulling the coat closed revealed that it was several sizes too big. "Did you lose a bunch of weight since you got this coat?"

"Nah," Pete said. "It was Bull's. Mine is covered with blood. He won't mind if I borrow it."

Vic came with the saddled horse. He and Dan helped the injured man mount the animal. Pete lifted the wounded arm and slipped it into the looped belt. "Hanging down hurts the arm," Pete explained. "I will use the belt as a sling."

Zac came out with the man's saddle bags and blanket roll. He tied it to the back of Pete's saddle and then climbed onto the bay they had gotten from the rustlers.

"You try anything, we will shoot you and leave you lying where you fall," Dan warned the rustler.

"I understand," he promised. "I won't do nothing that will put you boys in danger. After all, you fixed me up when I was shot."

Vic said. "Let's go get Burdick."

The cousins and the rustler left the cabin. The tracks of J.P. Burdick were plain to see. They kept Pete in the middle of the group, to keep an eye on him. Dan took the lead, glancing at the spot where Cal had fallen the day before. He had landed on his back, leaving two red streaks of blood on the snow.

The sun was bright, creating a blinding glare off the snow. Knowing that they were unable to spot danger ahead caused concern. Zac rode up beside Pete and hissed, "If you let us ride into an ambush, my first bullet will be into you."

The men rode with their hats pulled low over their eyes. Following the trail in the snow, which extended as far as they could see, made staying alert difficult. Vic stayed to the back, leading the extra horse, while Zac moved wide of the group, trying for a vantage to spot danger.

The snow was knee-deep on the animals in the valleys, while many areas on the hills were blown clean. Dan was pleased to see the exposed grass. The cattle would have grazing on the trip back to the ranch.

The cousins held up when they rode over a rise and saw another set of tracks cutting across J.P.'s trail. Zac rode ahead and was halfway down the slope when he waved the others on. He recognized them as an elk.

They rested the horse near a line of

cottonwoods along a small stream. Zac built a small fire and made a pot of coffee. They dunked hard bread into the hot brew. Luke Peters complained of an aching in the wound on his arm. His face was pale under the salt and pepper beard.

Leaning against a gnarled tree, he informed the cousins, "The ranch has a wagon we can use for the trip back to Casper. It will beat the hell out of clinging to the back of a hay burner."

Vic glanced up at the high clouds. "If a storm comes in we might need a sled to get back."

The men helped Pete back onto the sorrel and continued after J.P. and the cattle. The small butte came into view about four miles away when the men were going over a rise. Just below the crest, the party stopped. They looked for any visible access to the top of the butte. If there was one, it would have to be on the far side. The top would be a good place for a lookout.

"What are we waiting for?" Pete asked.

"I don't like the looks of the butte," Dan informed him. "It would be a good place to have someone watching for us."

"There ain't no way to the top," the wounded man replied. "We didn't need a lookout out on the butte anyway. When you cut toward the ranch they will spot you a mile away."

Vic moved his horse next to Pete. "Is there a way to approach the ranch without being seen?"

"Not without crossing the river twice," he replied.

Unsure of the wounded man, Zac said, "He

may be setting us up for a turkey shoot. How do we know we can trust him?"

Before anyone else could give their opinion, Pete reminded them, "I been straight with you. I warned you that if you ride in from the butte, they will be waiting for you with rifles ready."

The cousins realized that they were getting advice from a man who had tried to kill them at the cabin. The toughest part was that what he was saying sounded like he was being straight. So far, everything he had told them had been the truth.

"You were saying we have to cross the river," Vic prompted the man.

"Just over the next rise, you will come to the north fork of the river. Stay on this side and ride east until you reach the Little Medicine Bow River. Cross it and ride south. When you catch sight of the butte again, cross back and you will come up on the back side of the headquarters. You will be at the ranch house before you're spotted."

"You lead the way then," Dan told him.

"I can't," Pete stated. "It is a rough ride, plus two river crossings. With a bum arm I just couldn't do it. It will take a good man and a good horse to make it. But I promise you on my mother's grave it is the only way to get to the ranch without being seen."

"Where will you be while we're crossing the river?" Dan challenged.

"I will take the extra horse and ride to the butte and wait for you."

"I think we should tie you up right here. If you're lying and it's a trap, you will freeze to death before you're found," Zac suggested.

"I can't even get on the horse by myself. I couldn't make it anywhere alone. I need your help to get back and to a doctor," the wounded man pleaded.

Daylight was getting short and Pete was baggage that they didn't need. Dan knew a quick decision had to be made. "Vic help him off the horse, he can wait here until we come for him." Then to the wounded man he warned, "If anything you have told us is a lie, you best hope all three of us die, because if one survives you will never see another day."

Pulling Pete off of the horse, Vic ordered "You stay here until we come for you."

Dan was the last to leave the wounded man. The cousins rode to the north fork and then followed it to the Little Medicine Bow River. They crossed the river and went south. The foothills of the Laramie Mountains ran along the river, making the ride more difficult. There were steep ridges to navigate over, and narrow ledges that dropped straight to the river, that tested the cousins' nerves. Most of the way there was good cover offered by the aspens on the hills.

An hour after winding through the foothills above the river, the butte came into sight. The cousins stopped long enough to check their weapons. When they were ready, they rode down the slope to the river, the horses sliding on their haunches part of the way down.

At the bottom, the horses plunged into the river, splashing chilling water onto the riders. Belly-deep in the river, the horses crossed to the other side. After they climbed up the far side bank, the cousins dismounted and gave the animals a brief rest.

The land between the river and the ranch was covered by a mixture of aspen and evergreens. So far the shady Pete had been straight with them. The approach from the other side of the river had given them the cover that they needed.

"We don't know what to expect when we get to the ranch," Dan reminded the cousins. "J.P. has to know someone will come after him and have his ranch hands on alert. We have to expect to be riding into an armed camp."

"Pete said that those at the ranch will be local ranch hands," Vic added. "They will fight for the brand, but most won't go against the law."

"Vic is right," Zac agreed. "We best wear our badges on the outside of our coats."

Pinning the badges in plain sight and with another check to make sure that the water hadn't splashed on the actions of their guns, the cousins mounted their horses and rode toward the unknown. The three carried their rifles at the ready, and their coats were unbuttoned to give them access to their holsters.

As the trees thinned, they began to see cattle grazing. The ranch building stood just beyond the trees. Dan pointed at two animals with the Circle A brand. They counted five different brands, including the Bar H as they closed in on the ranch.

Zac pulled to a stop and motioned with his rifle to their left. It was a rider with a deer across the back of his saddle. The cousins sat on their horses among the thinning tree cover, watching the man. All of a sudden, he turned his horse toward them.

Stopping a short distance away, he called to

them, "Can I help you with something?"

The cousins rode toward him, closing the distance. "We are deputies from Casper. We're looking for a man and some stolen cattle."

"The names Joseph. We got a mixed herd here, but the boss has paper on all of them," the rider assured them.

The man carrying the deer appeared relaxed, but they noticed the rifle across his saddle could quickly be brought into action.

The meeting had become a standoff. Being outnumbered, Joseph couldn't get all three of them before return fire would kill him. Either way, the cousins would lose because the rest of the ranch would be alerted by the gunfire.

It was time to tell the man what they knew and find out where his allegiances lay. "You say the boss has paper on the cattle. We passed several with the Circle A brand. They were stolen from my ranch earlier this month. One of my hands was shot in the back, and then had a second bullet put in his head. The other had our bunkhouse burned down around him and barely escaped with his life."

Dan saw no change of expression on the man's face. "Three days ago, your boss, J.P. Burdick, shot Sheriff Winslow and then lit the building on fire, attempting to hide the crime."

Joseph's face paled. "Winslow is dead?"

"He's not dead. The man from the saloon saw the fire and found the wounded sheriff. He pulled him out and got him to the doctors. We were deputized to bring Burdick back for trial."

The man shifted the rifle away from the cousins. "Saul Winslow served with me in the army. He's a good man. Why the hell would J.P. want to shoot him?"

"The sheriff learned the names of a couple of men that rustled my cattle. He also found out about a man named Jackson Prince that had a set up in Texas, similar to what was happening around Casper. Sheriff Winslow began to wonder if there was any tie between Burdick and Texas, figuring J.P. was short for Jackson Prince. He was shot when he went to question J.P."

"What were the names of the rustlers?" the hunter asked.

"Cal Duncan and Tex Porter."

"Son-of-a-bitch!" Joseph exclaimed. "I figured those men were trouble. Them and a man named Bull that ran with them."

"Did Luke Peters run with them?"

"He was part of the bunch, but was a regular guy. Most everyone got along with him."

"We have to go and deal with J.P.," Dan told the man. "Are we going to have any trouble with you or any of the other hands?"

"No, I'll let the other hands know to stay clear. I should mention, though, that a few days ago Porter took two of the Texas boys and rode out. Word was they were after another herd that the boss had purchased."

"We figure they are after the rest of my cattle. We plan to cut them off and take the herd back along with the ones you got here," the rancher told the man.

The cousins left Joseph and rode toward the

ranch house. It was turning dusk and there were lights in the back of the building. It was away from the other structures, built on a knoll overlooking the ranch. Several large oaks helped to cut the wind and offer shade in the summer.

The cousins left their horses tied to the corral behind the barn. Using the sparse cover of the trees, they moved toward the ranch house. If J.P. was watching from the darkened front window, he would easily spot the cousins. They were banking on Burdick being in the lighted back room.

It was unlikely that he thought this remote ranch could be found, or that his men at the cabin could be overcome. As far as J.P. knew, his office had burned down, covering the shooting of the sheriff. The cousins froze as they saw someone stop in front of the window. As quickly as the person appeared, they moved away again.

Dan turned to his cousins. "I am going to go in, and want the two of you to watch out here in case anyone from the bunkhouse decides to help J.P."

"There is no way in hell I'm letting you go in alone," Vic replied.

"It's my fight, I can't ask you to risk your life in that house."

"And we haven't already risked our lives for you on this trip?" Zac reminded Dan.

Vic moved in front of Dan. "I am going in with you. Zac would be best watching out here."

The decision made, Dan and Vic stepped onto the porch. Their first instinct was to smash the door down and enter the house, guns blazing, shooting anything that moved. Both men knew that such a move could end up killing the wrong person. Also, they would be shooting in the dark, hoping to see a target. Burdick could sit, waiting for them to enter the lighted area of the house, then pick them off.

Dan tested the door. It was unlocked. Turning the knob, he carefully pushed it open. Stepping inside, he looked around the darkened kitchen. A large table and some chairs sat in the middle of the room. A stove to their left warmed the place. Light from the flames flickered from the ash pan.

Across the floor, light showed from under the door of the back room. They heard the sound of a glass being placed on a table or desk, then a cork being pulled from a bottle. It was the room their quarry was in. Dan crept across the room, his Colt drawn. Behind him, Vic carried a rifle. They tested every board as they stepped, fearing that one would creak and alert Burdick.

The door opened into the kitchen. The two cousins took a deep breath and nodded to each other. Dan grasped the knob and jerked the door open. They burst into the room, guns leveled.

Sitting behind a small desk was the shocked J.P. Burdick. "We are deputies from Casper and you are under arrest," Dan informed the man.

J.P.'s face suddenly broke into a smile. "Why, if it isn't Dan August! I figured you'd be at your ranch."

"You figured wrong, Burdick," the rancher snapped. "Keep your hands in sight."

The sound of a gun being cocked behind them caused Vic and Dan to halt. "You do anything but shuck those guns and this shotgun will blow you to pieces."

Realization that there was another person in the room sent a jolt through the cousins. Carefully, they placed their guns on the floor. "The one in your holster too," J.P. said, pointing to Vic.

Dan looked at the man who had the drop on them. He was a lean, chisel-faced, with a scar that went from his forehead, across his eye, and down his cheek. The man had come from a side room to the right of the cousins.

He had them covered with a W. H. Greenfield double-barrel shotgun. "I'll be damned. You must be important to have the law come clear out here," the snarling gunman said.

"Easy now," J.P. cautioned. "That buckshot will mess up the wall paper. We don't want that. I think introductions are in order. This is my younger brother, Bobby, with the shotgun. He arrived here from Texas just today."

"Damn good thing I did," Bobby pointed out.

Dan realized now that the sound he had heard when coming through the kitchen had been the brother pouring himself a drink in the side room.

"I don't believe I know the man with you, Dan," Burdick said, enjoying the rancher's dilemma.

"This is my cousin, Vic," Dan said, his mind racing to find a way out of this. "There are people back in Casper who know where we are. If you kill us there won't be any place in Wyoming or Colorado that you will be able to hide."

"Oh, you heard about the move to Colorado,"

J.P. chuckled. "That's where we'll sell the cattle. After that, Bobby and I will just disappear to live the good life. Of course, you will be dead."

Stalling for time and hoping that Zac would come in, Dan told him, "Your boys in the bunkhouse won't back you. We already talked to them. They know all about what you've been doing."

"I can keep those sheep in line," Bobby bragged.

"You know, Dan August," J.P. said, sighing, "you are beginning to bore me. Let's take them outside and finish this."

Dan and Vic stood trapped by the man they'd come to arrest. J.P. had a wild, almost insane look of pleasure on his face. He turned to take the revolver from the custom holster hanging on a coat rack behind the desk. As Burdick's hand touched the gun, a shot went off next to Dan. Instinctively he dove for the Colt lying on the floor. The sound of the shotgun rocked the room.

Grabbing the Colt, Dan continued to roll to his stomach and fired at J.P., who was aiming his revolver at the rancher. Burdick's bullet burned across Dan's side. J.P. fell back into his chair, his revolver falling to the floor.

At that same moment, Zac was talking with Joseph, who had come from the bunkhouse to warn them that J.P.'s brother had come to the ranch.

"His brother . . ." The crash of gunfire cut off the sentence. Zac drew his revolver and raced into the house crossing the kitchen and diving low as he entered the room. The haze of gunpowder hung in the air. Lying with his gun ready, Zac desperately looked around the room, trying to determine what had happened.

Dan and Vic were on the floor to his left, another man was on the floor on his right. There was a groan as Dan sat up, holding his side. Vic raised his head and muttered, "That was too damn close."

"You guys are alive!" Zac exclaimed with relief.

"It appears so," Vic said. "Something hit my legs and knocked me off my feet."

Zac, with his revolver ready, stood up and saw J.P. The man sat in his chair with his arms outspread, blood spreading across his white shirt, struggling to breathe. The other man, whom he guessed was the brother, lay outstretched on the floor. He had a neat hole between his eyes. A double-barrel shotgun lay on the floor. J.P. was trying to say something when he gasped and died, his vacant eyes open.

Returning his gun to his holster, Zac went to check on Dan. There was blood oozing from between his fingers. "How bad are you hit?"

"It's just a scratch, Zac. Check on Vic, I think he caught some buckshot."

There was the sound of someone in the kitchen. Zac drew his gun and stepped to the side, waiting for the man. "Can I come in and help? It's me, Joseph."

"You can put some water on and find me some bandages. Also, make sure no one else comes in." Zac instructed the man.

Kneeling next to Vic to check on his wounds, Zac asked, "What the hell happened in here?"

"Hell if I know," Dan admitted.

Cringing as Zac pulled on his boot, Vic explained. "The fellow with the shotgun had the drop on us and they were about to take us out and kill us. When J.P. reached for his gun, Bobby here looked in that direction, so I pulled the sneak gun and shot him. When he dropped the damn shotgun it went off and I caught some. I heard some more shots as I hit the floor, but then it was over."

Removal of Vic's boots revealed that the right leg had been grazed, and his left calf and boot had been hit. Zac withdrew the "good knife" from the nape of his neck and slit both legs of Vic's long johns just above the calves. He then found some alcohol in the side room. Picking up the bottle of rye, he brought it to his cousin. "Take a couple drinks, and then give it back so I can pour it over the knife."

"What the hell are you going to do?" Vic demanded.

"The buckshot cut through the calf and is just under the skin. I am going to take it out," Zac replied.

"You ruined a new pair of long johns," Vic complained. "You could have just pulled them up."

As Zac slit the skin with the razor-sharp knife, his cousin yelped in pain. "Damn, that hurt! Just take out the shot, not the whole leg."

Joseph came in with hot water, towels and strips of cloth for bandages. "Here, clean up these wounds and put on some bandages. You might want to give the patient some more of the rye or he might bite," Zac kidded.

While the ranch hand went to work on Vic, Zac went to assist Dan. Opening his shirt and long johns, he checked his side. It wasn't deep, but might have bruised or broken one of his ribs. He cleaned and bandaged the wound.

Joseph had finished with Vic. He smiled and said, "Grab the bottle. I put on some coffee in the kitchen. I figured you folks could use it."

Before leaving the room, Dan walked over to each of the men they'd killed. He picked up the handgun and shotgun. Closing the office door, he joined the others in the kitchen. Exhaustion swept over the cousins. The pace of the last week had left little time for sleep. They drank the coffee laced with rye.

Joseph gulped his coffee and went to put his cup in the dishpan. He headed for the door and then hesitated. "I just remembered, you have horses near the barn. I'll have them taken care of for you."

"Leave the sorrel," Zac requested. "I'll go and get Luke Peters."

"You brung Pete with you?" Joseph asked.

"He was wounded at the cabin and he talked us into taking him with us," Vic explained.

Joseph returned to the table and sat down. "You were at the cabin? You didn't mention that earlier. If you brought Pete, what happened to Cal and Bull?"

With a half-smile on his face, Zac answered, "They are waiting for us at the cabin."

"Damn! Who are you guys?" the baffled ranch hand asked.

"You mentioned taking care of the horses," Vic reminded the man.

"Come on, Joseph. I'll walk with you." Zac

said putting on his coat.

"He won't be there," Dan informed him.

"He won't be there?" Zac asked. "How do you know?"

"I told him to go, and keep going, before we left," the rancher replied.

Zac chuckled, "I'll go make sure he got back on his horse. I need the air."

The frigid night made the snow crunch under their feet as they used the moonlight to guide them along the path. "Tell Dan that I will have the men start cutting the Circle A animals out of the herd first thing tomorrow." Joseph told Zac.

Vic and Dan sat at the table. They had abandoned the coffee and were drinking the rye straight

"Thank God you're good with that derringer," Dan said.

"Thank God he looked away for a second," Vic said.

Zac returned to the ranch house an hour later. "No sign of Mr. Peters. He was leading the extra horse and never even slowed down at the butte. His wounds must have improved."

"I kind of liked that fellow," Vic admitted.

The cousins went to the bunkhouse and found beds for the night. The thoughts of sleeping in the house after the gunfight didn't appeal to the men.

CHAPTER FIFTEEN

It took four days to round up the cattle. One day was lost due to a storm. The wagon used for bringing in supplies would be used to carry the bodies back to Casper. Dan found $3,000 in J.P.'s office safe along with several forged bills of sale.

He asked Joseph to be in charge of his ranch until someone from Casper could come to bring the rest of the stolen cattle in. That would happen in early spring. Dan used money from the safe to pay the cowhands their winter wages in advance. He hoped that they would still be at the ranch in the spring to help drive the cattle. It would be hard to determine if the Bar H cattle were rustled or not, but that would be up to the courts to decide.

Joseph had the team hitched when Dan and his cousins finished collecting evidence from the ranch house. "I want to thank you for everything you did," the rancher told him. "I took the rest of the money and will turn it over to Sheriff Winslow. You have plenty of supplies to last you. If need be, butcher a Bar H animal."

Smiling, Joseph pointed at the Circle A cattle and horses. "I added a couple of J.P.'s horses to take the place of the ones they shot."

Vic chose to drive the wagon to favor his leg. Dan and Zac would push the cattle. The wagon would lead the herd. With everything ready, the cousins sat on their horses, saying their goodbyes.

"Joseph, you may want to use the ranch house," Dan suggested.

"No," the man replied, "I will stay with the others in the bunkhouse. I want you to be careful. Tex Porter is still out there, and the men with him will do anything he asks."

"If he took the cattle," Dan said, "we will stop him. If he hurt anyone in the valley, he may not live to see Casper."

"Knowing you, I'm sure he will arrive to be hung," Joseph replied. "May the saints watch over you and guide you back home."

Vic pulled out with the wagon. After passing the herd, Dan and Zac began pushing them. After a little stubbornness from some of the cows that didn't want to leave, they finally got them moving. The first stop would be at the cabin to collect Cal and Bull. Dan could imagine what would be said at the inquest when none of the prisoners were brought in alive. Maybe they could take Tex and the others alive.

It was the second day before they reached the cabin. The bodies were where they'd left them. The cousins spent the night in the cabin, appreciating sleeping out of the weather. Being shorthanded, they let the cattle out on their own to wander and graze.

Vic had gotten some maple syrup from J.P.'s ranch house and made up stacks of pancakes for everyone. They sat around the table eating the cakes and drinking coffee.

"I worry about those that went to the ranch. Amos may not be expecting Tex and his men," Zac feared.

"Amos can handle himself in a fight," Dan assured his cousins. "Unless they surprise the men, he will give them more than they can handle."

While his words were filled with confidence, he didn't feel nearly as sure that his men couldn't be caught off guard. Tex would try and kill from hiding, or sweep in if he felt he had the upper hand.

The cousins awoke early and ate cold leftover pancakes with coffee. It was still dark when they readied the team and saddled their horses. The shaggy silhouettes of the cattle could be seen against the snow. Their heavy coats protected them against the winter chill.

Vic headed out while Zac and Dan rode around the herd, slowly getting them moving. By the time the sun broke over the horizon, they were miles from the cabin. The cattle seemed to know that they were headed back to the valley. It was taking little encouragement to keep them moving.

Dan figured that it would take less than a week to reach his ranch. Zac would range around the herd while the rancher rode drag. The advantage of the snow-covered ground was that there was no dust. The first drive the cousins had participated in had been bringing a herd up from Santa Fe to Wyoming. Riding drag had left them covered with dust from head to foot.

Each night they would rig a tarp from the side of the wagon and build a fire near the opening, trying to capture some of the heat inside. Meals were simple. Whenever possible, they would stop near a flowing stream lined with trees. Extra firewood was carried in the wagon with the dead rustlers, in case they had to camp away from a source of wood.

The monotony of pushing the cattle across the endless white expanse of rolling hills was finally rewarded when they reached the line shack. It was early afternoon, but they planned to stop for the day. This would bring them to the valley at mid-day tomorrow.

Not having seen the rest of Dan's cattle being rustled gave them hope that Amos and the hands were safe. The plain was large, and there was always the possibility that the herds had passed out of sight of each other. Dan paused when passing the red ridge, remembering being ambushed by Hurley. If Tex was around, it would be a style he would use.

They found evidence that someone, most likely the rustlers, had been at the line shack on their way to the valley. Tins of dry goods were stored for use when working the area. Several had been left open, and a tin of rice was dumped across the floor.

Sitting in the line shack that evening, the cousins dined on beans and corn bread. They discussed arriving in the valley.

"I should ride in ahead of the herd and determine if there is any danger," Zac suggested. "I am sure I can get in without being seen."

"We should leave the wagon here and I can ride in with the herd," Vic recommended. "Being on horseback, I will be able to react more easily."

"How is your leg, Vic?" Zac asked.

Grinning, Vic said, "You did a fine job. For a while I was worried I would lose the limb, but then you quit cutting."

Dan listened to his cousins. He appreciated the humor. They were going into an unknown situation and it helped to relieve the tension.

He said, "We'll leave the wagon just short of the valley. Rather than scouting things ahead of time, we will drive the herd in on the run. Then we will hold back and wait to see who comes out. It if is Tex and his men, we will go in fast and try and take them out."

The rancher didn't have to say it, but they knew that if Tex was alive then Amos and the hands were most likely dead.

Before leaving the next morning, Dan and his cousins readied the line shack for the next visitor. It could be someone from the ranch, or a passing cowboy. Line shacks across the west were shared by travelers, and most often left ready for the next arrival.

There had been a couple inches of snow during the night. Zac saddled three horses while Vic and Dan readied the wagon. The frozen corpses under the tarp left Dan with an uncomfortable feeling. They had been given no option but to defend themselves, but taking a life would haunt his dreams for some time.

The herd moved slowly in front of them, trampling the newly fallen snow. Vic followed them with the wagon, his horse tied to the back. Dan and Zac rode on the flanks. The rancher strained his eyes looking for any tracks or movement. As the hours passed, the only other living things he saw was a fox hunting rodents and a hawk.

The walls of the valley opening came into view. The cattle, realizing that they were coming home, picked up the pace. Vic climbed off the wagon and limped to his horse tied to the back. Once in the saddle, he trotted to catch up to the herd.

As the cattle entered the valley, the cousins stayed back a safe distance. Zac glanced back and saw that the team pulling the wagon continued to follow them. He grinned, suddenly having the vision of a stranger coming across the driverless wagon, only to find four frozen bodies in the back.

"There in the valley," Dan whispered. "We can go on the right side and be in the trees before anyone in the building can see us."

All of a sudden there was the report of a rifle shot! Ducking low over the horses' necks, they spurred the animals into the trees. Coming up behind the ranch house, they dismounted. There was another shot.

"Who are they shooting at?" Vic asked.

Dan moved to the corner of the house, peering around, then stepped back. "I don't see anyone. Let's go around to the front. Zac, you go around the right side, Vic and I will go around the left."

In a crouching run, Dan headed alongside the house. "Slow down, damn it! My leg!" Vic hissed.

Dan reached the front corner and glanced at the ranch yard. He stepped back, his mouth open in disbelief. Vic, catching up, looked to see what had surprised Dan.

Next to the corral, he saw Ralph and Kelly saddling their horses to go after the cattle. Even more surprising was the partially completed bunkhouse to the left of the burnt remains. The rancher stepped out from the house just in time to see Amos come from behind the barn, carrying a rifle. Spotting Dan, the old prospector waved wildly at his friend.

Zac was standing on the porch of the ranch house. "I think all is well in the valley."

Dan looked over at his cousin. Again, he was surprised. The windows of the ranch house were repaired. He looked at the door. The bullet holes were plugged, and it was ready for painting once the weather warmed up.

Amos approached the house. "Damn glad to see you. I was beginning to worry that things didn't go too good."

"Good? We got a wagon load of dead rustlers with us," Vic boasted.

Not appreciating his cousin's humor, Dan frowned at him. "We were worried about Tex. We understood that he and a couple of men came after the rest of the herd."

Grinning, Amos nodded. "That they did. We were working on the foundation logs of the new bunkhouse. They came in, guns blazing. I picked up my rifle and shot Tex's horse. He fell ass over teakettle and was out of the fight. Kelly and Ralph got their guns into action and the other two men just gave up."

"Since then they have been spending nights

tied up in the root cellar and working with us on the bunkhouse during the day. That is, except Tex. He broke something during the fall. We tie him to a log and let him watch."

"We heard shooting when we came in," Dan said.

"A couple of wolves were chewing on the horse carcasses beyond the pond. I was doing a little hunting."

"Any luck?"

"Got them both," Amos replied. "I best get back and skin them out before they freeze." The old prospector started to leave, but then turned. "By the way, the prisoners are in the barn. Kelly trussed them up when the cows came in."

Vic volunteered to go find the wagon. Zac went to help Kelly and Ralph settle the herd they'd brought in. Dan walked down to the barn. Sitting in a horse stall were the three men. Tex was pale and sweating from the pain caused by a broken shoulder.

"I need a damn doctor," Tex complained. "Something is bad broke in my shoulder."

"You'll be out of pain soon enough," Dan promised the rustler.

"Yep, Tex," a slim, young rustler muttered. "Maybe when they stretch your neck it will fix the shoulder."

Tex's two companions appeared to be brothers. Both boys had a meanness about them. They were lean, and both had sandy-colored hair and ruddy complexions. Dan learned that the older one was Slim and his younger brother was Billy Bob. There was no doubt that the brothers' future was a rope when they got back to Casper.

A light snow was falling when the day's work was done. Everyone, including the prisoners, were in the kitchen devouring a meal put together by Amos. There was a large pot of hardy beef stew, sourdough biscuits, and a plate heaped with doughnuts.

The prisoners' feet remained tied together with pigging string during the meal. Amos carried his .45 in his waistband. It had been made clear to the rustlers that if one of them tried anything, the old prospector wouldn't stop firing until they were all dead. The wagon outside with the other gang members was clear evidence of their willingness to carry out the threat.

With more men to watch Tex and the brothers, they were allowed to spend the night in the house. Blankets were spread out in the corner of the kitchen and the men lay there, bound hand and foot. Tex struggled to find a position that didn't increase the pain in his shoulder.

Kelly and Ralph decided to sleep in the barn. They offered to have both wagons ready by first light to head for Casper. The cousins and Amos sat at the table, smoking and drinking coffee. Zac honed the edge of the "good knife" while Vic changed the bandages on his calf.

"After a winter in the valley, you are welcome to stay on in the spring," Dan offered to the old prospector.

"I don't want you to think I don't appreciate the offer, but when there's enough green grass for my mule, I will be off to find riches," Amos replied. "I believe Kelly and Ralph would like to stay on."

"I would appreciate if they would," the rancher acknowledged. "I will check on Curly when I get to Casper. He might be able to make the return trip with me."

"I noticed some sawed lumber next to the barn," Amos said. "We used logs for the walls, but need the boards for the roof and floor."

"Use what you need," Dan said. "I imagine the stove was pretty well ruined in the fire. I will bring one back from Casper. Will you need anything else?"

"Nope," Amos answered, then changed his mind. "Well, yes I do. I am running short on my chewing tobacco."

"I tried the stuff as a kid," Vic said, shaking his head. "I was sick as a dog. I don't see how you can chew the stuff."

Zac wiped the knife blade clean and put it back in its sheath at the nape of his neck. Amos excused himself and headed out to the little house.

"Don't be falling asleep in there with your pants down. We'll end up adding you to the wagon of frozen stiffs in the morning," Dan joshed his friend.

Vic sat with his chair leaned back against the wall. He glanced at the rustlers lying on the blankets across the room. All of a sudden, he rocked forward and stood up. "Yes!" he exclaimed. Motioning for his cousins to follow, he stepped out onto the porch.

"Yes, what?" Zac asked.

Smiling at his idea, Vic spoke in hushed tones. "I say we give a copy of grandpa Oli's map to Amos."

"What good would that do? We took all the gold from the cave," Dan replied, confused over what

Vic was getting at.

"All the gold except the three coins," Vic reminded him.

"And the Spaniards' other map," Zac added.

"That's what I am talking about," Vic continued, excitement on his face. "We found the gold and headed to Cheyenne, leaving the Spaniards map in the cave. It looked like it might have shown where they mined the gold. We left it there because we were anxious to get back to deposit the gold. I think we should show Amos where the cave and map is. If he finds the place where they mined it, there may be some left."

"I like your idea, Vic," Dan agreed. Amos had been a good friend and he was always looking for places to find gold. The sound of the snow crunching announced the return of the old prospector.

The rancher went into his bedroom and returned with the well-worn, leather bound ledger that was carried by their grandfather, which had a sketch of the map and several notes during his search for the canyon containing the cave with the gold.

"Amos, come spring, you plan to go back to prospecting, right?" Dan asked his friend.

"I figure on working the streams north of here toward Montana," Amos told them. "By next fall, I will be back in the Dakotas."

"We got a place you can start from," Dan said. He then opened the ledger and told him the story of Grandpa Oli's trip and discovery of the cave. He told him about the second map left in the cave that might lead him to the old Spanish mine.

When the cousins finished regaling him about their adventure in finding the cave, it was well after midnight. Amos' eyes sparkled with excitement at the prospect of finding an old Spanish mine. On separate paper, he drew the map and added several notes from the ledger. Folding it carefully, he placed the information in his pocket.

"I want to thank you boys," the old prospector said. "If I find the mine and it still has gold, I promise to send you your shares."

"A note of your success is all we ask," Vic replied.

Dan and Zac nodded their agreement.

They had stayed up later than they planned and the stories of gold would make falling asleep difficult. Dan noticed that Slim was awake. He wondered how much he had heard. They had tried to talk in hushed tones, but during the excitement their voices might have risen.

The four men each took turns watching the prisoners. When not watching the rustlers, they slept on the bed or floor in the other room. Zac was on the last watch. He sat against the wall near the door. Years of hunting and stalking game had taught him to remain motionless for long periods of time.

Billy Bob lay on his blankets in the dim kitchen. He had worked his hands loose. He reached over and poked Slim. He then pointed at the unmoving cousin. "Sleeping," he mouthed.

Taking great pains to make no noise, the brother began to worm his way across the kitchen, his eye on the rifle leaning near Zac. A mouse scurried away to his right and he glanced over. Billy Bob never saw the movement of the cousin as he drew and threw the "good knife". The knife flew just inches in front of the rustler's nose and pinned the rodent against the wall.

The sound of the knife hitting its target caused the brother to jerk back. He looked at Zac, then back at the knife. "If you are even thinking about going for the knife, I wouldn't," the cousin threatened. "I have been watching your attempt to get away for the past ten minutes. Your next move anywhere but back to the blanket will get you a bullet through the head."

The sound of the rifle being cocked sent the brother scrambling toward his blanket. Zac walked over and pulled the knife free, shaking the mouse off into the ash pan. After adding some wood to the stove, he went back to his station near the door.

Billy Bob lay there, expecting to be tied up again. "If you are waiting for me to re-tie you, you're wasting your time. If you even look at your brother, I will put this knife in the back of your neck and save the work of the rope."

An hour later there were the sounds of the horses being hitched to the wagons. Amos came out of the bedroom and turned up the lamp. While putting on coffee he noticed that Billy Bob's hands were free and the young man was laying rigid on the blankets.

"It will be nice after you boys quit cluttering up the place," the prospector growled.

The cowhands came in, rubbing their arms to warm up. "It's damn cold this morning. The only ones that won't be complaining are the four in the wagon," Ralph said.

The sun was just coming up on the plain when

they rolled out of the valley. Vic led with the wagon of dead rustlers, and the livery's dun tied to the back. Dan drove the second wagon with Tex and the brothers. Zac rode the chestnut, staying behind the wagons to keep an eye on the rustlers.

The plan was to drive straight through to Casper. They should reach the town shortly after midnight. Amos had packed them plenty to eat. The cousins kept the food and their canteens under their coats to prevent them from freezing. Tex groaned every time the wagon hit a bump.

The wind swirled snow across the plain and the wagons cut through the frozen crust. At mid-day Zac switched his saddle to the dun. Tex and Slim sat with their heads hanging while Billy Bob sat in the wagon, his eyes wild with fear knowing that he was heading toward a noose.

Later that afternoon, Vic pulled up near an open stream to give the horses a breather and a drink of water if they wanted. Dan pulled alongside and climbed down from the wagon. There was a shout and Billy Bob leaped from the back of the wagon, knocking Dan to the ground.

As he went down, the rancher caught the rustler's ankle and tripped him. Billy Bob leaped back to his feet and faced Dan. The rancher had the Colt leveled on the rustler. "You move and I will put a bullet in you!"

"Shoot me! For God sake, shoot me," Billy Bob begged. "I don't want to be hanged." With that, he turned to run. Zac cut him off with the dun and struck him with his gun barrel, knocking the brother out.

Looking over Dan saw that Vic had his rifle on the other two in the wagon. Zac swung off the horse and helped Dan toss Billy Bob back into the wagon. "You best tie the bugger tight. He is a slippery one. He got loose on me last night," the Ho-Chunk cousin said as he led the dun to the stream.

The sun slid behind the mountains and darkness engulfed the plain. It was close to the shortest day of the year. The night air was clear and crisp. Soon after sunset, the moon rose, bathing the snow covered plain in shimmering light. It was almost full and would provide enough illumination to travel faster.

Finally, the lights of Casper came into sight. A lamp was burning in the jail. Pulling the wagons next to the building, Dan went inside.

Harry Anderson was sitting in the sheriff's chair, dozing. Dan stomped the snow off his feet, waking the man. "What the hell . . ."

"I got some prisoners to put in a cell," the rancher explained. He opened his coat to show his badge. "Sheriff Winslow deputized my cousins and me to go after J.P. Burdick."

"I been covering for the sheriff since he was shot," Harry said. "I got a couple of drunks in the cell on the right. You can put J.P. in the one on the left."

"J.P. won't be needing a cell, but three others will."

"You didn't find J.P.?"

The rancher replied, "We found J.P., but he won't be needing a cell."

Zac and Vic came in with Tex and the brothers.

Billy Bob was sobbing and struggling. Vic had him by the back of his collar. Tex looked at Hal and pleaded, "I need a doctor. My shoulder is busted up something awful."

Deputy Anderson led them to the cell. Then, to Dan, he said, "I'll have Doc Morgan look at the shoulder come morning."

"We had a long day and will put the horses up and then get some sleep," Dan told Harry. "We got four more under the tarp in the wagon. J.P. is one of them."

Leaving the office, they unhitched the team and led the horses to the livery. Waking the hostler up, they asked if he would strip the harnesses off the animals and rub them down. They turned over the dun and explained that the mustang had been shot.

Leading the chestnut, the cousins walked up the slippery, rutted street, packed hard by wagons and sleds. The moonlight cast shadows from the buildings across the snow. The main floor of the mercantile was dark. There was a low lamp burning in the room that he and Mary used on the second floor. The saloon offered an abundance of welcoming light.

Vic and Zac continued to the saloon to get a room. The store only had two bedrooms on the second floor. They kidded Dan that he might want to be alone with his wife after the long trip. He could hear their laughter as his cousins walked toward the saloon. Dan led the chestnut to the barn behind the mercantile. Although he was exhausted, he gave the animal a quick rubdown and some hay. He promised the animal a bait of grain come morning.

Dan tried the back door of the store. It was

locked, so he knocked. He heard the sound of someone coming downstairs. "Can I help you?" It was Bert.

"It's me, Dan. We just got back with the rustlers."

There was the sound of the door being unlocked. Swinging it open, the merchant said, "Let me get a lamp lit. Damn, I am glad to see you. Your wife has been worried something awful."

The rancher promised to tell Bert all about their trip at breakfast. As the two men climbed the stairs, Dan realized how hungry he was. Other than the biscuits and meat that Amos had sent with them, he had only had water.

Mary was standing in her nightgown and robe at the top of the stairs. "Dan!" She flung her arms around him and clung to her husband as they went into their room. "I was so scared something would happen to you." For a long time, they stood in the middle of the room and held each other.

* * *

It was 9:00 a.m. before Dan arrived at the sheriff's office. Zac, Vic, and Sheriff Winslow were inside. Digger was checking out the tarp-covered wagon. "Dang it! It will take two buckets of coal to thaw these buggers out so's I can straighten them enough to get 'em in a box," the undertaker complained.

Smiling at the man's dilemma, the rancher went into the office. He placed his badge on the worn desk.

"I shouldn't be needing this anymore."

The pale sheriff, still sporting bulky bandages under his shirt, accepted the badge. Dan noticed two others lying on the desk. Vic and Zac sat near the potbelly stove, drinking coffee. Vic poured another cup of the strong brew and brought it over to Dan.

"You had a little trouble getting up this morning?" he kidded Dan.

The sheriff cleared his throat and then coughed. "The damn stuff the doc has been giving me dries my throat up. Your cousins have already given me information on what happened. You can look it over and add anything you think needs to be included."

Dan handed a bag to the sheriff, "This contains the money and papers we found in J.P.'s ranch house. We left a man named Joseph in charge of the ranch until you can send someone to bring in the rest of the cattle. They have been paid through the winter."

There was the sound of a cell door closing and Doctor Morgan and Harry came from the back. "He's got a broken collar bone," the doc informed them. "Not much I can do. He'll be hung before it would heal anyway."

With his shift finished, Harry left with the doc. The cousins drank their coffee in silence while Dan looked over the statements. Nodding, he added his signature to the bottom. "It's pretty much how it happened, sheriff."

"I expect some rewards will be in order," Winslow told them. "I found a couple flyers on them. After I get word from Texas, I'll get the money to you."

"Dan will hold ours, he can give it to us on our

next visit," Vic told the sheriff.

Zac stood and looked out the window. The undertaker was moving the bodies to his wagon. There was a light snow starting to fall. "There is a train Vic and I can catch this afternoon," he said.

Dan knew that his cousins had to get back to their families. After seeing each other almost every day when they were growing up, they hadn't been together for too long. The rancher hadn't realized how much he'd missed them until they'd come to help him.

"I'll be around town a few more days, taking care of things before Mary and I head for the ranch," Dan informed the sheriff. "Meanwhile, my cousins and I need to finish catching up before they leave."

The three men walked down the street toward the mercantile. "We need to figure out how to visit each other more often," Vic suggested.

"It has to be when it's warm," Dan said.

"The trains should make it easier," Zac said. Then he added, "Our children need the time together and so do we."

"And no chasing after bad guys," Dan insisted. "Just fishing, hunting, and visiting."

Vowing to start a tradition of annual visits, the three cousins walked tall and proud down the main street of Casper.

EPILOG

The sun was bright on the Colorado plains as the Ford Model T labored toward the foothills behind Denver. Vic and Carla sat in the front seat, enjoying the view of the mountains. They had just gotten the new Flivver, which proudly supported electric headlights. Vic had insisted on driving down from their potato farm in Idaho for a reunion in Boulder.

Dan and Mary looked out on the plains from the train window. Smoke billowed out of the steam engine. Dan had read about the development of electric and diesel engines. He knew it would only be a matter of time before he would be shipping his Wyoming cattle on trains powered with these engines.

Zac rode his horse into the yard and turned it loose in the corral next to the barn. He had just returned from guiding a group of fishermen on a successful trip. The screen door slammed shut on the house and he turned to see Eva smiling and waving. She held a cold root beer for him.

"Anyone arrive yet?" he asked.

"Vic is picking up Dan and Mary at the Denver station," she said. "The kids are out picking berries."

The kids were three cousins who spent the month of July, exploring the valleys and mountains around Boulder. They had ridden out on three of Zac's trail horses early that morning.

Zac and Eva sat on the front porch, enjoying their pop, when the sound of the four-cylinder Model T engine reached their ears. They stood and watched as it rolled into the yard. Vic pushed off the ignition switch and set the parking brake as he watched Eva running toward the car.

Everyone talked at once, hugging and welcoming each other. They turned to the sound of horses trotting into the yard.

Waving to the riders, they watched three of the prettiest girls swing down from the horses. Behind them the golden sun was sinking below the mountains.